KT-226-424

JOHN LYNCH

Falling Out of Heaven

FOURTH ESTATE • *London*

First published in Great Britain in 2010 by
Fourth Estate
A division of HarperCollins*Publishers*
77–85 Fulham Palace Road
London W6 8JB
www.4thestate.co.uk

Text copyright © John Lynch 2010

1

The right of John Lynch to be identified as the author of
this work has been asserted by him in accordance
with the Copyright, Designs and Patents Act 1988

A catalogue record for this book is
available from the British Library

ISBN 13 978-0-00-734870-1

Page 143–5, quotations from Louis MacNeice's 'Sunlight on the Garden'
from *Collected Poems* by Louis MacNeice, Faber and Faber, 2007,
reproduced by permission of David Higham Associates

All rights reserved. No part of this publication may be
reproduced, transmitted, or stored in a retrieval system,
in any form or by any means, without permission
in writing from Fourth Estate

Typeset by Palimpsest Book Production Limited,
Grangemouth, Stirlingshire

Printed in Great Britain by
Clays Ltd, St Ives plc

FSC is a non-profit international organisation established to promote
the responsible management of the world's forests. Products carrying the FSC
label are independently certified to assure consumers that they come
from forests that are managed to meet the social, economic and
ecological needs of present or future generations

Find out more about HarperCollins and the environment at
www.harpercollins.co.uk/green

To my parents Finn and Rose

Counting in the Dark

He was told that he had a month. Nineteen days later he was dead. It was his back. It had been bothering him. It was strange, he told a friend, it was like someone had stabbed him. He went to masseuses and chiropractors and they bent him and pulled him like he was a bendy toy but nothing seemed to help. Eventually his wife suggested he go to a doctor. It's nothing, he had said to her, something is out that's all, or maybe a muscle is in spasm. Go and see a doctor, she had said. They took X-rays, they took blood. When can I have the results, he asked? You can have them now, was the reply, you see, what you have has already taken you without you realising it. The doctor then showed him the X-ray and said that his spine was rotten, that the cancer had eaten it from the inside out. There's nothing we can do, I'm sorry. He went home and closed the curtains and sat in the dark. He counted. He began with seconds, moved on to minutes, then hours and then days until he reached a month. He spoke to his wife, he told her that he would be leaving and that she had to be strong. She demanded a second opinion, he told her that would be a waste of time, and time was something that he didn't have much of anymore. His name was Thaddeus and he decided to work one more week at the one thing he was good at, counselling, but he didn't say anything to any of them, he didn't look for anything in any of his patients' eyes. He gave as he always did. The pain stopped him after four days and after that he was given morphine and confined to bed. A Macmillan nurse was with him to the end, she was young and attentive.

It is moments since I got the news. A lot has happened since I first met him, much has changed in my life since he first stood before me five years before. A man sees his life in another's death and as I sit here and gaze out the window of my living room I think of my own story and how it nearly broke me. The man who called me to tell me the news is a part of that time when the world splintered before my eyes. He cried as he spoke, telling me how much we all owed him. I agreed and cried too. I imagined his last days alone with the knowledge that the clock of his life was ticking down more loudly than ever before. I am sure that he faced them with courage, although you can never be sure. When my wife comes home I tell her. Come and sit down, she says. She looks at me and shakes her head; everything is going so quickly, she says. He was a good man, Gabriel, like you.

I look at her, at this woman that I nearly lost and I smile. She asks me if I'm okay. Yes, I reply, she then asks me what I'm thinking. I tell her that I am back in that hospital where I was forced to claw back what was left of my life.

'Don't,' she says. 'It's the past . . . Let it go . . .'

But I'm no longer listening. I am back in that time when the ground rose to meet me. I am five years younger and I am falling.

The Last Thing to Go

I remember how the room they had put me in smelled of disinfectant and crisp sterile sheets. I was wearing a white gown. I knew that I was in trouble, that I was in a place where broken men like me came to be mended. I had lost track of time and I recall being grateful, but I also knew that there was a price to be paid, there always is when a man renounces the hand he has been given to play. They left me alone for long periods, calling in only to make me swallow a pill or to readjust my bedding. But I knew that they were never far away. I was high-risk and they were watching, they always were. When I see him now, that man lying in that white room, his mind tearing him apart, I have trouble believing that it was me, but it is something I must never forget. His forehead glistens, his mouth is dry and he craves the one thing that has almost destroyed him, a drink. He is shivering but it is not from the cold. He believes he is in danger, but he will not ask for help. He will not admit that he is beaten, no matter what they say or do to him.

How I came to be there and the prisoners I took along the way was not something that was available to me as I lay in that bed. My curse will be that as the days pass I will fall in and out of memory, good and bad, terrifying and benign. My name was the last thing to go and as I sit here now five years later, healthy and in good spirits, I feel pity for the animal I had become.

A doctor came to see me shortly after I was admitted, she

was young and I remember her breath falling on my face as she bent down to me, it was cool like summer lemonade.

'You seem a little better,' she said to me. 'A little less agitated.'

I saw that she was not alone, two men stood behind her, their arms folded.

'Please . . . Try not to upset yourself . . . It serves no purpose . . .'

Then she wiped my brow and smiled at me, and for a moment I wanted to trust her, but my heart was too sore and too poisoned.

I didn't want her to leave. I wanted to tell her that I feared my mind and that when I was alone I lost sight of myself, and that I was at the mercy of the past with its dark assassins. That's why they tell you to live a good life, because there is nothing worse than a bad memory, it will grow a mouth and sing cruel songs.

Stronger than Pain

My mother loved butterflies and she loved God. She was a tall woman; He had made her like that, she said, because her mind would be closer to the sky and His love. She had been gifted by His divine power, she had one of the fruits of the holy tree, she could speak in tongues. When she was young God had moved through her. He had laid His joy across her heart and asked her to move forward to spread His Word. She said that she had been standing in a field that overlooked her house and she could see her mother and father moving about their garden tending to the flowers. It was an autumn evening and the land around shimmered in the fading light. She was sixteen and she wore a dress that had small butterflies embroidered on it. Her father had bought it for her, just after he was told he had cancer. He had gone into the town one day and returned with it. As he handed it to her, they both knew that he was saying goodbye, and that it was a gift that she must treasure. She told my sister and me that she had been sad all day as if her world had come to an end. As she stood in there above her house she watched the shape of her father in the garden below and she said she knew from looking at him, the way his back was bent and the way he held himself that he had hardly any time left. He had lied when he had said that it could be a year or so before he left, she could tell that it was only weeks. She remembers how the certainty of it moved through her and she said that in that moment something happened that changed her life forever. A monarch butterfly landed on her shoulder and nestled next to one of the embroidered ones stitched into her dress. She said she knew that it was a sign that God was saying that our lives were just the same, as brief and as beautiful as a butterfly's. Just then she felt a power move across her heart, she said she knew immediately that it was God's love, reassuring her, letting her know that no matter what happened she would be alright and that her father was going to a better place. She said she knew that God was touching her for a reason, and that she was being prepared for something. Two weeks later to the day her father died, he collapsed in the garden, just as the weather was beginning to close down for winter. He was waked in his favourite suit, the one he wore for special occasions at the bank of which he was manager. It was for special customers, so it was only right that he should go to meet God in it. It was as she stood over his open coffin that she felt the force come to her again. This time it brought language, an ancient tongue that the first apostles had spoken when the Holy Dove had touched them on the brow.

It happened when she placed her hand on her dead father's forehead; she said that she felt a rush deep inside her like the sea spilling onto a shore and she knew that God had chosen her. She heard a voice, it spoke deep inside her next to the place where she kept her dreams. She saw the hem of her Lord's gown as she bent to wash His feet, she was among His disciples. She was favoured and loved. She saw the blood on His brow and the wound in His side as He gazed down at her from the Cross. She tasted His despair on her tongue. She said that the passion of His final hours filled her heart and flooded her mind. Such pain, she told us, excruciating and unending, but through it all His love shone through, she could feel it sitting like a small sun in the darkness of her grief. As her fingers felt the cold of her father's dead flesh, she knew that she was chosen and that she must speak, to tell the world. So her tongue spelled out the code of his love in that room where the mourners had gathered. Some thought her mad, because they would not or could not be open. Others fell to their knees and praised God in His wonder. Her mother was not so pleased; she thought that she was making a show of herself in front of the mourners and pulled her away from her husband's dead body, spitting at her to be quiet. She told us that her mother may as well have been trying to halt a spring flood; God was in her as surely as there was breath in her body. One of her mother's friends followed them out to the hall and tried to reason with her, telling her that this was a sign that the Lord's own hand was behind this. But our grandmother wouldn't listen, telling her friend to mind her own, that this was family business and didn't concern her.

Mother said she was saddened by this and that when they buried her father two days later she felt God knocking on the door of her heart again, but this time she had to refuse Him entry for fear of angering her mother. She said that as she stood there in the new soil of the opened grave she vowed never to betray Him again.

When she met my father, he told her that God was his friend and had steered him through many lonely periods in his life. He had been a sickly child who disappointed his father, and had spent his childhood toughening his body and building muscle so that he would be accepted by him, of course he never was, his father died still cursing him for being frail. So when he met my mother he became what she wanted him to be, he presented her with a caring, Godfearing man. He was used to being what he wasn't.

She got married in the butterfly dress. She had it altered

slightly to fit the occasion. It was her way of staying committed to her calling, she said. Her mother, by then broken by old age and a failing memory, didn't put up much of a fight; she wasn't able to, she said. Some people thought that it was inappropriate, that a good Catholic bride should get married in virginal white not in a faded mauve dress with the butterflies of the world dotted all over it.

My father, she said, never objected, he wanted her and would do anything to get her, even betraying his own nature. It was all done so he could possess her, and when she accepted the wedding band he offered her he changed almost overnight it seemed and the world darkened. Later she would have to hide the dress from him. God was now a threat to my father. He resented his hold on my mother's spirit. He began to taunt her belief and hunt down the goodness that she was trying to bring to their home. He began to ridicule the butterfly dress saying that my mother was cracked in the head and that if he had his way he would have them married again properly this time, in a white wedding dress, like normal people. We are a laughing stock, he would say in later years, the whole place is laughing at us. When he was drunk he would rifle the drawers and the cupboards of our house searching for that dress. He would grab her by the shoulders and shake her, his eyes locking with hers. Where is it? he would say, where did you put it? She would never tell him.

'I will ask God to guide you, Johnny.'

'Don't. Don't,' he would say.

I would see fear in his eyes, and sometimes his anger would subside.

'God loves you, Johnny . . .'

'Don't.'

'He wants you to put down your anger towards him . . .'

'No. Stop . . .'

'It doesn't have to be this way . . .'

I would watch from the top of the stairs as this big man was made small by my mother's words. His arms would fall from my mother's shoulders and he would stand there like someone under a hypnotist's spell, his body swaying from the booze, and the soft murmur of my mother's speech.

'He knows you try to be good . . . He knows your heart is wounded . . . Just as He was, Johnny . . . Just as He was . . .'

'I'm no good . . . I'm no good.'

'There is goodness in everyone . . .'

'No.'

I remember sitting there in the dark, drawn by the noise, watching as my father struggled with the blackness that sat across his soul. I saw how my mother's heart was reaching out to his, asking it to join her in the sunlight that she had found. There was something else in that moment when they held each other's eyes, a moment when something hung in the air between them. It was as if my mother was waiting for him to complete a sentence he had started, to get to the bloody meat of what was bothering him. He never did. Those moments when he let her in were rare, and then he only did it partway. Most of the time though he would tear himself away from her gaze and stumble away like a man who had just been blinded by the truth of something.

'God's love is stronger than any metal,' she would say. 'Stronger than stone . . . Stronger than pain . . .'

She had to choose her moment to work her way around my father's moods. Once he picked up a glass full of milk and hurled it at the kitchen wall as we were seated for dinner one night. My mother had suggested that she help out at the church on Sunday mornings, handing out communion. Without a word my father had stood and lifted the glass and smashed it above the heads of my sister and me and then calmly sat down again and continued eating.

Sometimes she would come and sit with me, and pray over me as I drifted off to sleep.

'Close your eyes,' she would say. 'They are all around us . . . The saints . . . God . . . Can you feel Him?'

I would nod, but it was a lie.

'He loves you, Gabriel . . . He loves you . . . God adores you.'

I would squeeze my eyes shut and beg my mind to make them appear to send them from her heart to mine, these warriors, these guardians from the gates of heaven.

'Close your eyes, Gabriel . . . See them there the host and soldiers of our Lord.'

Try as I might, wish as hard as I could, all I could see was darkness; a black endless emptiness that I knew was waiting for me when my time on this earth was done.

'Your father doesn't understand . . . He said he did . . . Once . . . He told me many things . . . Soft things . . . That make a woman feel special . . .' she said almost to herself. 'He's had a hard life . . . It was tough for him . . .'

'Mammy . . .'

'Ssh . . . Concentrate . . . God needs patience . . . needs gentleness.'

She had been beautiful my mother, but belief in God had made her ugly. There was plainness to her, and greyness in her eyes as if she was weary beyond words. She became smaller when my father was around; she shrank as if his presence ate into her spirit. I watched her skirt him, trying to double-guess his moods from the shape of his shoulders or the look in his eye. It took me a long time to realise that my sister Ciara and I did the same thing, that we were stunted, that our hearts cowered when he was in the house.

I knew that the black dot of pain that lay in the centre of his eyes also lay in mine, and that it was a stain that no amount of washing or praying could shift. I think of my loneliness, how it coils around the centre of my being like a long thread of steel and realise that he must have been the same, he stood on the outside of our family condemned as an ogre, just as I do now.

The Horizon

They were telling me to calm down. I watched as they moved about me. It was my second or third night there, I can't be sure. I was doing quite well until I dreamt about you. There was sorrow in your eyes and you turned me away. I stood there and pleaded with you but you walked away and kept walking until the horizon claimed you and you were gone forever. I woke up screaming and in a moment I was surrounded by nurses and doctors. I think that I fought them, I can't be sure. I remember how they smothered me, laying their bodies across mine and I was sure that my heart was going to explode through my chest, spewing blood across the pristine sheets. I wanted to tell them that I wished them no harm, that I was dying from a lack of love that's all. But they weren't in any mood to listen.

There must have been four of them, all men and though they were being physical with me, they kept talking, whispering reassurances, saying things like relax, Gabriel, try and relax, we're here to help you.

Needless to say I didn't believe them, and somewhere I didn't trust that I was awake, and then I thought that maybe you had sent them to make sure that I stayed away from you and our child. That made me cry, and for a moment everyone stopped and waited.

'It's okay,' one of the younger nurses said. 'Everything will be alright. You'll see.'

Part of me wanted to believe him but all I could see was everything that I had thrown away. I needed the one thing that I knew they wouldn't give me, the hot fire of whiskey on my throat. It was the only thing that had the power to burn the memory of you from me. It was then that I saw the syringe and I began to fight them again. The young woman doctor had it in her hand as she made her way to me.

'I need his forearm,' I heard her say. 'Quick. Quick.'

Someone else speaks. I hear the words sleep and trust, but my hearing is going, it is mixing with sounds from the past, my first baby words, and my mother's voice, as soft as surf spilling onto a beach, plates being stacked, the hollow chime of our hallway clock, my sister's laugh, and then my father's hard bark like a seal demanding fish.

The Firebird

I watched as he patrolled the house, his eyes flicking periodically in my direction, sizing me up, daring me to shatter the silence he had spent the best part of the morning setting in place. It began with the way he responded to my mother's request that he run her into town. He stared at her as if she had just insulted him and then walked the length of the kitchen and looked back at her, disdain in his eyes. She knew better than to say anything, that she had to let him posture and sulk his way through this latest mood otherwise there would be war.

From her he moved on to me. I remember I was drawing at the table, it was the picture of a bird in flight, a red bird with bright orange flames for wings. I had spent most of the morning on it, enjoying the feel of the crayons between my fingers. I could feel the heat of his presence as he stood over me; I could smell tobacco and diesel and hear the sharp running of his breath.

I recall sitting there, my hands frozen in the middle of their task, my brain desperately trying to read the situation. Should I look up at him and smile, careful not to make it too sure or confident, or should I continue drawing? I knew from experience that the best thing was to do nothing. After what seemed an age he moved off and sat by the door of the kitchen and lit a cigarette. I watched my mother, her eyes keeping track of him; aware at all times where he was, and most crucially who he was looking at.

I felt sorry for her that morning. I loved her; I wanted to kill for her, to smash down the grey walls of her life and to free her. Anger clutched at me as I looked at the man she had married as he sat there, the smoke from his cigarette climbing lazily, his legs crossed.

He saw it in me as I looked from her to him, my eyes meeting his, in that second he had me. He knew it; I had revealed myself to him. I remember him smiling as if to say go on, let's see how long you can hold it, let's see how big you are.

'Seen enough?' he asked.

I nodded carefully and took my eyes from him, wondering if he would pursue it, but he didn't. I was easy prey. I was a pushover.

My sister broke the silence that morning. She rushed in from playing outside, her hair strewn across her face, her doll Lola pressed to her breast. She threw open the door and yelled.

'Mammy.'

The wind rushed in, blowing apart the game my father had been playing. It ran through the kitchen like a storm of freshness, banishing the silence, busting it into a thousand little pieces.

'Sssh,' my mother had said. 'Your father's thinking.'

'What? What did you say?'

'Nothing. I meant . . . '

'Don't take the piss.'

'I'm not. Please, I'm not.'

'Yes, you were.'

'No, I wasn't. It just came out. I didn't mean it that way. Ciara, come here, do this dress up, what have you been doing to yourself?'

'Don't fuck around with me,' my father said as my mother fussed over my sister, running her hand across her face, gathering the snot from her nose between her fingers and shaking it into the sink, then running the tap.

'Don't speak like that.'

'I'll speak any fucking way I please.'

'Alright. Alright.'

'Is that clear?'

'Yes.'

'What?'

'I said yes.'

'Good.'

As he left he slammed the door behind him. I remember sitting there looking at my hands, they were shaking. Ciara began to cry, dropping her doll as she put her hands to her face. My mother bent down to her and pulled her close as we heard the sound of my father's car pulling out of the garage in the yard and roar away from the house. I could imagine him sitting there, his hand ripping through the gears, his eyes blazing with anger, his world small and cold.

The Fall

I believed that I was falling. It was as real to me as my next breath. As I lay there in that hospital bed night after night all I could see was the tumble of my body through space. I could feel the moisture of the clouds bathe my face and the wind tugging at my clothes. I could see my life spread out before me like a half-assembled jigsaw. Sometimes I was glad and enjoyed the sensation, happy to be leaving everything behind. Other times fear held my hand as I fell and I would shake and moan as I saw the ground below hurtling towards me. I remember grabbing at the air, trying to find something to hold on to. I had left love behind and my only hope was these men and women who tended to me, whose job it was to bring people like me back from the brink.

I fell into my past. I walked the hard ground of my childhood again. I saw our marriage. I saw our love begin and end. I became a ghost walking the corridors of the living. They told me later that it wasn't uncommon for a man in my condition to believe strange things, to think that he is in peril. Some never return from the strange land that they find themselves in. Hell is alive and well in the minds of men such as me, one of the nurses said with a strange grin on his face.

There were times as I lay in that hospital room when I felt my fear subside, it was as fleeting as a bad man's smile. For a moment, I was embraced by a sense of peace, and my body's fever abated. It was in moments like these that I tried to ask God to forgive me, but I was still too angry with him and the words never made it past my lips. I still blamed him for all that my father had done to me. He died a long time ago but he still had a hold on the guts of my being. His hands are always there twisting and pulling. Sometimes when I was falling I could hear him whispering, taunting me.

I thought of my life, of how I had believed that I was a fortress, standing alone on the horizon of other people's lives. I saw how much of a lie that was. I had learned the hard way. Here I was, alone, dependent on the kindness of these doctors. I thought of all the pain I had caused, the misery I had brought to my door and the doors of others. At night sometimes when I woke I would call for someone to come and sit with me. If no-one came I would lie there shivering in the dark hoping that my fall was almost at an end.

The Pier

I see you as I first saw you, your eyes shining, your face offered to me as I bent to kiss it. We were in a bar in County Clare, behind us people were celebrating New Year's Eve, and we had slipped away and left them to put the old year to bed. We stood on the small wooden pier that fronted the pub and watched the night sky turn in glitter and ice high above us.

How long ago that New Year's Eve seems and yet sometimes in a moment when my weary spirit is caught off-guard, I taste your sweetness once more as if it was all about to happen again. I'll be ready this time and meet you on the long pier, which divided the sea and held us and our dreams that night long ago.

'I love you.'

'I know,' you said.

'Do you?'

'Do I what? Know that you love me?'

'No,' I said.

'Oh you mean . . . ?'

'Yes.'

'Do I love you? What do you think?'

'I think yes.'

'Then you think right,' you said.

Just after, you smiled and quickly closed your lips over your teeth, and a slight embarrassment flickered across your eyes.

It was because one of your incisors was crooked, I'd seen you do it many times, most especially in company. It gave you a vulnerability that made me want you more. I remember I put my fingers to your lips and ran my thumb across them, holding your eyes.

'But . . .'

'Love isn't just saying. It's doing too,' you said.

'I love your mouth.'

'Gabriel, I'm serious.'

'The wow of your mouth.'

'Gabriel?'

'Yes?'

'Are you listening?

'Yes.'

'Then show me, Gabriel. Show me.'

'Your lips . . . so beautiful.'

'Gabriel.'

'Yes?'

'Words are easy. I don't want that, do you hear, I don't want that.'

Eating God

I see her holding my young body down, her hand on the nape of my neck, forcing me to spit out the prayer. I remember her body shaking as she implored heaven for release.

'Holy Jesus, we implore you . . . Holy Christ, fruit of the vine . . .'

'Holy Jesus,' I said, echoing her.

'Holy Jesus . . . The one true Lamb . . . The one true God . . . Enter me, Lord . . . Fill me with the sweet Glory of your Love . . . Come to me, Jesus, in Love, in Sorrow.'

'Mammy,' I would say. 'Mammy.'

Her eyes would glaze over, the look I used to see in the eyes of fish I caught, as they lay on the riverbank and death passed over them. Her head would move from side to side and a film of foam would cover her lips. I would hold her hand and squeeze it until my knuckles whitened. I felt as if I was holding on to her as she dangled above a steep drop and that I was her last hope.

Then I would feel her leave me, it passed through her body and into mine, the feeling of absence, of flight. She was no longer mine; she was beyond me. She had passed into trance. Then the noise would pour from her. Words half known, bastardised and tangled, child words, woman sounds, all fell from her lips, and God, always God, the word that kept coming, kept shining through like a flame on a dark hillside. It would last for minutes sometimes, her mouth working, sweat forming in the small well between our clasped palms.

I knew better than to say anything, I just kept my head bowed and waited for the storm of words and emotion to pass. Then she would fall silent, her body flopping forward as if she was a puppet whose strings had just been cut. The first time she did it, I panicked, thinking her dead. I had grabbed her, pulled at her white face and tugged at her hands.

'Mammy, Mammy, I'm frightened.'

Then she would sigh and open her eyes and regard me. I would see myself reflected there, I looked so small and scared.

'Don't worry,' she said. 'The Lord is with us . . . All these things, son . . . All this pain . . . It's sent to try us . . .'

'Yes, Mammy.'

'God sees it all . . . Remember that . . . There is nothing He doesn't see.'

'Yes, Mammy.'

I wanted to tell her that I understood even though I didn't. As I knelt over her like a doctor tending a patient I remember wondering why I couldn't see what she saw, feel what she felt. Why was I different, why had God excluded me?

'Don't tell your father,' she said. She always said it.

'I won't.'

'Promise?'

'Yes.'

'Good boy.'

'What's it like?'

'What, son?'

'That. The . . . praying.'

'It's like . . .'

'Does it hurt?'

'No, son . . . It's beautiful.'

'Do you see angels?'

'Well, not really . . . I see light . . . I see the light . . .'

'What light?'

'It's hard to explain.'

'Try.'

'Well . . . I see . . . I feel the power of God's love . . . It's like the summer sun on my face, only it's forever, not just one season, or one day . . . And deep down in my heart I know that everything happens for a reason . . . That all the good things and all the bad things they all enter our hearts for a purpose. I suppose I feel safe . . . Like I'm on a big white cloud.'

'Is Daddy there with you?'

'Sometimes . . .'

'Why only sometimes? Does God not like him?'

'Don't talk like that, son . . . God loves all his creatures, bad, good or otherwise.'

'Does he like him even when he . . .'

'When he what?'

'I don't know.'

'What are you trying to say?'

'When he does really bad things?'

'Son, that's when God loves him most of all.'

Code, that's the way we live, tapping out cloaked messages to the ones we love. We never say it, the thing of something; we never tear the secret from its cave and lay it at the feet of the ones nearest to us. All those years ago as I sat with her she told me that God was by us, that He knelt with me. I felt the rage rise in me, and I wanted to tear down her belief, smash the altar of her faith. I wanted to stand and tell her that God didn't exist and that if He did He was more like the devil than anything else. How could He be all love? How could He love the pig man who ruled our house as if he was an agent of the damned?

What You Don't See

'You can either do it yourself or I will have to do it for you. It's your choice.'

I say nothing but hold her with my eyes. I am in a bathroom of some kind but it is more industrial than personal, all chrome bars and wide porcelain sinks. I am sitting on a small folding steel chair. I am still wearing my white gown and I can see the goosepimples on my exposed arms and legs.

'Hygiene is very important,' she says.

I don't feel as alone as I did, maybe it's the long sleep or the fact that I am getting used to these people who surround me every waking hour telling me that they only have my best interests at heart. She is pretty this young girl in front of me and her face is open and rounded. She has a small plastic basin full of soapy water.

'My name is Naomi.'

I know she's trying to get me to speak, but it's so long since I have that I'm not sure if I can.

'I know that this is difficult . . . That you feel alone . . . But you are in good hands . . . This is a good place, you must trust that . . .'

She gently takes my feet and puts them in the basin. I feel the warmth spreading up my legs. She begins to move the sponge along the line of my calves.

'You'll feel better for this, you'll see.'

Her hands are small like a child's and I watch as they slide up and down my shins.

'You're from the North, aren't you?'

Still I don't reply but look at the suds forming in soapy rings on the hairs of my legs.

'It's great what's happening up there now. Let's hope it holds. It must have been tough for you all those years, all that violence . . . I'm from Waterford. I think sometimes that we had it very easy down here. You know, what you don't see won't hurt you . . . Now I'm going to put this mat on the floor and I need you to stand on it so I can give the rest of you a good scrub. That's it . . . Who's a good boy?'

May

Often I would meet her at night on the road as I walked home. She would appear out of the darkness, her shape moving towards me with that jaunty, disconnected gait that I would come to know so well. She lived alone in a crumbling farmhouse about a mile from us, fronted by a line of ancient trees. The only company that meant anything to her were the cats and dogs that she gathered to her like a princess collects suitors. They would follow as she moved about her garden, waiting for titbits or an affectionate ruffle of their coats. They were like her, rejects from their own kind. They huddled together in the face of a violent world, depending on each other for protection and warmth.

When I met her late at night she would always ask me if I had seen one of her animals, that it had gone missing and that she was worried about it, fearful of foxes or even larger predators that she believed lurked high in the mountain's undergrowth. She never washed and her face was a large smudge of dirt and wrinkles. Her hair hung together in tangled clumps and her eyes looked at you as if they were regarding you from another world, one that only she had access to. I was attracted to her in spite of her strangeness, because of her strangeness.

The Dead's whispers are heard more clearly at night, she would say to me, as we stood on the road, the moon bathing us in its ghostly light. She would stand close to me and indicate with her head that I should listen. I remember the wheeze of her breath and the smell of dog and cat that had overpowered her own human smell.

'Be careful what you say. Be careful what you think because they are always listening,' she would say, her head upturned, her mouth slightly parted. When I was a child, she told me stories of old Ireland, the one that grew strong on the meat of poetry and the spoken word, the one that gave the world its dreamers and magicians. She looked as if she had been moulded from the woodland that surrounded her, carved into being with bark as her spine and moss for flesh and a bird's nest for a heart. At night as I lay in bed I could hear her as she moved across the fields searching for a lost cat, using a high-pitched feeding call to try and attract it.

My sister and I accepted her as only children can, wholeheartedly and without prejudice. My parents were not so accommodating, believing she was mad, or worse just plain evil.

I would often sneak off, running the distance to her house, my heart longing to see her.

'Who is it?' she would demand as I stood at her front door.

'Me,' I would say.

'Which me? There are a lot of mes in this world.'

'Gabriel me.'

'Ah . . .'

Her door had an old cross on it, with a peeling Jesus nailed to it. He looked so forgotten and so tired. Every time she opened it either to let herself out or to usher someone in she would touch him gently on the wounds of his feet and pause for a second, her eyes closed, saying something I couldn't quite hear.

'Why do you do that?' I asked her one day.

'Because it only takes a moment,' she said. 'And besides, he's in trouble.'

It was dark in her house; the windows were so grimy and

dirty that they only let in a pale wash of daylight. Her sitting room was a muddle of broken chairs and discarded clothes. The floor was covered with old newspaper and magazines, and everywhere there was movement, small shapes lurked in the corners, their eyes flashing in the darkness. The place smelled of stale piss and warm bodies. Ashes from the fire were strewn in front of her fireplace like a grey beard. I remember the first time I went a small tawny cat sidled up to me and ran its tail across the tops of my knees. It only had one eye, and its good one ran with yellowy pus.

'Don't be afraid,' she said to me. 'He's only new here. I found him on the mountain a few days ago, he has a cold in his eye, but it will be alright. All he needs is a bit of love like the rest of us.'

I was mesmerised by her, by this child-woman who lived in the cracks of life that the rest of us avoided. I could see what had once been a beautiful young woman beneath the coat of filth she seemed to wear like a suit of armour.

I felt comfortable with her and her troop of sick and wounded animals. I would watch as she spoke to each of them in a language made up of coos and tuts. Sometimes she would break into a strange banshee wail, beginning softly, her head thrown back, her tongue disappearing in and out of her grimy mouth then building to a screech which filled the whole house. Her animals would stand pert with attention and as the noise built would move to her, quietly circling her, rubbing her with their bodies, their heads upturned and their eyes glowing.

She talked to me as if I was a grown-up, as if I had something to say. I would listen to her as she spoke of the magic that lived in the hills around us, how each breath of wind had its own message. She told me that on every hand we were being watched, that God had filled the air with spirits that noted how we were doing, and that animals could see what we couldn't see, that they held a key in their souls that we had lost a long time ago.

I would walk the countryside with her, watching as she stopped now and then to sniff the air, her hand raised, her head stock still.

'There's a wee one in trouble,' she would say.

I would stand beside her and look around me, desperate to see what she saw, scouring the hedgerows and the ditches. Sometimes she would say: 'He doesn't want to be found. It's his time and he wants to go on his own and in peace.'

Now and then on the way back from school we would see her, as we sat in the back of Dad's Hillman Imp. He would shake his head as we passed her and mutter something like *no good lunatic* under his breath. We would watch as she raised her hand to us in greeting as if she was conducting some unseen choir.

It was only later in life that I discovered that she had lost her brother when she was in her early twenties. He had been taken out and shot nearly thirty years before; local men had arrived in the dead of night wielding a rusty gun and iron bars. She had answered the door. They pushed their way past her and dragged him from his bed out into the front garden where they beat him senseless and then shot him twice in the head. His blood seeped into the grass and onto her nightshirt as she held his broken body. He was an informer, or so a man told me, running titbits of information to the local police in return for a few shillings, for blood money, was the way the man put it.

The man also told me that when she was younger she would have broken your heart with her beauty. She had many suitors, him included; they would follow her like the strays that she subsequently collected. When her brother was shot the young men looking for her hand fell away, melted back into their own lives. The world shut her out, banished her to the wild scrub and the fluttering heather of the mountain behind her house.

She stopped washing maybe out of protest, maybe out of shame, maybe rage. She shoved herself into the face of an indifferent world, the stains on her face put there by the good people of the parish. She buried her brother and stood in the wind alone as he was put in the earth, and an anger must have begun in her, it must have moved within her with the force of a detonating bomb shattering every dream, every hope, every prayer. Maybe as she stood there watching the coffin being lowered she thought about leaving, setting out for England or America. Instead she looked to the night; she moved to peer through the cracks that border this world, the place where fury lived and where the lonely spin in eternity, friendless and without love.

She began collecting strays, broken beings who knew the taste of disappointment just as she did. She held them to her as the world lay sleeping and told them that she was one of them, that she had left her own kind behind. She would shield me too when I was with her, her grimy features following every move I made. She made me listen to the whisperings of nature at work, from the heavy hum of bees seeking pollen to the flick of a trout leaving the water to take a fly.

Sometimes we would just sit there on a hill, the clouds hovering above us, and hold the silence between us, believing that we were close to unearthing some secret that lay hidden just beneath the wings of the breeze.

I would look at her in profile and see the fine beauty she once had, the ghost of it still lying across her bones and in the corner of her green eyes and in the gentle plunge of her long neck.

'What do you want to be when you grow up?' she asked me one day as we sat there.

'I don't know.'

'Maybe you could be my gardener.'

Then she laughed, throwing her head back.

'Would you like that?'

'Maybe.'

'Then you could listen every day to the worms and beetles moving in the ground, happy and free in the wet muck, eh?'

'Yeah.'

'Or you could be a wizard or a warlock. Do you know what a wizard is?'

'Yes.'

'What about a warlock?'

'Not sure.'

'A warlock is a male witch. He has powers that can frighten a man and bring him weeping to his knees. What about that for a notion?'

'What?'

'You . . . A warlock. That'd be something.'

'I don't know . . .'

'What are you a man or a mouse?'

'I'm frightened,' I remember saying.

'Of what?' she asked. But before I had a chance to answer, she said, 'They've put that there.'

She waved her long arm at the middle distance as if an army rose on the crest of the hill in front of us, poised to take us apart.

'The world and its wife.'

I remember nodding, unsure what she meant.

'No-one listens anymore. They only plot and fiddle with other people's happiness. They take and take. Everyone says they're owed . . . Don't you think?'

She plucked up a long stem of grass and put it between her teeth and sucked at its end.

'There's goodness in these. Try one.'

She handed me one, and I put it in my mouth.

'The thing to remember, wee one,' she said. 'It's they who are frightened, not us.'

As the sun set that day, throwing up long threads of fire as it disappeared, I remember looking at her and her lioness profile, part animal part woman, and my heart was calm and full of love for her.

Locals from the town, young boys fed on a diet of Republicanism and sheer fuck-you hardness, used to circle her house in the dead of night like wolves scenting the weakness of a fallen prey. They would call to her and taunt her, throwing rocks at her doors and windows. Inside, her animals would howl and beat the deadness of the night with their cries. Sometimes one of the boys would force a window latch and try to climb in screaming abuse at her, but none of them ever made it in, the largest and strongest of her dogs would always be there, fangs at the ready, his eyes blazing with fierce loyalty to his owner.

Stories began to circulate that one of the youths had caught a glimpse of her lying naked in front of her fire, a fine ridge of animal hair running down the length of her back, her eyes glowing with wildness, her teeth bared, as she was mounted from behind by one of her dogs, an old grizzled Alsatian called Ahab after the sadistic captain in *Moby Dick*.

One night they came armed with baseball bats and chains, one had an axe, a kid called Hardface. He was known for it; at dance halls up and down the country he would produce this small wooden axe to impress and frighten, to let the world know that he had come prepared. They were about twenty strong and this time they were determined to get beyond the threshold of her small house and her pack of loyal guard dogs. Four or five of them led the charge, rushing at her door, busting it down with a blow from their boots, swinging their baseball bats at anything that moved, catching dog and cat in equal measure, their barks and shrieks filling the house. Old tables, chairs and pots were thrown to the ground; kittens scurried between their feet like rats caught in a flood. The youths wore heavy combat jackets, thick motorcyclists' gloves and balaclavas. One after another they poured into her house, thumping and kicking their way down her small hall. They heard her calling to her animals; she was in the room at the back where she lived most of the time by the guttering fire. Ahab was the last animal they met; he stood by her, growling at them as they burst into the living space. He looked like a lion of the savannah, proud and ferocious, daring any of them to make the next move.

Hardface, who up until now had been using a baseball bat like the rest of them, pulled out his small axe from inside his coat, it glinted like a devil's eye in the gloomy candlelit room. Youth after youth squeezed into the tight dark space. One of them spat on the floor as he looked around. Their heavy violence filled the air and for a moment they just looked at her, as if she were some kind of soiled queen about to be deposed, being given one last moment of deference before her execution.

Ahab inched forward when he saw the axe, his coat bristling, his eyes filled with hatred.

'Ssh, Ahab,' she said. 'Ssh.'

She stood slowly and faced them, her eyes shining with a quiet defiance. One by one she looked at them.

'At least have the decency to show me your faces,' she said. 'Let me see who I have the pleasure of welcoming into my house at this late hour.'

As Ahab leapt I saw the axe move past my head in a downward swoop, its blade gleaming. It struck the dog across the muzzle, drawing a long line of blood across it and almost separating the nose from the snout. I let out a cry and May's head snapped in my direction and her eyes burned into mine. The dog managed to get a hold on Hardface, biting into his wrist, causing him to drop the axe. He tried to shake his attacker from him, but Ahab just bit deeper. I grabbed the axe and swung it high above my head, bringing it crashing down across the dog's back. I could hear the dull thud of steel on bone and fur. Its body buckled but still it held on, its teeth shining, its blood mingling with that of its attacker. In I struck, my breath coming in quick grunts.

'Fuck,' I said. 'Fuck.'

I remember fumbling with the handle, how it slipped in my gloved hand. I felt May's eyes on me, I knew that I had crossed a line, that I had committed a treason against the beauty she had laid at my feet, that I was taking an axe to the strong tree of poetry she had grown in my heart. I wanted to explain to her that the stain had always been there. Even when I first came to her, my small hand beating on her door to let me in, the mark lay across my heart like the shadow of an upturned cross.

He had put it there. He had placed it between my legs where all good things come from. He had put his hand there and in doing so he had taken any chance I had. He had told me it was alright, that the night was made for secrets and that this was just one more to add to the ocean of secrets that the world was made up of. The seed was already in me as I stood in her front room for the first time; I was lost to her even before she began to talk to me of the world of magic and wondering. I was a hard ball of hate and so immune to her. I was one of those she had spoken about, who felt that they were owed.

As I killed her dog that night, pounding it until its carcass was a mass of fur and blood, that's what I was trying to tell her, that she shouldn't have bothered with me, that all along I was a spy, sent to peer into the workings of her soul, and that like my father I was built for betrayal.

All of this and more rose in me that night as she watched me smash her last friend into the earth. I pounded his hand on my balls, his mouth on mine, and the seam of sweat he brought to my skin every time I thought of him.

The dog was dead and with it any hope I had of crossing back from the wasteland I now found myself in. I no longer cared. I remember removing my balaclava and looking at her and that was the moment I put my signature to the crime, not caring that the moon had dimmed and that the lights that guided me had begun to fade. She didn't say anything and made no sound as we dragged her into the front garden and stripped her. Then we hunted her, giving her a head-start, listening as she crashed through the hedges and fields that surrounded her house, her dirty nakedness flashing through the moonlit night. We chased her, calling to her, taunting her, making animal noises. I remember revelling in the power of my hold over another human life. We spread out, calling to each other in owl hoots when we spied her, the cider we had downed only hours before giving us madness and a violent clarity.

Higher and higher up the mountain we pursued her, the grassy hills giving way to scrub and tufts of wiry heather. Through pools and brackish water, past half-slumbering cattle and bearded silhouettes of goats, eventually she gave up, collapsing only minutes from the top, her breath leaving her body in a little pleading whine, her arms lying about her.

When we reached her we stood in a circle around her. I ignored the look in her eyes that told me she knew me. I tried not to pay attention to it because I was someone else; I had worked very hard at it, day and night, minute to minute, and hour to hour. I had killed the dreaming child, the one who had talked of the courtship of butterflies, who had opened himself to the world like a daisy reaching for the sun.

The rest of the gang wanted to rape her, but I put myself between them and her. I knew that as an act it was complete, it was pure. We had taken everything from her, and that what was left of her dignity was hers, and not ours to brutalise. Some of them said I was chicken but I challenged each of them to back what they said with action but none of them did. They had seen what I had done to her dog.

So we left her there, in the pool of her sweat and her misery, her strong profile broken by the shadows that grew up around her, her eyes a mist of confusion and sadness.

Blue-grey

'Your episodes will come and go, that's normal . . . You will panic like you did yesterday . . . We will have to restrain you . . . That's normal too . . . You have divorced yourself from reality . . . And these dreams . . . notions that you have are not unusual for someone in your state . . . At the moment I believe you can hear and understand me though you are still refusing to speak . . . So I am taking this opportunity to let you know what's happening . . . You must try and trust us, we deal with cases like yours all the time . . . We are set up for it and have a great deal of experience . . . The most important thing to remember is that you are not alone . . . In spite of what you may think there are a great deal of people who care about you . . . As the days pass it will be our job to see that you sleep . . . That's where your mind will repair itself . . . And if you trust us gradually you will come back from where you've been until you will wonder if it ever happened at all . . . My name is Doctor Rush and I will be in charge of you while you are here . . . Any questions?'

It is the young doctor from before, the one with the syringe. She is sitting on the side of my bed. I look at her and want to ask her if she is real but I just lie there and shake my head.

'What's wrong? Tell me. I know that you understand what I'm saying to you . . . By not communicating you only make this process longer and more painful for yourself.'

She waits. Her eyes are blue-grey like the sky on an October morning. She wears a wedding band and her fingers are long and slender.

'Very well,' she says.

As she moves to get up I take her hand and hold it. I see a slight fear rise in her eyes. I watch as she decides what to do. Eventually she sits back down.

'You don't want me to go . . .'

I don't say anything.

'My first name is Moira.'

I blink, and then I close my eyes. When I open them she has gone. Time has passed.

The Boys

I'm telling myself that I care. But I don't. The truth is I liked the Troubles that held sway in this tiny state of ours for so many years. It told me that the terror I felt in my bones since the day I was born had a name, and everywhere I looked I could see it in action. Man killing man, killing woman, killing child. I resent the glee I can see in the faces of the people around me, some I know, and some I don't care if I never do. I am in a bar on the outskirts of town. I thought that I could escape the bleating horns and the flag waving but I was wrong. Everywhere I look it seems as if the streets are blooming tricolours, they hang from open windows and passing cars. They line the roads like over-eager trees showing their blossoms before summer has arrived. I am trying to get drunk quickly to disappear into the past where the bogeymen still wore balaclavas and shouldered an Armalite or two. I read somewhere that there is no such thing as victory and that both sides lose when they decide to engage. I feel like spitting it into the face of the man who is grinning at me across our half-empty pint glasses.

'We showed them,' he says. 'Don't fuck with the boys,' he continues.

I nod and look away, hoping that when I look back he will have found a new victim for his vainglory.

'The boys will do you every fucking time,' he says.

I look back and stare at him.

'What boys?'

'The boys in green.'

'You mean fucking elves. Or sprites or some fucking thing . . .'

'What?'

'Elves.'

'You taking the piss?'

'No. Are you?'

'Oh fuck off.'

'No, you fuck off,' I say.

I can see him debating whether to drop it. I can almost read each thought as they pass across his beady little eyes. It's when he nods at me, his eyes full of anger, that I know that he's decided to pursue it. But he's drunk and I'm not yet so I wait, knowing that I have very little to fear from this small man who wants the world to be full of fanfares and victory parades. He sits there and I know that he's working up his next line of attack. I feel sorry for him, he looks comical and I know that somewhere he realises that no-one has won, no-one ever does. I wait, holding him with my eyes, watching for any sudden movement. But when he speaks all he can say is: 'Fucking elves. Are you with us or are you not?'

'I'm not with anyone,' I spit back.

'People like you don't . . .'

'Don't what?'

'You couldn't give a fuck. But when there's a knock at the fucking door and some fucker's there, wanting to do you and your family damage . . . then . . . then . . .'

'Then?'

'Then you'll come running.'

'Oh please . . .'

'You know. You fucking know . . .'

'You've been watching too many fucking films.'

'You'll see. You'll fucking see. They thought they had us, the cunts. They thought that they could fuck us up. Think again, you bastards.'

As he says this he gets to his feet and raises his pint glass above his head and looks around the bar. Someone gently taps him on the head with a large green, white and gold inflatable plastic hammer. The people around us laugh, one of them a young man with spiky red hair nudges me in the back. I turn round to find myself staring into his eyes. They are hard, and glitter like frost on stony ground.

'I heard what you said,' he says to me.

'Did you?'

'Yeah. There's a word for people like you.'

'Is there?'

'Yeah. And a place too. It's not far from here. It's a small beach. Where fuckers like you can rest in peace.'

'Is that right?'

'Yeah.'

'Are you threatening me?'

'Yes, I am. That's exactly what I'm doing.'

Baby Man

How beautiful he was, like fresh snow on old tired ground. His eyes were wide, his small hands pawing at life. The doctor congratulated us, he moved with a businesslike air as if he was in a boardroom. He had seen it all before; I resented him, I wanted to push his nose into the miracle that was before him. You sensed this in me and squeezed my hand and looked for calm in my eyes.

I hadn't drunk that day. I wanted to be present. I remember you were pleased and had given me a tight little hug when I arrived. You did what you always did, smelled me, and checked my breath as my head came close to yours. You were very good at it; after all you'd had a lot of practice. You gave me a smile and led me to our son. I said something like shouldn't you be resting, and you said no, that you were strong; you said it almost as a challenge, as if I doubted you. Anyway, you said the doctor was a practical man and believed in people getting on with things.

I said that the doctor sounded like an idiot and you said, why does everyone have to be an enemy? They don't, I said. Then you gave me that look that you wore more and more whenever I was around, that look of disappointment.

So I came to see our son as prepared as I could be. I was clean, I wore a jacket, the one you insisted I buy, and a fresh shirt that I had hurriedly ironed that morning. Yes, I was alcohol-free but my skin spoke of it every chance it had. It felt tight on the bones of my body. Fear lay across the palms of my hands, and my eyes questioned everything they saw, that is of course until I saw our child.

As we gazed down at him, and I looked to you and I saw the love in your eyes, we were briefly joined and the world we had built righted itself and hope fluttered like a flag in a sudden breeze. But that moment gave birth to another darker one, and I saw you move from me across the burning love you felt for our newborn child and look back at me as if to say that now you had found what you had spent your life looking for. Here was someone you could mould and teach. I remembered that night years before on the pier, when you told me that love was doing, not just saying. I never understood what you meant until I saw you look at our son. I knew then that I was losing you, and that the towers of our love were falling.

That night I lay with a prostitute. She was Korean, and younger than you, she was soft and fresh like a spring flower. She worked out of a house not far from the hospital, and her room smelled of old sweat and fading perfume. She called me Baby and for the best part of an hour fooled me into thinking she cared. She was good at the act, the one that involved touch and noises that women make to reassure men that the world is not as cold as they think it is.

An old woman had answered the door and brought me to the small room that had a massage table in it with a blue, worn towel draped over it. She looked at me for a moment, eyeing me up and down before asking me if I had been there before. I said yes, I lied.

'When?'

'A few months ago.'

'What girl?'

'What?'

'What girl?'

'A young one.'

'No, what girl you with last time?'

'Can't remember . . . She was pretty.'

'Hmm.'

'Is there a problem?'

'You police.'

'No.'

'Wait here.'

She left and returned two or three moments later with a young Korean girl who was probably no more than twenty-three or -four. She wore a short white lab coat, and underneath nothing more than a tight, green two-piece bikini. Her eyes were dark and shone with mild interest as she looked me up and down. Her lime green eye make-up matched her bikini.

'Forty for the room, mister,' the old woman said.

'How long?' I asked.

'Half hour, forty . . .'

'The hour.'

'Eighty.'

'You pay the girl separate. Between you and Cookie.'

'Who?'

'Me,' the young girl said. 'That's me, Cookie.'

'Hi, Cookie.'

'Hi.'

It was a few moments before I noticed that the old woman had left. She was good at leaving her girls to it with the minimum of fuss, without disturbing the client.

'You want massage,' Cookie asked me, her large eyes smiling at me.

'Yes, massage,' I said as if it was the answer to all my problems.

'You tired.'

'Yes, tired . . .'

'You look tired. Life hard.'

'Yes.'

I was almost twice her age but I had become her child.

'Undress from your clothing, please.'

I looked at her for a moment and then obeyed, peeling off my jacket and the freshly ironed shirt, the one I had worn to see our newborn son. I remember the stab of guilt that caught me in the chest, causing me to wince.

'You okay?' Cookie asked me.

'Yes, okay.'

She watched me as I undressed; I suppose to see what she had to work with. I tried to hide my belly from her with its small bulge of sadness and approaching middle age.

'Don't be shy,' she said. 'You nice body.'

'Thank you,' I said, stammering like some fool knee deep in embarrassment.

'Lie down, Baby Man,' she said.

The massage table creaked as I lay across it, and I felt her hands on me as she guided me down. I felt a twitch of desire begin in my groin as I looked up into her face.

'Other way.'

I turned over onto my front and felt her run her fingertips the length of my body, stopping briefly as they reached my buttocks then continuing on down to my heels.

'Massage hard or soft.'

'Hard,' I mumbled.

Her hands moved across my shoulders and dug themselves into my neck and began kneading. Her fingers were firm but gentle and I drifted with them as they moved across the broad of my back. I saw your face briefly and dismissed it as quickly as it rose in my thinking. She made noises as her hands touched me, delicate sounds like a breeze tugging at trees in a meadow. I wondered at all the bodies she had seen, that her young eyes had sized up as they undressed in front of her. I wanted to see behind the mask of sweetness she was careful to present to me. Did she leave herself behind every time she crossed the threshold to greet another customer? Outside in the grubby corridor that I had walked to get to this room, I imagined her soul sitting in a small jar waiting for her to return after she had done what she was paid to do. I saw it gleaming like a berry after a rainfall.

I imagined rows and rows of jars lining the corridors of every brothel in the world. I wanted to ask her how many times she had put her soul out of harm's way, locked it down as she walked into another man's arms, knowing that she was the fantasy that he had dreamed up in the sewers of his mind. She is getting bolder with her hands, spending time around the round flesh of my rump, her fingers separating and coming back together. Then she wipes the hair back from my brow and asks me if I am okay. I grunt and shift my face and realise that I have been drooling like an ape on the point of sleep. I know now that I died in that room, a part of me left and walked free of the suffering I was heaping on myself. I couldn't tell you, I couldn't tell anyone, how her hands became his, tough needy hands digging out the badness in my hide.

She took off her coat and began to move across my body, climbing gently up onto it as if it was a tilting boat. I could smell her cigarette and chewing gum to hide it. It reminded me of school; it also reminded me that I was an older man wearing a younger girl's skin. Her knees began to walk my back, tentatively digging into any resistance it found there.

She asked me again if I was alright, I nodded this time. I was used to being at someone else's mercy; I was well-schooled in it.

Eventually she got off and asked me to turn over. As I rolled onto my back I saw her take off her bikini, facing towards the door, away from me. Then she turned and I saw her nakedness. Her body was brown and her breasts small. She didn't say anything but moved slowly towards me, her hips swaying slightly.

I saw so many things in that young girl's nakedness, as she stood before me. I felt the jaws of the world close around me like a dog that has found a bone. I heard the baying voices of my childhood, the ones that told me I was no good, the ones that told me that I deserved everything that was happening to me.

'You okay, Baby Man?'

'Yes, fine.'

'Relax.'

'Yes, relax.'

'You want everything?'

'Yes, I want everything.'

'You want fuck?'

'Yes, I want fuck . . . Cookie . . . I want fuck.'

She was astride me slowly bringing me to orgasm, her hands moving down to play with my nipples, her fingers slowly circling them, tweaking them. Yes, her body was young and for the next few minutes it was mine. I looked at her as she lifted her head back and closed her eyes. I saw the long graceful sweep of her neck and the small gulp in her throat. I tried to fool myself that it meant something, that I was the stranger that she had been waiting for, the one that would change everything for her, but I knew that she couldn't give a fuck, literally. Now and then she threw a look my way, and nodded her head as if to say, you're doing well. She reinforced it by bending down slightly and running her hands along the sides of my body. Everything she did had a practised sensuality to it, seamless, full of purrs and coos. I didn't think of you, I didn't even think of me. I thought of nothing, you see, it entered me and swallowed me whole.

The Gift

We have a chance, you said to me. We have a gift from God. He is beautiful and he has your eyes, you said. Let's begin again. Stop the visits to the bar after work and come home to us, your son and me. I remember nodding like a twelve-year-old who had just been reprimanded. Yes, I said, I would like that, yes. You are a teacher, you said, be one, act like one, show yourself and your family the way. I remember listening to you and how the tears rose to sit in my eyes. You placed your hands on mine and smiled and for a moment all the pain and all the filth of my past fell away from me. It was the closest I ever came to telling you. I could feel the dark truth of what he did to me begin to move through my body and rise to sit on my tongue. Maybe if I'd said something then as we sat in the garden beneath the canopy of autumn leaves, things would have been different. But I didn't, you see he had told me not to, he had made me promise deep in the belly of the night when the rest of the world was asleep. You talked of when we had first met, of the young man who spoke with the bright fire of a poet. I was kind, I was generous and I had love, you said, such love to give not only to you but to the world. You told me you wanted that young man again. He still exists, you said, I am sure of it and you smiled and for a moment I believed.

That night we celebrated and you did your best not to notice how much I drank as we ate our meal in our favourite Italian restaurant. We talked of the future and the fine life our son would have. I did as you asked me to, I acted. I pretended that the world was suddenly mine and yours again. I humoured you and nodded when I thought it appropriate and smiled when you made a joke or told me you loved me. I tried, I really did, but I still wore the perfume of the brothel, it smelled of shame and sex. You suggested that we go home and light some candles and make love in the shadows they threw against the walls of our bedroom. I nodded but somewhere I knew that our time had gone.

The next day you woke and looked at me and the disappointment had returned to your gaze. We hadn't made love the night before, we had barely touched when I had got up and made my way downstairs to open a bottle of wine to find the touch that I knew lived there. I am sorry but you see my heart was only strong enough for one. Your mother called round and you both found me passed out on the couch in the living room. When you tried to wake me, I said that I had no need of you. I don't remember saying it, but then again I don't remember you trying to waken me.

Peter

He was his pipe. It defined him, it was an extension of the measured, watchful way he approached life. He would stand there and pack its bowl and ask me how I was doing, his eyes squinting as he lifted the moist, peaty tobacco from the battered tin he carried and placed it in his pipe. I would watch as his fingers prodded and padded before he lifted the stem to his mouth and began to light it. No words would pass between us as he did this; I knew better than to interrupt his ritual. I would watch him pull on the pipe, his cheeks being sucked in and out as he tugged. His eyes would close as the small knots of smoke began to rise. He would then take the pipe away from his mouth and regard it, as if he was seeing it for the first time and then gingerly pack the glowing embers at the top of the bowl down a little deeper, and place the pipe back in his mouth. When I was very young it impressed me, how he would stand there and take the time he needed, as if to say the world can wait until I have this thing going. As I got older I began to resent it, and I would quietly shift my weight from one foot to the other as I waited for him to get through his routine. He was my mother's self-appointed guardian and somewhere I know that she welcomed it, was flattered by it although she always had one eye on the watching God in the skies. They both attended a monthly prayer meeting together. He considered himself a proper man, a man of principle and fortitude. He viewed the world and its events with dispassion and quiet resignation. He was strong, you could tell from the way he carried himself, with a slow, studied amble. He had a short thick neck and hard, tight shoulders and he was bald except for two wiry tufts of hair that stood up on either side of his head. He had removed himself from the real business of life, he had his pipe and his ways, but he never read a newspaper or watched the news, what's the point, he would say, it's all going one way, and that's down. Jesus was his news; he gave him all he needed to know, he would say, He's the biggest newspaper of them all. Then he would laugh, it was more of a wheeze, full of old smoke and burnt tobacco.

He told me he had boxed when he was young and he said that all the fight had been beaten out of him. He loved to tell me of one bout when, for the first time in his life, he met someone who had the measure of him.

'Up until then I'd battered anything put in my way . . . I'd let the fists fly and not stop until the fella in front of me went down . . . And if he was stupid enough to get up Bang . . . Bang . . . Bang . . . Not that fighting solves anything . . . But like anything else there's a science to it. For a while there when I was a kid I believed I was it . . . You know, Ali, Foreman, all that gang . . .'

'Right.'

'Aye, this night anyroad I was in with a young buck and he had a tight guard . . . watertight . . . I think I got one good look at him all night and that was when I was flat out on the canvas looking back up at him. I'd gone in all guns blazing like some mad thing . . . Boom . . . Boom . . . Nothing, not a thing. He was as sealed as a tortoise shuffling here and shuffling there. The more he hid the more I looked for him and the more I slackened. Everything went to pot, my breathing . . . my stance . . . my power . . . I think it was round five about a minute from the bell when suddenly he hit me with this combination. His hands were so fast I'm still not sure if he threw them. All I know is one minute there I am banging away like a good 'un and the next the ref's standing over me giving that look . . . You know, are you still with us? To this day I'm effed if I know what that fella did. I tried to get up but the legs didn't want to know, and the brain had gone to mush. It was then I knew there's cleverer bastards out there than us. There's bigger and there's smarter. It's like life, you just don't see it coming . . . You never see it coming . . . Best you can do is keep the old snout clean and mind your own . . . How's the old lady?'

'She's fine, Peter.'

'Good. Hell of a woman. Hell of a gift she has . . .'

It was always the same with him. He would tell a long tale of daring-do from his youth, itching for the moment when he could enquire about my mother.

'How's the boss?'

'Who?'

'The old fella.'

'Aye . . . Alright.'

'Good . . . Good.'

'Does God see everything, Peter?'

I remember he looked at me when I asked him this, for what seemed an eternity, smoke rising up his face like long grey fingers.

'Every damned action and every damned thought,' he said.

'Right.'

'What's on your mind, son?'

'Nothing.'

'God is here, son, it's only a matter of opening your eyes.'

'I can't see Him, Peter . . . I've opened my eyes . . . And I can't see Him.'

'See these, son?'

He held his fists up to me until they were inches from my face; I saw the knuckles, and the scars.

'Yes.'

'On their own they're no good. Just weapons. I learned that the hard way. Left to my own devices I'll misuse these feckers. I'll start a war in a paper bag. I had to learn to lie Jesus across them, son. To put Him between me and them. That's what I learned in that ring. No bugger can do this life on his own. He'll get seven kinds of shit kicked out of him every time. After that fight I spent a long time just looking into my heart asking myself what I wanted. And everywhere I looked I saw the same thing. People throwing punches. Catholic at Protestant. Protestant at Catholic. Mother at daughter. Father at son . . . You know?'

'I think so . . .'

'Jesus came to me, son.'

'Yeah?'

'As surely as there's breath in these old lungs of mine.'

'When?'

'At night. You know when the fear sits across a man's heart. I was in the bed and I had a compulsion. An urge to get up and drop to my knees and pray. Unknown for someone like me. Always said no, you can keep religion, it's messed the whole show up in this country of ours. But . . . it was as if a voice was working my thoughts. Had no choice, son. So up I leap . . . And onto the knees . . . And for some reason I didn't join my hands. No, something told me to make fists with them. So I hold them out. And the voice says . . . Christ says . . . the living Christ says . . . Those scars are mine . . . Those fists are mine and they are to do my work. It was powerful, son. I haven't struck a man in anger since.'

I remember how he closed his eyes as he lost himself to the memory of it and I stood awkwardly waiting for him to come back to me. He loved my mother, I knew that, my father knew that too and he would often tell me that the moment would come when Petey would have to raise his fists once more because he had him marked. My mother would never have done anything to hurt my father, but I know now that a woman doesn't have to sleep with a man to make him her own. They met in secret, attended prayer meetings together, and my mother would always fudge the issue if my father asked her if she had seen Petey. They behaved as if they were lovers even though they weren't. I felt sorry for them; I knew that in a different world, beneath different skies, it would have been different.

The Lacewing

'Aren't they magnificent?' she said.

'Yes, Mother.'

'Truly God's own children like us, Gabriel . . . Just like us. Praise them, Gabriel . . . Praise them, son . . . Just like they praise us with their presence.'

'I do, Mother.'

'Say it with me, Gabriel. . . . I praise you, Lord, and your golden children . . . I praise you.'

I remember how hot it had been in the place where they were kept, how the heat stuck my hair to my neck and brought me out in a prickly sweat. I grabbed her hand. I wanted her to stop, to tell her I was feeling uncomfortable, that I felt sick.

'Say it with me, son . . . Let's hold Jesus to our hearts in the presence of these His finest creations.'

'Mum . . . I . . .'

A couple on the other side of the butterfly sanctuary had stopped briefly and stared as she grappled with me, trying to get me to kneel. I knew that they were thinking about saying something, I could see it in their eyes. I looked at my mother on her knees in front of me, her hair wild and unkempt.

'Please,' I remember saying quietly. 'Please.'

'Don't turn away from the holy heart of Jesus . . . Don't betray Him as so many have done.'

I looked back to the couple. The woman now had a child at

her side; it was a girl of my age, and roughly my height. She was looking at me; there was pity in her eyes.

Eventually I knelt, my mother's hand on mine as tight as a vice's grip. I conceded as I did so many times with her, I laid my heart at her door, and told her I no longer had need of it.

'I praise you, Lord . . . I praise you, Jesus . . .' I remember saying the words, forcing them from my lips.

'Good boy. Good boy . . .'

I remember looking at the butterflies as they moved from plant to plant. Some were the colour of a lion's back, tawny and speckled with gold. Others were the brightest, deepest green I had ever seen, with garish yellow dots. Some were as big as a man's palm and they moved slowly, their wings bearing them unsteadily from one large leaf to the next. They looked as if they had been hypnotised, fooled into accepting the glass cage that they were in. They reminded me of my home, a hothouse seething with heat and fervour. I felt sorry for them, they seemed tamed, and captivity had made them stupid and lethargic.

On our way out we stopped in the gift shop. My mother bought me a butterfly kite. It was a Malaysian Lacewing and its wings were a clash of reds and yellows, they looked as if they had been drenched in the hot fires of the sun and there were fine white lace markings on their edges.

All the way home I turned its large wings in my hands, marvelling at its colours. It cast a spell on me that day and all the embarrassment of the praying and the kneeling were forgotten as I held it in my trembling hands. I read the leaflet that came with it, my young mind devouring every word. I read how the butterfly could be seen in Indonesia and Malaysia, I remember turning the words silently on my tongue, tasting the hot continents they spoke of. I read about their fragile lives, and how the cost of the glorious garments they wore was two short weeks of life. My mother smiled over at me as I fumbled with the packaging.

'We'll fly it together,' she said.

'Okay. God is good, Mother,' I continued.

'Yes, son, God is good . . . Never forget that.'

I remember looking across at her and wondering at how quickly my heart could change, only moments before I had hated her and now I looked at her with love, pure and as varied as the wings of the large butterfly I was holding.

Standing in the Mouth of Love

My brother-in-law loved my sister. That was clear. He was her minder, her strong arm. She often told me that she didn't know where she would be without him, that he was the still point in her heart. Ciara didn't lack confidence, she had a bloody-mindedness that I recognised in myself, but Seamus gave her the quiet surety that I know she had been looking for all her life. He wasn't a tall man, but had a presence that belied his height. He didn't say much but when he did people tended to listen. They had met at a local dance when she was a young woman of nineteen or twenty. At first she had dismissed him as just another local, a hard man without a cause. He had asked her to dance with him and she refused and kept denying him for the next month, but he persevered, telling me later that the first time he had seen her he knew that she would be his wife. I remember being jealous when he told me this, I wasn't sure why, but now I know. It was because somehow I believed that she was mine.

I envied him his strength. I wanted it for myself. He could see that in me, always looking at me as if I had a part missing and I suppose he was right. In the early days they both included my wife and me in what they were doing. We went on short trips together, shopped together. But I could always feel him watching me in quieter moments when the conversation lulled or when the others were preoccupied with other things. For a long time I resisted looking him directly in the eye. When I did summon the courage to meet his eyes I saw that he had a hold on me, that he knew something, it was apparent in the slight smirk that lay across his gaze.

It reminded me of the way my father used to look at me, that same penetrating stare that said, I have your number, I have you marked. I knew that there would be trouble between Seamus and me, but then again trouble was something that I was accustomed to.

He was bright though he was at pains not to show it, he had more success that way, he could surprise people, but he didn't fool me. I knew his game. He worked with brass, fitting out bars and clubs in the area. He had a small foundry just outside the town and worked there five or six days a week. The business was his; he had started it with a friend and then bought him out when they fell out over money. It did reasonably well, but he said that he would rather be his own boss than work for some idiot and earn twice the money. He could do what he wanted, think what he wanted, you can't fucking buy that, he would say to me. When he'd had a bit to drink, he said that working with brass was just like life, that there was a mould for everything, we could be anything, we could go anywhere but you couldn't buck the mould, the shape that your heart had to fill. That's how he had wooed my sister, I remember thinking, with talk of shapes and hearts and the moulds that house our souls.

He was legendary for his obstinacy. He had received a visit from some hard men shortly after he had taken over sole ownership of his business. The ceasefire hadn't been long in place, and the violence that had gripped the province for so long had mutated into a different kind of threat. Self-appointed vigilantes sprang up like weeds across a wasteland. Gangs of youths roamed the dark, armed with baseball bats and chains, telling anyone who would listen that they had been appointed by the powers that be to keep the peace. As always there was a price, usually a weekly payment made in used readies into one of their grubby little paws. Seamus said that one day he had been pouring molten brass all morning, as he had a rush order to get out, so he wasn't as aware as he should have been, he was distracted and hadn't noticed them creep into his workspace until they were almost upon him. They were young, no more than nineteen or twenty and there were about six or seven of them, and they were wearing scarves across the bottom halves of their faces, you know, like the fucking Lone Ranger, he said. He looked up and there they were, like starving dogs with that same desperation in their eyes. He knew it was important to stay calm, and that probably the leader would not be the one who spoke first, but the one who was the quietest, they're always the most dangerous. So one of the little runts begins yapping about the price of keeping the peace and that they were attached to such and such unit of such and such brigade of the fight for Ireland's freedom and all that bollocks. There was a price to pay for this new dawn, he was told, a weekly stipend, to be collected by them. Seamus said he didn't say anything; he just listened and nodded, scanning the eyes of the others to try and find the one he knew he would have to bring down. He said he knew him as soon as he saw him: he was standing at the back of the pack and he was slightly taller than the rest and he quietly nodded as his colleague delivered the speech about freedom and money.

'Fuck's sake, boys, I have fuck all money here. I'm behind on my orders. I'm owed money . . .'

'When can you get it?'

This time it was the tall one at the back who spoke, and Seamus knew he had been right.

'I can have it for you tomorrow evening.'

'What time?'

'About six.'

'We'll be back at six tomorrow evening,' the tall one said.

Then he made a motion with his head, indicating that the rest of them should leave. As they did the tall one moved towards Seamus and said, 'Don't fuck us around.'

'Wouldn't do that, son. Wouldn't do that.'

'Good.'

That night Seamus made two phone calls. The first one was to a friend of his who was connected. He checked that these kids were who they said they were. Never heard of them, his friend said. Right you are, Seamus replied. The second call was to a mate of his who was a bouncer at a local dance hall. He had a face that even his own mother wouldn't kiss, Seamus said. He told him what had happened and that he needed his help the next evening. His mate was called Bulldog mainly because he looked like one and he had the neck to go with it. Do you need any more bodies? he asked Seamus. No, just yourself, Bulldog, just yourself. I need you there at five.

There was a small hall at the front of Seamus's foundry with two doors, one opening out onto the yard outside and the other opening into the workspace. Above in the ceiling there was a small roof space cover, the kind you give a slight push to and slide on and off. That's where he put Bulldog, crouching up there in the dark, his large body scrunched over, his fists poised. Both doors had strong brass pull-across bolts on them and when the bandits arrived Seamus was sure not to glance upwards as they moved past him.

He watched as they filed into the work area, the tall one as usual at the back, a baseball bat dangling from one of his arms. As Seamus joined them the tall one looked at him and said: 'So?'

'Aye.'

'Good.'

Seamus reached into his pocket and counted out the notes into the young man's palm. The others gathered around them as he did this like orphans in a soup kitchen at feeding time.

'Right. Knew you had sense,' the young one said as he pocketed the cash.

'Who wants any more trouble. We're all sick of it,' Seamus said.

'That's why we are here,' the youth said.

Seamus said it was laughable the way he said it, as if he was in some daft American movie. He said he wanted to rip his face off, but he knew he had to play the stupid older man, make use of his smallness by standing close to him so that the kid would feel empowered by his greater height.

'Next week?'

'Right you are. Next week, son . . .'

'Good man. Let's go.'

Seamus watched as they began to file out, the leader waiting until the end before starting to leave. He stayed on his shoulder and moved with him towards the front door. As the others cleared the threshold Seamus waited until the tall one was about to leave and said: 'You're Owen McCarthy's son, aren't you?'

He said it was comical the way the kid swivelled on his heels to meet his gaze, the look of surprise in his eyes was powerful. Before he knew it Seamus had bolted the front door, trapping him one way and at the same time Bulldog had dropped from the attic, like a stone of doom was how Seamus put it, and had locked the other door leading back into the workspace. He was trapped both ways. His mates were on the outside looking in, and he was inside about to have his skin rearranged.

'Let's talk fucking freedom now, son,' Seamus said.

They took back the money and kicked him all over the fucking place, bouncing him off the walls like he was a child's football. Seamus said you could have heard his screams in Fermanagh they were that loud. When they had finished, Bulldog picked up the youth's baseball bat and smashed it to smithereens on the concrete floor. Then they hauled him to his feet and delivered him to his friends outside. They didn't say much, they looked kind of sheepish as they took him from the two men.

'One more thing,' Seamus said as they walked away. 'My fucking generation invented violence, son. Don't ever forget that.'

The Room at the End of the World

I am being led. I no longer think about resisting them, the drugs they have given me have seen to that. My mind swims with the images that I know have broken me. I realise that my salvation now lies with them. I no longer have any choice in what happens to me. Somewhere I welcome it. I am weary. There are two of them and their hands are clutching my arms so that I don't go anywhere. A man walks ahead of us; he is wearing a suit and now and then throws glances back our way. We reach a door at the end of the corridor.

It is reinforced with steel slats that run all down its sides and there is a codelock on it. Beyond is a small holding area that connects to another door. Both have tiny windows in them. The suited man punches a code on the buttons beneath the door handle, and after a moment I hear a click and the door snaps open. He pulls it wide and beckons to the two men holding me to place me inside. I step into the small space between the two doors and watch as they shut me in. One of them raises his hand and makes a gesture as if to say it's okay, you're okay. I nod back and see them retreat down the corridor. After a moment I walk to the other door and try it. I don't expect it to be open, and it's not. A voice inside me laughs and says, so this is it, this is what has become of you.

Now and then someone comes and peers through one of the windows at me. They look at me dispassionately as if I was a specimen in a Petri dish. I mustn't panic. I must stay calm. My sweats are beginning again. I try and remember what the doctor had said to me, she had said that they were just episodes, that they would come and go and that my mind needed rest, that's all. I slide down to sit on the floor. My brain is racing. I try to ignore it and breathe deeply. Then I wonder if anyone will come and save me, then I realise that they won't, that's why they have put me in this room at the end of the world.

The First Man

I am lying on the living room floor of my house, willing my eyes to open. A vicious headache sears across my thinking. My mouth is dry and my hair stuck with sweat. I try to remember the events of the night before but all I see is the taunt of my father's walk. He moved as if it was a challenge to the watching world.

It is the first thing I remember, it's the image I always see when nothing else will come, and sometimes it forces its way through like a jilted lover breaking down his ex's door. He is by a river; I hear its throaty rush, swollen from the spring floods. I see his bare midriff, blue-pink from the cold, his braces hoisting the waistband of his trousers high across his belly. I hear his snorts in the cold morning air, as he looks for a place to wade in. In his left hand is the carcass of a freshly killed rabbit, its head nodding lifelessly against his legs. I see him take on the water, pushing his body against the current, until he is almost thigh deep in it. He looks like a prophet, his head proudly tilted towards the heavens, his eyes fixed on some better place. He dips the rabbit into the water and then produces a long thin knife from his pocket. He holds the rabbit up to look at it one more time and then plunges the knife into it just below its sternum and draws it down its body, leaving a crimson line. I can see the gum-coloured entrails peeping out. He then shoves his hand inside and pulls at the shit and the intestines, ripping them free. I see them squelch and squirm in his grip, he then lets them drop and they are taken by the current.

The hide is next; he strips it from the body and then begins to pull it free. The rabbit is now unrecognisable, its furry bobtail look gone forever, in its place a long veined mass of sinew. Its eyes are large black opals, shiny and unseeing. Then he douses both himself and the rabbit, tilting his body forward so that his head and neck disappear into the swirling current. I remember the slight panic that ran through me the first time that I saw him do it, but then both he and the carcass would reappear, the water falling from them both, his large head shaking it free from his hair and his neck.

'Bring that in to your mother,' he would say, handing me the rabbit.

Then he would piss in the water, taking his dick out and watch as the yellow liquid arced into the river's rush. He would grunt with relief, and his shoulders would drop as he relaxed. I knew that sound; it usually lived in the dead of night when the world was asleep, when his hands took another piece of goodness from my hide. I remember looking away, forgetting about his order to bring the rabbit indoors, my body quivering as the last drops of piss left his body. Then he noticed I was still there and quickly zipped himself back in, his face bloodying with anger.

'What the fuck is wrong with you? Are you bloody perverted or something?'

'No, Dad.'

'Then do what I told you to do.'

'Yes, Dad.'

Later that morning he punched my mother. It was so swift like a striking snake and suddenly my mother was flat on her backside, blood spreading across her chin, her eyes glazing over from the force of the blow. They had been arguing, or rather my mother had been trying to argue, my father just ignored her. We had crept to the doorway of the kitchen, my sister and I holding on to each other's bodies. We watched as the scene unfolded, my mother criss-crossing back and forth across the kitchen after my father, hectoring and badgering him. I remember the slight flinch in his face as she shouted and postured around him. It was about money or the lack of it and the fact that my father had only just returned home clutching the skinned rabbit, having been missing all night.

The hills beyond the kitchen glowed with the beginning light of day. Neither parent saw us lurking in the shadows of the doorway. My mother said my father smelled of another woman, she said he was disgusting like all Irish men, a waste of time and space, and then he just turned and unleashed his fist, driving my mother's body across the kitchen floor, her nose busted, and her eyes wide with surprise. For a moment I thought that she was going to laugh, her mouth made the shape, but then it turned downwards like a doll's face being eaten by fire. My sister pissed herself. I looked down and could see it pooling on the floor between her legs. It spread to my feet and then a trickle began to work its way into the centre of the room.

To this day my sister will query the events of that morning; she buried it deep inside of her, like so many things in her life. When I have pushed her, she only pays lip service to it, leaving the meat of what happened on that kitchen floor where her piss mingled with our mother's blood. For me that morning is a brand seared on the flesh of my heart. I carry it with me. I wear it. I honour it. I drink myself sick to it. It tells me that the only prayer that works is violence. That one action, my father's fist on my mother's face that one moment sits like a lion in the jungle of my thinking.

Pieces of the Day

My eyes are asking them to tell me even though I don't really want to know. I'm afraid. I can see that it's bad because they are looking through me, not engaging with me. I turn my head away from them and begin to cry because I realise that I have nothing left to pray to. My face hurts, it stings and I wish I was dead. I am in hospital, I have no idea how I got here, or why I feel this shame, it sits on me like a curse. I can taste it. My brother-in-law asks me how I feel but I don't answer him, my sister looks away. A nurse bends over me and tinkers with the bedcovers, I think she's embarrassed. I put a hand to my face and can feel the long thin scabs running down my cheek. A man comes in and stands for a moment, looking at me; I can't read what he's thinking so I know that he must be a doctor.

'How are you feeling?' he asks me.

I look at him but don't answer.

'The police are here. They've been waiting for you to come round.'

Still I don't say anything. He bends down so that he's within touching distance of my face.

'Listen to me. You need help. At the moment we have you on Librium to keep you calm, but you can't go on like this.'

He looks to my brother-in-law as if to say it is his turn to speak.

'She says she's going to press charges.'

'Why?'

'What do you mean why? You fucking bounced her off every wall in the house.'

'Seamus,' my sister says. 'Losing it is not going to help anything.'

I close my eyes and her face is there, her eyes widened in terror, her mouth open and screaming. I shudder because I know as the day goes on the image will grow and that snatches of the previous night will shoot into my consciousness like sparks from a bonfire.

'She says you raped her.'

'Fuck off,' I say.

'No, you fuck off. What the fuck is wrong with you?'

As he says this my brother-in-law lunges at me, my sister grabs him and the doctor stands up, blocking his route to me. They calm him down. I watch as they put their hands on him and soothe him. He leaves the room, he doesn't look at me. My sister comes and sits on the edge of the bed.

'This is what we're going to do,' she says. 'We're going to talk to the police and tell them everything . . . everything we can remember, after that there is someone else who wants to talk to you, who could maybe help you. He runs a place just outside Dublin where they can help people like you. You can't keep this up, Gabriel, it's tearing us apart . . . Then you can sleep.'

'I don't want to talk to anyone,' I say.

'Gabriel, this is not a playground where someone has grazed their knee or tripped over a ball. This is grown-up serious stuff. We're all worried sick about you. Seamus is at his wits' end, he loves you, we all do . . . but this can't go on.'

She stops suddenly and for a moment just sits there gulping quickly as she tries to stop herself from crying. I watch the battle in her and admire her for her strength, always the strong one, always the pragmatist. When I was younger I used to marvel at how she sewed together the threads of her life, how she marshalled her children and steered her husband's every move. Nothing was a problem; all were only solutions waiting to happen. I often joked with her that we couldn't have come from the same womb. She didn't seem to have the same echo of defeat running through her brain that I had. I reach out to take her hand, and for a moment I can see her debate whether to take it or not, but in the end she does.

'I just want to sleep,' I say. 'Sleep.'

'First we have things to do. People to talk to. Gabriel . . . Gabriel . . .'

I open my eyes. For a moment I try and remember where I am. I look at my sister and realise. She still has that look in her eye, the one that said trouble.

'The police are here to see you.'

I think about my father and the curse he slipped to me one day when I wasn't looking. He hid it in my mother's milk and watched as I downed it in one greedy gulp. I wonder at the insanity, at the violence that sits brooding in me like a spurned lover. I know that I have nowhere left to go, that I have backed myself into a corner, and that I stand on a cliff edge and below me is the black sea where the lost fall, never to be seen again.

'Gabriel O'Rourke?'

'Yes.'

'Gabriel O'Rourke of Temple Avenue?'

'Yes?'

'I need a statement from you, sir, concerning the events of yesterday evening.'

There's pity in his eyes and a faint glint of disgust, but he is doing his best to hide it. I shift in the bed, my sister lowers her head, and the doctor quietly leaves, nodding in my direction as he does.

'You don't like me, do you?'

'It makes no difference what I think, sir. I'm here to take your statement, I already have your wife's.'

'She lies.'

He takes his cap off and places it on the bed beside me and runs a hand across his forehead. I can see the line where his flesh has been dug into. He is balding and what's left of his hair is the colour of straw. He looks at me and waits.

'Talk to him, Gabriel. It's for the best,' my sister says.

I tell him what I can, I describe the screaming and pushing, I talk about the anger rising in me and about the hate I felt for her, but no, I didn't rape her, she's my wife, for God's sake, how can a man rape his own wife. He tells me that doesn't make any difference, that sex between two adults has to be consensual, married or unmarried. When he tells me this he talks to me as if I am a child. He also says that my wife believes that I have some kind of personality disorder, that she was genuinely worried about my sanity. This stops me and I feel a burning begin inside me, I feel it start in my gut and it begins to spread until it has me by the throat. He asks me if I'm alright, but I can't answer him. I feel the tears begin to fall; they rush down my face. I want to tell him about the blackness that surrounds my thinking, how it eats into any image my heart offers to my mind.

My head feels heavy. He asks me again if I'm okay and this time gestures to my sister. A sound comes from my mouth, a grunt of defeat. I curl up in the bed, pulling the bedclothes to me like a beaten child, my knees up by my chin. The cop stands and for a moment hesitates, unsure how to react or what to say. Suddenly the doctor is there, I can make out the white coat and the glisten of sweat on his face. Something is stuck into my arm, it stings and for a moment I try to fight it but then a wave of soothing washes over me and I am lowered down to sleep.

'Son?'

'Yes, Daddy?'

'Has Ciara been talking to you?'
'What do you mean?'
'You know what I mean.'
'I . . .'
'It's alright, son . . . It's alright.'
'A little bit.'
'A little bit?'
'Yes . . . A little bit . . .'
'Well she mustn't do that . . .'

The Shifting of the Earth

The principal is a tidy man. He is known for it. He regularly holds inspection parades in the classrooms, surprising the students, checking them over for hair length, nail chewing and any other lapses that show a boy of weak disposition. He will lecture any culprit in full view of his classmates and recommend detention; the days of beatings are long gone, but I know given the choice which one he would plump for. His name is Jarlath Boyle and he walks as if he is always on his way to some emergency, briskly and with barely concealed panic. He has never been sure of me, I know that, it's something I live with, but if the truth be told it's something I take quiet satisfaction from. Flaky is a word he loves to use when something or someone is not up to his rigorous standards. Another is loose, the world is loose and loosening further by the minute and it is our duty is ensure a general all-round tightening. Often he looks at me when he says this, holding my eyes longer than he does anyone else's. The other teachers on the staff have him read, have him sussed, but I hate games. They tell me I should be more careful, that he has me in his sights, but like so many things it passes me by like an aircraft screaming off to some foreign clime. He dresses neatly, he says it is a reflection of a man's mind, the outer links the inner is another of his catchphrases. I know he is stalking me, waiting for me to fall, to trip over the long leash of my arrogance.

I know I'm good at what I do and that the kids find me interesting and unconventional, not moored in the dry dust of academia and syntax as some of my colleagues are. I spend time getting to know their interests, the passions they have. I consider some of them my friends; I like their eager minds and unstained hearts. They confide in me, they tell me of other teachers' methods and the way some of them bully them into learning. This is nothing new to me; I know for example that Mr Farrell the tall County Clare man will stand over a boy breathing threats into his ear until he breaks down in tears. I have often thought of calling him on it, of telling him I find his methods repulsive, but that's the one thing a teacher must never do, pull his colleague up on his ways of schooling.

I saw it for myself once. I was passing his classroom one day on my way to the staff room when I heard a boy cry out. It stopped me dead in my tracks and brought a cold shiver to the back of my neck. There was something about the sound the boy made that opened something deep within me. So I stood in Mr Farrell's doorway looking at a scene that had been described to me many times: a young student smothered by the large brooding presence of an older man, his face inches from the boy's, his large head bobbing imperceptibly as his lips issued their threats. I saw the redness in the student's face, which I recognised as McKillen, I saw the humiliation, and my blood began to boil. I decided to try charm and coax the big man away from the kid, without alerting either the teacher or the boys in the classroom.

'Mr Farrell.'

I watched as the man's head froze and turned slightly in my direction, and then he said without looking directly at me: 'Mr O'Rourke?'

'Forgive me for interrupting, but I wonder if I could borrow one of your students for a moment.'

He straightened himself and turned to face me, a slight look of puzzlement on his face.

'Which one?'

'Er . . . Pettigrew . . .'

'Pettigrew?'

'Yes, I just need to remind him of something. Something I didn't get to tell him in class this morning.'

His face briefly darkened and for a moment I thought he was going to challenge me. He took a step forward, and raised his hands palm upwards as if to say what is this all about? He was caught and he knew it.

'Pettigrew?'

'Yes, sir?'

'Mr O'Rourke beckons.'

'Yes, sir.'

I watched Farrell as Pettigrew came to join me in the doorway. He seemed at a loss. I could see him thinking about turning back to McKillen, the boy he had been terrorising, but then thought better of it and strode to his desk and sat, his long limbs sticking out from its sides. He looked like a long insect that had just settled unsteadily on a large summer leaf. He was pissed off with me I could tell. I took Pettigrew outside into the corridor beyond the jamb of the door. In my mind I could still hear that cry, although I wasn't sure if it was from me or from McKillen's lips.

'What's going on in there, Pettigrew?'

'Sir?'

'With that long streak of piss?'

'Sir?'

'With Farrell?'

'McKillen didn't know what x was worth, sir.'

'What?'

'He hadn't done his equations.'

'His homework?'

'Yes, sir.'

'Tell him to do it from now on.'

'Sir.'

'Good.'

'What did you want to see me for, sir?'

'That was it, Pettigrew . . . I've said it.'

'Right, sir.'

'Now go on, get back in there. And if Mr Farrell asks you what I wanted tell him that I've given you extra homework for being late this morning.'

'But I wasn't late this morning.'

'What?'

'I wasn't late, sir.'

'Pettigrew, have you got rocks for brains? Pretend you were, for the sake of McKillen, for the sake of all of us.'

'Yes, sir.

'Goodbye, Pettigrew.'

'Sir.'

As Pettigrew rejoined the class I popped my head around the door and thanked Farrell. He nodded and said any time though I knew he didn't mean it. McKillen looked at me with what I could only describe as pure love in his eyes. As I walked away something stirred in me, like a small shift of earth after a rainfall. It was the cry that McKillen made. I hated bullies but then again bullying was something that wasn't beyond me either. I remember that night I got drunk. I blamed Farrell for it, but then that wasn't a hard thing to do, I had been programmed to blame.

Fishing

I remember once my father took me fishing. He told my mother to make some sandwiches and a flask of tea. I was in the field opposite the house enjoying the warm tumble of one day into the other, as school had broken for summer. I saw him standing in front of the house and when he saw me he didn't say anything, he just held his hand out at me as if I was a troublesome motorist that a traffic cop had just pulled over. I stopped what I was doing immediately, dropping the sticks I had been collecting to build a fort further along the fields where the river met the earth and swelled into a large pool.

I waited for him to speak, squinting in the sunlight, careful even at that distance not to make any sudden movements.

'Dig some worms,' he said.

I didn't hear him properly and knew not to ask him to repeat what he had just said. So I just waited stock still, rigid with attention that I knew he expected every time he spoke to one of us.

'I said dig some worms. We're going fishing in the morning.'

And with that he turned and went back into the house leaving my mother looking over at me. She made a gesture with her hands as if she was apologising for something.

That evening he asked to see the worms I had gathered. We were kneeling together in the garden. I could feel his heavy breath on my neck as I stooped down to rake through the dirt in the bucket exposing them for his approval.

'Give me that,' he said.

He dug his fist into the black soil pulling out the worms, holding them aloft in the dying light as if he was a jeweller appraising a batch of diamonds. I saw them wriggling in his grip, lengthening and coiling around his fingers.

'Not bad,' he said. 'There's a couple of scraggy fuckers but they'll do.'

Then he looked at me and nodded, and I felt my face reddening.

'The purple-headed ones are the best,' he said. 'The fish love them.'

'Right,' I said.

'Good,' he said and threw them back into the bucket. 'Put a drop of water on them tonight to keep them moist and a bit more earth, do you hear?'

'Yes, Dad.'

'And no fucking about in the morning. Out the door at six.'

'Okay.'

'Okay? What sort of a fucking word is that?'

'Sorry, Dad.'

'Fucking Yanks have ruined everything. There's no need for lazy language.'

'Yes, Dad.'

The next morning we set off for the lake. Mist sat like a fine quilted web over the fields. Birds swooped in and out of light and shadow beginning their day with calls and somersaults in the air. We drove in silence, the windscreen smattered with the remains of flies and gnats, their squashed bodies smeared across its surface.

At one point a rabbit hopped out into the middle of the road and my father stood on the brakes for a moment before saying 'Fuck it' and stepping on the accelerator. I remember the countdown of the moments as I waited to hear the thud of the rabbit's body beneath the car. I was relieved to see its tail flash goodbye as it cleared the far hedge seconds later.

By the time we reached the lake the sunlight had broken the back of the hills that bordered it, and the mist had melted away. My dad stood and looked at the sky for a moment as I got the rods and tackle out of the back of the car.

'We could do with some cloud,' he said.

We walked across the fields to the lakeside, me slightly behind him as usual watching how he strode across the ground as if it belonged to him, cursing now and then if his Wellington got snagged in ragweed or a tangle of bramble.

I watched as his fat hands held the hook, I noticed they were shaking, the fishing line vibrating wildly as he tried to thread it through the hook's eye. He stopped and looked at me and shook his head. He didn't say anything but turned to gaze out across the water, its surface as pure as polished steel.

'You couldn't buy that, could you?'

'No, Dad.'

I wanted to tell him that he should thread the float onto the line first but hadn't the nerve. I knew that it was best to let him discover it for himself, I knew that I'd still get the blame but not as much.

'Fuck it,' he said when he realised. 'Hand me one of those floats. No, not that one, you moron, the other one. The thin one.'

I watched as this bear of a man crouched over the tackle, his shoulders rounded, his head buried in his chin. I saw the bulging of his muscles through his clothes, the powerful fuck-you body. I felt so puny in comparison, so weedy and girlish. I knew he'd wished for a stronger son, someone who could bounce others out of his way, someone who could take on the world and still have strength left for the fight at home.

As I stood and looked at him grapple with the fishing line I knew that his patience was ebbing from him so I began to inch my way to the water's edge to peer into the hidden world beneath.

'Where the fuck you going?'

'Nowhere.'

'Well come here and thread this bastard line. I have to take a piss.'

He shoved the rod at me and marched off to a bunch of reeds that lay in a clump behind us. I heard him grunt and mutter as he turned his back on me. Then when I looked over I saw him reach into his coat pocket and pull out a small bottle. He put it to his head and I saw his body relax for the first time that day as he took a swig. He then took his piss, whistling as he did so.

For the next two hours or so we fished, watching the bob of our floats on the water's surface as the sun rose like an angry tyrant beating its hot displeasure down on our heads.

'It's too fucking hot,' my father said at one point as if it was my fault.

As the morning wore on he no longer hid the bottle from me, and I knew that the day was taking a very different turn, one that would need me at my most vigilant. I took comfort in the water and its long calm shine, enjoying the bounce of the sunlight off it. I watched swallows coming in low, their wings working furiously as they grabbed quick sips, and then saw them climb again into the blueness of the sky.

Now and then I reeled in and checked the worm; once or twice I changed it, throwing the dead one into the water. I imagined it tumbling into the depths, its torn body wriggling and twisting down deeper into the darkness. I felt sorry for it, I felt strange that I did, it was only a worm.

'What's up?' my father asked.

'Nothing.'

'You look a bit puce in the face.'

'I'm okay . . . I mean . . . Sorry . . . Fine.'

'Come here.'

'I'm alright, Dad.'

'Come here when you're told. Come here.'

I remember how I picked my way across to him, stepping between reeds and small pools of stale water until I stood by him.

'Sit . . . Sit . . . Sit.'

He patted the grass beside him and I knew better than to hesitate more than I already had.

As I sat I felt the cold water seep through my jeans and run down the top of my legs. After a moment of us both looking out at the glinting water in front of us he put his arm around me. There was no life in it, it just lay across my shoulders like a large timber, and it was heavy and uncomfortable.

'Ah . . . It's all fucked, isn't it?'

'What is, Dad?'

'The whole fucking shooting match. Don't you think?'

He finished what was left in his bottle, burped loudly and threw it into the lake, then he drew me close to him, his large bicep tightening around the back of my neck, so that my face was buried in his chest. He smelled of old fish and chips and dried sweat.

'Trust no fucker. Man or fucking beast, do you hear?'

I muffled that I did. I could hear his heartbeat, it sounded steady and deep like the pounding of a large kitchen clock.

'Has your mammy been talking to you?' he asked.

'About what, Dad?'

'Oh you know. Me. Stuff like that?'

'No, Dad.'

'Good.'

I could feel his grip on me. I felt his breath; it was hot and heavy like the blast from an opened oven.

'You sure?'

'Yeah.'

'Yeah?'

'I mean yes.'

'What about Ciara?'

'Dad?'

'Has she said anything?'

I knew that I must answer quickly or that he would be onto me, but she had said something, the other night as we had lain in bed together listening in the dark as my father's rage shook the house. She had whispered it to me as we had held each other; she had told me that he had touched her in her private place.

'No, Dad.'

'Nothing. She's said nothing?'

'No.'

He let me go. I blinked as I sat back up and rubbed my eyes.

'Look at me,' he said.

His eyes had a faraway look as if he was watching something in the distance that he couldn't take his eyes from. They looked hard and flinty.

'You never knew your grandfather, did you?'

'No.'

'He was a hard bastard . . .'

He stopped. He searched his pockets; I knew he was looking for the bottle and that he'd forgotten that he finished it.

'Trust no fucker. That's all.'

He got up and gestured to the rods.

'Reel them in. Let's see what your mother has for breakfast.'

Clouds

How long have I been here staring into this man's eyes? I don't remember coming here, taking my place in front of him in this bare room, beneath the pale glow of the fluorescent strip-light. He can see my confusion because he suggests that I try and relax, to think positive thoughts. He tells me that I have been on a journey; that everyone has been worried about me. I can't hold his gaze when he says this. They obviously think that I'm well enough to be moved, but I still feel fragile and I recall the panic I felt in the small room they put me in only a little while before. He waits and then he begins talking again: he's listing the medication that I'm on and he's saying that I have been very sick and that they weren't sure if I would make it. I feel like telling him to fuck off but I know that's exactly what he wants me to do, that he will see that as a connection or some such bullshit.

I shift slightly in my seat and look at him. I think I frighten him because he stops talking and just stares at me. He then picks up a notepad that is by his feet and scribbles something in it. This annoys me, I feel like an animal in a zoo being monitored and noted. But I decide to smile at him, instead of showing my anger. This seems to unnerve him even more because he gets to his feet and goes to the door of the room we're in and knocks on it. After a moment it is opened and a young man sticks his head in. They whisper together, throwing me glances now and then. I like this even less and decide to make a sound to show my displeasure. They both stop and look at me as I growl at them. The young man who opened the door puts his forefinger to his mouth, but it doesn't make any difference, my growling has taken on a life of its own. It's a sound I have made many times before, it's one I learnt as I fell, it's the noise that clouds make when they collide.

The Stain

First the breathing, it fills the room. Then the hurried discard of clothing. I see his silhouette, it seems mountainous against the faint tablet of light coming from the window. I am peeping through the folds of the bedcovers. I pray for sleep, begging for it to pass over my eyes. I hear the snort he makes, like a bull staking territory. I watch as his shape bends slightly as his trousers drop. For a moment he stands there and then pulls a hand across his chest, scratching at the hair it finds there. I smell him; it is the smell of bars, of wet ashtrays, of piss and fading aftershave. My heart is pounding, my body frozen in fear; I am praying to a God I have no love for. I see him lurch towards the side of the bed, and hear him curse the darkness. I feel like vomiting. I gulp quickly, and still I implore heaven for sleep. His body makes the springs of the bed groan as he lies down beside me. Then his breathing again, it comes quick and fast now as if he has just run a race.

'No, Daddy . . . Please, no . . . Please . . . No . . . No . . .'

His hands are on my young skin, touch, dig, grab, on they come. Nipple and cock, balls and hair and the smell of man, the worst of man, it moves across me. I feel my softness respond, hardening against my will, the world is small and narrow like a closed fist. His grunts shoot through my heart like bullets tearing at the sweet meat of my goodness. I become a dead boy made of disappointment and dust, an eight-year-old clawing at the blackness descending into his soul.

'No . . . No . . .'

He is moving me, adjusting me, pawing at me. My whimpers rise in the air. I remember whispering that if God was nearby, to step in to halt the horror that was taking place under his gaze. I waited for the saviour to split my attacker in two like lightning striking an old oak. Instead it was me who divided, cleaved into two separate beings as I lay there, my father's breath of whiskey and death moving across my body.

I saw the butterfly kite; I saw it flit on the quickening wind like a spirit beyond flesh. I watched it in my mind as it spiralled and twisted, eager for the lift of the breeze. I saw it soar against the blueness and beauty of a summer's day, its long tail of ribbon swirling in the air. My heart sang to it, pleaded to join it. As I leapt free of my small body to move in the air with the kite I looked back at the child whose body was obscured by the writhing shadow that was his father. I cursed God and all his saints. The boy below me was no more than a husk, the facsimile of a child.

I remember being carried along on gusts and bursts of wind, wishing I could stay there forever caught in the world of birds and coming rain. I felt at home, at peace.

When he spilled across me, I plummeted back down into the flesh of my body, landing with a jolt into a pool of stickiness and the pull of his fingernails on my belly. I felt a great sadness envelop me, like a dark rain cloud, and in it shame and self-disgust lurked like assassins waiting to pounce.

Sometimes he stayed in the bed with me, falling asleep almost instantly, his snore shuddering through the bed, his large chest rising and falling, his hands twitching across my body every now and then, as if they still owned it, still claimed it. If he lay on his side facing me he would gather me to him in a hug. My face would then lie against the wiry hairs on his chest or my lips would find themselves pressed to one of his nipples. I can recall the soft pinkness of it against my mouth and how I gagged.

I knew then I was condemned, that later in life men would look at me with pity and women would sense my obscene history even before I had crossed the threshold of their hearts. Something died in me all those nights ago when the moon spied through the curtains, and that man took the child in me away and cast him into the wilderness.

He broke the thread in me, the one that holds on to life. It dangled within me useless and torn. I watched him as I grew older, followed him with my eyes as he patrolled our home, as he planted the flag of conquest in every bedroom of the house. I dreamt of picking him apart, of taking his flesh from his bones. My world was shaped in gunfire and thunder, and the sly reach of my father's hand across my balls.

Honour Him

This time there are three of them. One stands behind me, one at the door and the third is seated in front of me. The one in front of me is the one who was here before. He is speaking to me. He is asking me my name. I laugh, and then I'm surprised to find I begin crying in almost the same breath. I am annoyed with myself because this will only make him pity me. So I bang my head hard with my hand to stop the tears. The man behind me stoops down so that his face is inches from mine. It's alright, he tells me, everything is alright. He then turns to his colleagues and tells them that I was in a pretty raw state when I was taken from the holding room, that maybe it hadn't been such a good idea to leave me alone there for so long, that I was sweating and shaking when they found me.

I wave a hand at him as if to say you don't understand, none of you do. It has nothing to do with that.

I am angry because I know that if I'm crying it means that I am still attached to this world. I wait a moment and a part of me wants to speak to them to explain, but I don't. If I speak then I will be truly lost. I will be no better or no worse than them. I know that they are waiting, I can tell because their breathing is different. They can wait all they want.

I wish that these tears would stop falling. I must try and think of something else. I hold myself by clasping my arms about my body and I lean forward. Don't do that, one of them says, please sit up straight. I ignore him. Then I feel his hands on me pulling at me. Like she did a long time ago, her hand on the nape of my neck pushing those words out, those God words, those love words. 'Feel Him, Gabriel, give yourself to Him, honour Him, Gabriel, feel His love, can you feel Him, Gabriel?' His hand on my tiny cock, moving and pushing, digging and probing. Can you feel him, Gabriel? Can you feel the hardness of his sex? This is his love, Gabriel, and this is his gift. Honour him, Gabriel, honour your father in heaven.

The Seagull

I know that I must forget the events of the past few days, though pieces of it rise in me, like a dying man's last words, fighting to be heard. My wife decided not to press charges and the hospital released me on the understanding that I would get the help I needed. I nodded and assured them I would. My sister wasn't pleased and my brother-in-law even less, but fuck them, as the man said.

I have things to do today. I have arranged to take my class to see a production of Chekhov's *The Seagull*. It isn't on the curriculum but months ago it seemed like a good idea, I thought that it would stir the artists in them and give them an appreciation of theatre. Most of them have signed up to come; some have dropped out at the last minute. I have hired a minibus which I will drive myself. My body feels as if it belongs to someone else. It doesn't want to obey me, and I can feel the man at the car rental place looking at me quizzically as I bang my head when I climb into the cabin of the van. He asks me if I'm okay, and I look at him as if he's crazy. I have a couple of whiskey miniatures in my jacket pocket. I might need to press them into service later on.

The students are to be at the school ready to go at 6 p.m. It's a four- or five-mile drive from the car hire. I stop twice to throw up. The second time I am hunched over in the layby, heaving as the tea-time traffic screams by. A few of them honk their horns at this pathetic figure bent double in the brisk wind dredging up what's left of his insides.

Just before I reach the school I take out one of the miniatures and down it in one. I know that my body will want to reject it so I take short quick breaths until the feeling of nausea passes. I then stuff three or four mints in my mouth and suck furiously, trying to kill the smell of vomit and whiskey. All this has made me late and I know that I won't have time to splash my face in the school toilets before we go.

I take the turn into the driveway of the school at speed, cutting across an oncoming car. He bangs on his horn, and slows down, for a moment I think that he is going to follow me. That's all I need, I think, and am relieved when I see him decide to go on.

The students are all waiting for me when I arrive; some are with their parents, sitting in their cars. I slow down as I approach, a speeding teacher would not go down too well. I pop another couple of mints in my mouth as I pull on the handbrake and jump out. I smile and bang my hands together.

'Are you alright, Mr O'Rourke?'

One of my pupils' parents is standing looking at me. She is called Patricia Numby and I remember her from the parent-teacher meetings, she always had one question more than the others, always wanted reassurance that her son was doing better than the others. I knew that she found me a little flighty. I think it was because I tried to joke with her once that every mother wants a Mozart to tuck in at night. It didn't go down too well.

'Yes, Mrs Numby, I'm fine . . . Really fine . . . Looking forward to our little trip.'

'Well thank you for organising it. You look a little pale.'

'It's nothing, stomach upset . . . That's all.'

'Something you ate?'

'Exactly . . . Something I ate . . .'

'Right. What time do you expect to be back?'

'Oh I would say around 11.30.'

'Good. Are you sure you're feeling alright?'

'Terrific . . . Terrific . . . Obviously apart from the stomach thing.'

'Yes, there's a lot of it going round. My friend Mr . . .'

'Yes, well . . . We really should be going if we want to be on time . . . Sorry to interrupt, Mrs Numby . . .'

She moves to step forward; as she does this I take a little pace backwards. I realise that she's suspicious and wanted to get a smell of my breath. I smile at her and turn around to tell everyone to get ready to go. Before we leave I ask my pupils to behave on the journey down the M1, and pop another couple of mints in my mouth. One of them cheekily asks if he can have one, I tell them they're medicinal and that I need every one I have.

Once I get the students in the theatre and seated I can slip out and get myself together. I console myself with this as we travel down the motorway, the lights of the cars bleeding in and out of each other like long snakes of fluorescence. Part of me just wants to keep on driving deeper and deeper into the night.

I am staring into the mirror. The play has started. I am in the Gents toilet. I have just drunk the last of my whiskey. I left just as Konstantin's little play began. I have about fifty minutes or so before the interval.

I can see deep circles of blackness beneath my eyes. I am staring at a stranger. I no longer see the person I was. As I splash my face with water I get the feeling that there is something I haven't thought, a part of my mind that I haven't been to.

I don't remember the short walk back to the auditorium or the look one of my students gives me as I take my place beside him. One of the actors on the stage forgets his lines for a moment and I loudly snort my disapproval. A few people look round in my direction and tell me to be quiet. I tell them to fuck off. I was happy, I was sure I was, just for a second it rose within me like the sun in July. My mind was hazy and the hard thinking in my brain had eased. I no longer thought of my hands at her throat or the beast that roared inside me as I forced myself onto her. Yes, I was at peace; it was something that I had been looking for all day and I was grateful that at last it had arrived, it was the final miniature that did it, and the two or three nips I had at the theatre bar. Thank God for Mr Johnny Walker. I laughed, it must have been louder than I remember because one of the ushers came down and suggested that I go outside for a moment. I told her that was impossible as I was a teacher and a man of character and that I had some pupils in my charge and to abandon them would be beyond reckless. I think she looked at me as if I was mad. Fuck it, I was used to that. It was the same look my sister had given when I lay in the hospital bed and she told me that I had tried to rape my wife, what the fuck is the world coming to, how can a man rape his own fucking wife. Konstantin has just brought on a dead seagull, one of my students beside me laughs and says something under his breath to one of his mates. I hit him a dig in the ribs with my elbow and tell him to be quiet. This is Art, I say, do you understand, this is fucking Art, you moron.

I watch as the actor lays the dead seagull at Nina's feet and something begins to stir in me, something that has lain dormant for a very long time, it's like the first cry of love from a child's lips and it brings tears to my eyes.

I don't notice that I have stood up and am making my way towards the stage forcing my way through people's crossed legs. I think I shout something at the actors. I know that I feel sorry for the bird that lies lifelessly in front of them. I remember wanting to cradle it in my arms, to woo it back to life. I know that I am angry at the world for killing it, for ripping it from the sky, just like I was, I think, just like I was.

It takes the parents of my students some time to organise lifts to take them all back to Newry. They tell me that it took three men to stop me climbing onto the stage. I don't know, I say, when they tell me, I can't remember, I'm sorry, I can't remember. The manager of the theatre is standing in front of me; there is a man beside him. They both have that look on their faces; it's a mixture of anger and pity. The man is taking notes. He tells me he is head of security at the theatre and if he had his way he would throw the book at me.

I know that I have a better chance with the manager and it's him that I focus on, fixing him with my eyes whenever I can. It seems to work because through his speech about how he believes the theatre to be a sacred space, a church, if you like, where people come to pay homage to great works of art, his face softens until eventually he tells me that he has a brother who drank and that he knows the pain that lives in the hearts of people like me. I'll let it go, he says. He looks to the security guy who is disappointed not to have the satisfaction of charging me. I thank him, I think I even cried a little tear to emphasise my sincerity. Then I call my wife. I tell her that I need her help. Her voice is bloodless and cold and she asks me what it is I want. A lift home, I say. She asks where I am. Outside the Lyric Theatre, I say. Wait there, she says and hangs up. An hour or so later I see my brother-in-law's van pull up. I curse quietly to myself and think about hiding until he drives off, but I know that he has seen me. He parks on the other side of the road and barely looks at me but just sits there with the engine idling. As I get into the van he crunches it into first gear and hardly waits for me to bang the door shut before moving off. I think I thanked him as we travelled back to my home, I'm not sure, but he doesn't speak to me, keeps his eyes dead ahead, his left hand moving back and forth across the gear stick, his right hand flipping the steering wheel this way and that. So I settle into the silence that he seems so determined to put in place. In my mind I know that the ground is moving up to meet me at a greater speed than ever before.

Torn Down

'My name is . . . Gabriel.'

'Okay . . . Good.'

'Gabriel.'

'Good man.'

'O'Rourke . . . Gabriel O'Rourke . . .'

'Now we're getting somewhere.'

'Yes . . .'

'And how do you feel, Gabriel O'Rourke?'

'Strange . . .'

'It's to be expected. But don't worry. Please try not to worry.'

I can't help feeling disgust at myself. I have given in. It has taken a while but I have succumbed nonetheless. I tell myself to ignore the grin of victory on this young man's face; he's just doing his job. He had to pull me from the sky; he had to tear me down so that I sat across from him just as I do now, meek and full of yeses and nos. It feels strange to say my name; it tastes dusty and dry on my tongue as if I have just put a handful of dirt in my mouth. I know that I am back in the dull plain world that I have spent my life fleeing. I smile.

'What's funny, Gabriel?'

'Everything. Everything is fucking funny.'

'Really?'

'Yes.'

'Such as . . . ?'

'Such as not knowing when you're standing or when you're sitting, when you're crying or laughing or . . .'

'Or?'

'Or when you're falling and when you're not.'

Falling Together

There is that old familiar smell of bacon grease and the sound of the kitchen clock. My mother stands over me, she is concerned. I am crying. My tears are the kind that will not let anyone in, especially those closest to you. This angers my mother though she tries not to show it.

'Don't cry, son.'

Her hand is on my shoulder. I know that she doesn't know what to say next.

'Son . . . God is with you.'

'No,' I say. 'No, he's not.'

'Don't, son . . . Don't disrespect Him . . .'

My head is in my hands, I feel my hot breath against my palms.

'What is it, son? What has you so?'

I try to answer, to tell of his heavy touch and the thrust of his hand on my sex. I want to scream that the devil walked the gardens of the Lord and that no-one was safe.

'Pray with me, son . . . Let's pray for the touch of God's love, for His grace, for His compassion.'

'No.'

'Pray with me.' Her voice is more urgent now.

I look at her across these years that have fallen and I see the need in her eyes. Don't betray me, they say. She takes my hands in hers. Her eyes soften, and she rubs my forearm making small shushing noises.

'There's nothing so big or so small that God can't handle.'

A cow lows in the bottom field. My mother cocks her head and a tear rises in her eye. I watch it as it sits there, unsure as to whether to fall.

I feel stupid sitting there waiting for the prayer that I know will do no good. After what seems an age she focuses once more on me, her eyes searching mine.

'God loves everyone and everything that moves on the face of this earth, Gabriel; He makes no distinction, no exception.'

'Yes,' I say. 'Yes.'

'Good boy.'

'Mammy.'

'Yes?'

The words dance on the tip of my tongue, the black words that speak of sin, and defilement. But I stop short of uttering them.

'Nothing, Mammy.'

I want to tell her that there is someone else there crouching in the dark and that my body already belonged to him, and that the thief wore a husband's clothes. He had got there first and claimed me for himself. It was his skin I felt next to mine, man skin, broken and leathered. Sweaty piss-smelling skin. I want to tell her that God watched and did nothing. Maybe God enjoyed what he was seeing because he didn't stop it. I remember I began to rock in my seat, gently as the violence of the memory worked its way through my body and into my thinking. I wonder at her blindness.

'Gabriel.'

'Yes, Mammy.'

'Don't do that.'

'What?'

'Rock like that.'

'I have to.'

'Why?'

'Because I don't think that God loves me . . .'

Suddenly she drops her head. She looks away from me and I realise that she knows. That through all the smoke and fog of our unhappiness, she knows. She has kept it from us, from herself, and has looked for refuge in the high clouds of God's love, and the soft embrace of His saints and angels.

As I fall into that kitchen, into the tension of my mother's touch, of her hands, I see now that the secret lives in her too and that she has buried it deep within herself and looks out on the world with the eyes of a convert.

'Mammy,' I said.

'Yes.'

'It's alright.'

'Oh my God.'

This time there are no fireworks, no high language, just a simple plea, and for the first time stillness comes to her, it settles on her like a sea bird finding land, its wings weary from the hunt. She has found the end of love.

Take it Back

My father died trying to crack open Petey's head between his bare hands. I was seventeen and was with him in the town when he suggested that we have a drink before returning home. It was a hot July day and I remember feeling thankful for the coolness of the pub's interior. It was only after he had drunk half of his first pint that my father first noticed Petey. He was sitting in the far corner near the exit for the toilets tinkering with a crossword. I can still see the debate in my dad's eyes as he thought about leaving, but instead he ordered another drink. It was a while before Petey saw us. I could see him in the reflection of the large mirror that hung above the bar. He stared at us for a full minute before calling over one of the young students that worked at clearing up and taking orders from the floor. I saw him whisper in the young man's ear and indicate my father with a nod of his head. Two minutes later a fresh pint arrived in front of my father.

'What's this?'

'It's from your mate.'

'What mate?'

'Petey,' the barman said.

'Take it back.'

'What?'

'Take it back.'

'Fuck it, Johnny. It's poured.'

'So?'

My father then lifted the pint and walked over towards Petey. He placed the drink on the table in front of him.

'I don't want anything from you,' he said.

'Don't be like this,' Petey said.

'I'll be any fucking way I please.'

'There's no need for this.'

'She's my wife.'

'No-one's disputing that.'

'Stay the fuck away.'

I remember feeling relieved when my father turned and started to make his way towards me, but then something crossed his eyes. He turned and lunged at Petey, using his greater strength to drag him clear across the small table and into the middle of the floor. The barman called on my dad to stop but he just ignored him. Petey just sat there as my father's hands found the side of his head and began to squeeze.

'She's mine. She's fucking mine.'

'Johnny . . .'

'Fight me.'

'Johnny, no . . .'

I can still see Petey's head in my father's lap like a cradled lover and how his lips were puckered as if he was waiting for a kiss to be planted on them. A space cleared around them. A man at the bar started to laugh, an old drunk who spent every day in the same spot nodding into the debris of his past. One of Petey's mates tried to prise my dad's hands off the man's face. He then thumped dad hard across the head, I saw the blow register in my father's eyes, but it didn't shake his grip; he just spat out a grunt and applied more pressure to Petey's head.

I looked at the large splay of my father's fingers as they lay across the sides of his head and knew that Petey would be lucky to walk away. The barman asked me to say something, to intervene, but all I could do was shyly shake my head like a girl being asked for a first kiss.

Then suddenly my father looked up at me, there was something in his look that told me there was a problem. His hands left Petey's head and reached up to his heart and began tearing at the clothing that covered it. I still see him ripping at his shirt buttons before his upper body fell backwards his head landing with a smack on the bar room floor. For a moment no-one moved, and then Petey rolled free of my father's prostrate body, got to his feet and quietly said: 'Call an ambulance. For God's sake, call an ambulance.'

By the time we had reached the hospital he was already dead. I remember us waiting to see him, how my mother stood, her head slightly to one side so that she looked like a little girl, and my sister crying and holding on to her arm. I lit a cigarette and when my mother told me that you weren't allowed to smoke I said: 'I'd like to see someone try and stop me.'

When she saw him at last she was brief. She stood by his lifeless body and whispered something that none of us could hear and then she placed the tips of her fingers on the knuckles of one of his large hands and traced each one. She looked as if she was paying homage to the force that lived there, to the weapons that she knew he relied on.

We buried him. Sleet whipped through the air and cloud lay heavy and grey over the land like dark slabs of stone. That night I got drunk. I seemed to be carried by a black energy from bar to bar. People came up to me to pay their respects; some I tolerated, some I treated with disdain, others who were drinking pals of our father I hung on to, as if they were living Bibles.

'Do whatever you need to,' one of them said.

Two of them shadowed me for the rest of the night. I can remember them whispering to me, holding me upright. One of them rubbed the back of my neck as I threw up in the street on our way to another pub and said: 'Go on, kid, get the fucker out.'

He then asked me if I'd had enough. I remember shaking my head, and putting my fists up and swaying there in the cold night air, my head pounding.

'Okay, son. Okay.'

They told me that I drank for thirty-six hours straight that time. I stood there as night became day and then night again, the look in my eye hardening, my tongue wounding anyone who came near. Once or twice I was asked to step outside but my protectors ushered my challengers away explaining that my father had just died and that I was taking on what was left of the world.

The New Sun

After my father's death my mother became the person she had hidden all the time that she was with him. A new energy seized her now that the storm she had faced for all those years had abated. Petey was there more often. At first my mother told him to stay away but he nibbled away at her resolve until she relented. She prayed more, and spoke of God at every opportunity. She no longer had to whisper His name. My father's photographs were taken down and stored in the shed outside. His clothes were packed and given away or sold at a church jumble sale that took place on the outskirts of the town every second Sunday. I went with her and helped her set up the small stall and watched as people haggled over my dead father's suits and jackets, his old shaving kit, and his books on hunting. I felt like saying something, but thought better of it. I knew that my mother was claiming back her life, wrenching it back from the dead fingers of a man who only saw the world for what it could give him. My sister refused to come, she said it was obscene to stand in full view of the town and barter off what was left of our dead father. My mother just looked at her and said, it's time he left for good.

Some people who had known my father came and watched with displeasure as strangers rifled through his belongings. They were mainly drinking pals. A couple of them stood to one side and grunted or shook their heads every time someone asked the price of an item of clothing. My mother ignored them and told me to do the same.

Petey was a self-appointed bodyguard. He hovered by the stall and oversaw all transactions, keeping a watchful eye on any potential troublemakers.

'This our new life . . . Blessed by God's goodness,' my mother said. 'Now we move on under His guiding hand . . .'

Petey was careful around my sister and me because of what had happened in the bar in the town. The rest of the world he could face down, but he didn't know the rest of the world as well as he knew us. My sister refused to speak to him, and she would leave the room whenever he entered it. He would look to my mother and she would nod her head as if to say give it time, Petey, give it time.

With me it was different. I felt removed from it all and took refuge in the numbness that had settled around my heart many years before. I listened to his stories and jokes and smiled and laughed when I thought it appropriate, but truth be told I never really heard anything he said. I did it for my mother, because I knew how important the new world she was building was to her.

It was difficult to believe my father had gone. His presence had been so total, so overpowering that for a long time the house still wore his energy. You could feel him in every room. I felt it most especially in my bedroom, his spirit seemed to seethe in every nook and cluttered corner. I would come home and find my mother kneeling in the centre of the living room, praying. I knew immediately what she was doing, she was asking her dead husband to go, once and for all to leave, that he was no longer wanted.

I had begun to drink. At first it brought me a rush of freedom. I liked the warm reassurance that a couple of beers in my gut brought me. I was solved, complete. Two beers though brought a roaring hunger with them and I craved more. I would cram myself with whatever I could find and my friends would laugh at my greed and my recklessness. A bloody-mindedness would rise in me and sit across my eyes.

My mother noticed the difference in me. She would stare at me as if a changeling was sitting in front of her, not the son she knew and loved. She told me that she had an idea to set up a healing school, one devoted to faith and prayer and the easing of people's pain. I remember I laughed when she said it, and my sister slapped me on the arm, telling me not to be rude.

'Fuck off,' I said.

'Don't you dare talk like that in front of Mum,' my sister said.

'I'll do what I please.'

'Leave him. Let me talk to him,' my mother said. 'God is watching our every move, Gabriel. Remember that.'

'Don't I know it. He watches. But he does fuck all.'

'Stop it this minute.'

'Stop what?'

'This blasphemy . . .'

'It's not blasphemy if you don't believe.'

'I beg your pardon.'

'You heard.'

'What do you mean you don't believe?'

I remember how the colour drained from my mother's face. My sister got up from the table, shaking her head and moved to the window, standing with her back to us. I looked down at the table and could feel my mother's eyes on me.

'Don't do this to me, Gabriel . . . Don't.'

I raised my head and looked at her.

'I'm sorry,' I said.

'A lot has happened, son. Maybe you're not thinking clearly.'

'Maybe,' I said.

I recall leaving the house, walking out into the damp evening air and looking at the trees that lined the fields. They looked so stark and threatening like men made ugly by life. I remember the loneliness that rose in me.

I knew that somewhere I missed him. I sensed that every man's life needed an ogre, and that he had been mine.

The Healing School

Four months after my father's death the healing school opened for business. My mother stood at her front door and welcomed her callers. They were mostly fellow believers from the church and prayer group she and Petey attended once or twice a month. She was so happy that she no longer had to hide her faith, and her whole being lit up as she greeted her friends.

They made their way to the living room that my mother and sister had cleared and sat on the small school chairs that Petey had found. They spoke to one another about their week and the love that they had for each other and of course for God. Then they would hold hands and concentrate, my mother telling them to feel the power of the Holy Spirit as it moved across their hearts. They would intone Hail Marys and Our Fathers, their voices rising in pitch until the whole room thrummed with sound.

I sat in a couple of times to begin with; I had no choice as my mother made it clear that it was expected of me. It was strange sitting there in the stripped room watching these people pray to something they couldn't see. It made me want to laugh out loud in their faces and tell them how blind and stupid they were being. Most of them were there to see my mother do her act. I remember watching as she moved around the room stopping to place her hands on someone's back or across their face, her head cocked, her forehead lined with concentration, then she would say things like, 'There is sorrow across your heart . . . Give it to Jesus, He will take your burden . . .'

One woman began crying even before my mother touched her. She was an overweight lady with unruly brown hair. She ran the local sweetshop and had lost her husband Ned a couple of years before in a bomb blast that had ripped through a bar and butcher's shop in the town. It was said that the ambulance crews and police had trouble distinguishing the animal meat from the human. The butcher's shop reopened for business a few months later but closed quite quickly as no-one wanted what they had to offer anymore.

'Hello, Geraldine.'

'Hello, Theresa.'

'Is your heart open, Geraldine?'

'Yes, my heart is open . . .'

My mother's body seemed to slow as she approached her, as if she was a hunter approaching a dangerous beast.

'I see Him, Geraldine . . .'

'Do you, Theresa?' she said through her tears.

'Yes, He is standing beside you with a look of love on His face.'

'Oh God.'

'Don't worry, darling, it's alright . . . The Lord loves you . . .'

'I know, Theresa . . . I know . . .'

'The Lord says He is always with you . . . He is holding his arms over you . . .'

'You mean it's not Ned.'

'No, it's the Lord Himself.'

'I thought it was Ned.'

'No.'

'Where's Ned then?'

'He's with . . .'

'Can you ask him where Ned is . . . ?'

'Please, Geraldine . . . It's the Lord I'm speaking of . . .'

'I don't care. I thought it was Ned so I did.'

'Take a deep breath . . . Breathe, Geraldine . . . Let the Lord's love fill you . . . Let His radiance enchant your heart . . . That's it . . . That's it . . .'

I watched as Geraldine lowered her head as if she was falling into a deep sleep, her hands falling softly into her lap. Her hair tumbled across her forehead so that she looked like one of those nodding dogs you find in the back of cars.

'Let Him in . . . He is knocking, can you hear Him?'

'Yes, I can hear Him, Theresa . . . Thank you, Theresa.'

'The Lord is telling me you're hanging on to the past too tightly, Geraldine . . . That it's time to let go . . .'

'Yes. But I miss him so.'

'Ned?'

'Yes, my Ned . . .'

'Everything happens for a reason . . . Every falling leaf has its purpose . . .'

'No, I know. My faith is weak.'

'Don't say that.'

'It is. It is. I want to punish those bastards who did this to us. Hurt them like they hurt me.'

'I know . . .'

'They took my life from me. They took a spear and put it through my heart.'

Her hands were now two fists and she held them in the air, shaking them at her imaginary foe. Her whole body was shuddering so much that I was afraid she might have a heart attack.

'Please try and calm down, Geraldine,' my mother said. 'Give this pain to the Lord, He can take it. He is strong enough and big enough. Do you hear me?'

'Yes.'

'I want you to see this pain as a gift . . .'

'A gift?'

'Yes, a gift and I want you to wrap it up in a nice big bow and hand it over to your loving God . . .'

'Yes, Theresa . . . I'm sorry I don't understand . . .'

'Hand it to me . . .'

'My pain . . .'

'Yes . . . Hand it to me and I will give it to your loving God . . .'

I remember how my mother's eyes locked on Geraldine's. I shifted uncomfortably in my seat, I felt trapped. Geraldine's pain seemed to slip from her like an old skin, and a childish joy took hold of her as she gazed into my mother's eyes. Then she slowly raised her hands as if a burden lay across them and offered them to my mother who nodded and took the bundle of grief from her, smiling as she did so. Then my mother's lips began to move. Her arms rose above her shoulders as if they had a life of their own. Her head began to move from side to side; she reminded me of one of those wind-up toys I'd had as a child, a monkey that beat a small drum, a look of manic glee on its face.

I looked around the room at the fellow believers, one or two were crying, a young girl who was painfully thin was wringing her hands and moaning words like Jesus and Love. One man was on his knees asking God to forgive the sins of all gathered there and to wrap us in the web of his care. Petey was on his knees repeatedly making the sign of the cross and my sister was prostrate on the floor, her palms flat on the ground, her arms stretched out in front of her. The noise in the room built and built like the air raid siren they used to sound in the town when there was a bomb scare. I lowered my head and waited for the storm of praying to pass. I felt sorry for them, all this energy, all this belief hurled into the air like confetti at a wedding, what a waste of time.

Winter

I took my wife prisoner and held her back from life. I patrolled her sleeping body, watching for any signs of betrayal. I listened at her mouth for a name I didn't recognise, or for a phrase from a secret life she was living. I was a December cloud bringing her short winter's day to an end.

I banished everyone who came to her. I took apart every relationship she held dear. I watched with satisfaction as her sister fell away from her. I froze her out, until she was no more than a distant figure crossing the vast plain of my wife's memory. Her mother and father were tougher; they took me on and waged a war against me. My mother-in law would look at me as if I carried every badness this world was capable of holding. I didn't care, what she didn't know was that I was used to the wilderness, I had spent my youth in its burnt landscape. One day she said something to me when my wife was out of earshot. She placed her long hands across her lap and tilted her head back slightly so that she was looking down at me.

'Please stop,' she said.

'Stop what, Margaret?'

'Hurting my daughter.'

I didn't answer but looked away instead.

'Did you hear me, Gabriel?'

'Yes,' I said.

'This situation . . . The way you are . . . is so damaging to her.'

'Margaret, please. Mind your own business.'

I replied without looking at her and was angry at the plea I heard in my voice as I said it.

'My daughter is my business and so are you as long as you are with her.'

'I don't want your concern, Margaret, or your time.'

'You have no choice.'

'I think I do.'

'You need help.'

'Don't patronise me.'

'You're unwell. This drinking. This anger . . .'

'Save your breath.'

'There are people who can help.'

'When I need advice from someone who hasn't been fucked in a decade I'll ask for it.'

I remember how her mouth dropped open and how she sat there trying to come back at me in some way. Fuck her; I thought the world was full of 'Margarets', with their daylight God of gossip and pearls. I knew what I was doing; I was being everything she despised. I was good at that, making people peer into the winter of my heart, and letting them know that in a fight to the death there would only be one winner, because one of us was already dead.

I knew that I wouldn't be seeing her for a while. As she said a hurried goodbye to her daughter and left I knew that I should expect a visit from her husband at some point. He was a man who wanted to slip through the nets of this life unnoticed. He didn't look for anything. He smiled when he should have cried; he knelt when he should have stood. I always dismissed him, but then I think a lot of people did. He was a tall man with a stoop to him as if the ceiling of this world constantly brushed the top of his back.

So a few days after Margaret fled from our house, I opened

the door to find him standing there like a large bony bird that had just been blown down from the skies.

His eyes held mine for a second and then looked down at the ground. We had only just met and already he had conceded.

'Is Cathy in, Gabriel?'

'No.'

'Oh.'

I know that he expected me to invite him in, that it was only proper, that it was the grown-up thing to do, but I was happy to disappoint him, holding the door half open as if he was a troublesome salesman who had just disturbed my day.

'You see . . . I just wanted to . . . Margaret said you were quite rude to her.'

'Margaret and I always clash, you know that, James.'

'Yes, well. It's not just that. It's not just a question of personality.'

'Then what is it?'

'You said something to her . . . that I didn't like.'

I looked at him, at the small beads of sweat on his forehead and I felt sorry for him, but not sorry enough.

'Well maybe I was a little too graphic.'

It wasn't an apology and he knew it was nowhere near what he had been ordered to come and get from me, but for him it would do.

'Right, well, I just thought that I would say it.'

'Right.'

'What time is Cathy coming back?'

'I don't know. Do you want her to call you?'

'Maybe . . . No. No, don't bother. Let's keep this between us.'

As he walked away I did feel a pang of remorse for the way I had treated him but I had no choice. I was marked from day one, I was hostage to something that he and his wife could never begin to understand. I wanted to call after him to say that he deserved better, that he should expect and demand more from me but I knew somewhere that the fires I was lighting all around me would end up burning no-one but me.

Bring a Protestant

It is an open day at the school to coincide with the cessation of hostilities, as the official flyer for the event put it. I am in no mood for it; I called it Bring a Protestant. The idea was to get everyone at the school including myself to invite a person of the other persuasion to a fête to be held in honour of the new dawn in our little state. Farrell was particularly pleased with the idea, but that was no surprise to me, he was a Southerner, his lot had had seventy years where they sang themselves to sleep beneath peaceful skies. To him the North was just like one of his maths equations, add and/or subtract equals peace. I resented the jaunty grin he greeted me with when the news of the big day was released. We had met in the science corridor; I was on duty to make sure that pupils made their way to class without any fuss and to apprehend anyone who was shirking.

'That's more like it,' he said to me.

'What's more like it, Mr Farrell?'

'Peace, Mr O'Rourke. Reconciliation.'

'Those are big fine words for a maths teacher, Mr Farrell.'

'Always the joker, Mr O'Rourke.'

'There aren't just two religions in this country, Mr Farrell. I now realise that there are three: Catholic, Protestant, and Southerner.'

'Droll, Mr O'Rourke. Very droll. It will be interesting to see who you bring to our open day. Men like you never look beyond their own . . .'

'Men like me?'

'Yes, men like you.'

As he walked on, I wondered about what he said. It was true I would be hard pushed to find a Protestant who was a friend. I told myself that it just never crossed the radar of my everyday life, but I knew that this wasn't true. We all lived on top of each other as if we were two colonies of termites fighting over one small hill. I also knew that I had marked Mr Farrell for what he had just said and that one day I would make him pay for the superior way he had looked at me when he had made his last remark.

The next day I went to the secondary school that lay on the outskirts of the town, where the kerbs changed from green, white and gold to Union Jack red, white and blue within a matter of feet. Above, from every chimney, the red hand of Ulster told anyone who cared to look that they had just crossed into another territory, one where everything was opposite and contrary to the place you had just come from. I knew a teacher who worked in the school; we had trained together many years before. His name was Jeffrey. We had fought the first time we had met; we had got drunk together and had ended up on the floor, our hands trying to rip the opinions from each other's throats. We had to be separated and calmed down, me by my Catholic friends, he by his Protestant.

Afterwards we had settled into an uneasy peace with each other, avoiding subjects that could bring us to blows again. If anything we became close, as close as we could given the war that raged in the streets of the city we were studying in. We had both ended up teaching in the same town and now and then over the years our paths would cross. Sometimes we would stop and quickly catch up, at other times if things were tough and dangerous we would nod and move on, knowing that it wasn't the time for pleasantries, the blood on the ground beneath our feet had seen to that. Our relationship, if you could call it that, was complicated like the place that we both called home.

I decided that I would ask him if he would like to come to our open day as my guest and maybe even as my friend. I stood in the small office of his school and asked for him. I was told to wait as he had a class but that it was nearly finished. I tried to chat with the school secretary to pass the time, but she just smiled as I rambled on about the weather, gently raising her hand when the phone rang or when someone came in to ask her a question. In the end I gave up and stared at the large photograph of the queen that hung above the door.

When Jeffrey arrived, he paused in the doorway and looked at me as if he had just seen a ghost.

'Well this is a surprise.'

'Jeffrey.'

'Gabriel.'

He agreed to come to the open day, he smiled as I asked him as if he had just won an argument I didn't realise we'd been having.

I have a hip flask in my pocket. It is my friend. It will guide me through the day ahead just like it has always done. I am outside of the main building of my school waiting for Jeffrey to arrive. Now and then the principal scurries past, full of urgency, his face smiling, his arms outstretched as he greets another arrival. I know that he is pleased with himself, with the big idea of the open day. He had told me it had come to him when he was asleep; it had been a gift from God. So was Hitler, I felt like saying, but I knew better as I was already on thin enough ice as it was. Pray for sunshine, he had said, pray for the clouds to part. So it is with some satisfaction that I watch everyone hurry from their cars trying to get inside as quickly as possible without getting drenched. The event has made the local newspapers and the North's TV stations, and a couple of journalists and cameramen hover around like flies over a half-eaten meal. I watch as parents arrive with their sons and their Protestant friends. I am taken aback by the glow of optimism in their eyes. I resent it. I feel like telling them that just weeks before we were tearing at each other's flesh. Jeffrey, when he arrives, warmly shakes my hand and stands with me for a moment before we go inside. We smoke a cigarette together and watch as the smoke rises to join the grey heavy clouds above us.

'There are two ways to view today,' he says.

'I know,' I say.

Peace and Reconciliation

My hip flask is empty. One of my students is standing in front of me. The boy has just asked me a question but for the life of me I can't remember what it was. So I just stand there grinning at him, muttering something about it being an auspicious day. I was fine until the wine had appeared. I was pleased with myself, I had faked it very well, telling anyone who I happened upon that I was glad that the fighting was over. Jeffrey had left around an hour before. He had done his bit, applauding politely when the speeches were made about all of us being one and that love and not hate was the way forward. When he left he had come up to me and looked deep into my eyes and asked if I was okay.

'Fucking sure, my old friend,' I had said.

'Come outside with me.'

'Why, do you want a kiss?'

'Don't be a prick. Come on. Why don't you have some coffee? A couple of cups,' he said.

'I don't want coffee.'

I got the feeling that Jeffrey wanted to say something else as we stood there in the damp air. I remember looking into his eyes and realising that they were different. They used to be clouded like mine but now . . . It had bothered me all afternoon that he had drunk nothing except water.

'I don't drink anymore, Gabriel. I had to stop.'

'So?'

'So I'm saying maybe go easy. It doesn't help anything, it only makes them worse. I should know. I nearly lost everything, Gabriel. Believe me.'

I knew it, the bastard was weak, couldn't handle it. I looked at him and I remembered that night long ago when we rolled in the slops of other people's beer and discarded cigarette butts.

'I don't need help from your kind,' I'd said.

'What do you mean my kind?'

'Your kind . . . Your side of the fucking street . . .'

'Oh fuck off, Gabriel. That's such a load of bollocks, Look at where we are, look at what we're celebrating. Listen . . .'

But I didn't wait to hear anymore, I turned and walked back into the hall. You see, I didn't want to miss the local politician's speech about peace and reconciliation.

Black Daffodil

My sister is feeding her. I watch as the spoon pushes at her closed mouth. I see the look of surprise in her eyes as the baby food oozes across her pursed lips and drops in blobs onto the kitchen table.

'Come on, Mammy. You must eat.'

She nods as if she just about understands what's being said, like an infant who is hearing language for the first time. We had been told that this would happen, it was my sister who first warned me as she had seen it time upon time at the hospice, and the doctor had confirmed it. Her brain would begin to shut down motor functions such as swallowing, walking, even smiling. Her illness had entered a new deadly phase and neither my sister nor I was quite ready for it.

I join my sister, moving from the doorway of the sitting room to kneel by her side.

'Talk to her,' my sister says. 'It'll help. She likes it when you talk to her . . .'

'Mammy. It's Gabriel. Mammy?'

'Gabriel?'

'Yes, Mammy, Gabriel.'

'Sweet little daffodil.'

'Yes, Mammy . . .'

'Sweet . . . Sweet . . .'

'Yes.'

'Is it time?'

'For what, Mammy?'

'For the game to end?'

'What game, Mammy?'

I see her look at my sister, her eyes widening in disbelief. She shakes her head and then chews on her lower lip.

'There are angels in the television, son . . . They talk to me at night . . .'

'No, Mam . . .'

'Yes, I hear their wings beating . . . I see them glow . . . They glow, son . . .'

'If you say so . . .'

'God loves me . . .'

'Yes, Mammy, he loves you . . .'

'You don't know, do you?' she says.

'Know what?' I ask.

'Tut . . . Tut . . . Tut . . . Wee fella doesn't know . . . Wee fella never knew . . . Wee fella lives in a pie . . . Tut . . . Tut . . . Tut . . .'

We look at her. We've lost her, whatever moments of lucidity we had from her have gone and in their place is the childish gibberish that breaks our hearts.

'Wee fella . . . So serious . . . So angry serious . . . Wee black daffodil . . .'

'Mammy . . . Mammy . . .' my sister says.

She cocks her head as my sister speaks and puts one of her fingers to her mouth as if to say, I will be quiet, I am all yours. In her eyes there is that open trusting look she puts on when she thinks we want to talk seriously to her.

'You can't stay here any longer, Mammy . . . It's too dangerous . . . Too upsetting . . .'

'Right you are . . .'

As she says this she tries to get to her feet, her eyes scanning the room for potential threat, her mouth widening in terror.

'No, please, Mammy. Please,' I say.

She sits back in her seat, gently puts her head back so that she is looking up at the ceiling. She breathes through her mouth, long deep sighs going in and out, in and out. The tears when they come run quickly down her face, and down the creased folds of her neck.

'This is bloody impossible,' my sister says.

I don't look at her; my eyes are fixed on my mother. I know that she is back with us, that somewhere she is aware of what she has become.

'Oh no . . .' she says. 'Oh no.'

Farrell's Undoing

I knew that he had been watching me. He was fascinated by my fuck-you attitude. I was everything he wasn't and it drove him up the wall. I suppose it began when I interrupted his class to stop him terrorising one of his pupils. For weeks after that, now and then, I could feel his eyes on me as if I was one of those cryptic puzzles that you find at the back of the serious newspapers. I knew that he wasn't sure whether he wanted me as his friend or his enemy. I didn't have the same quandary. I was good with people; Farrell knew this and it irritated him. He would watch as I encouraged students to think, to write, to express themselves in any way that they saw fit. I would tell them that rules were there to be blurred, what was important was that they took life by the balls, grabbed a hold of it. I talked like that once. I thought that I was fearless. Now I know better. So it became Farrell's mission to get to know me, to find out what made me tick. I knew all I needed to know about him, he was a bully. It took him a couple of weeks but eventually he worked his way up the teachers' dining table until he was sitting beside me. He would crack jokes about teaching, about Gaelic football, women, anything that would give him an in. He suggested that maybe we spend some time together, maybe have a meal to chew the fat so to speak. I said that was a good idea. We went to a Chinese restaurant in the centre of town and ordered sake with our food, that was my idea. Before long he had loosened up and the starchy Farrell gave way to a sloppy, vain man who talked about all the women he'd had. It was because he was over six feet tall and that well, you know, he said, leering at me across our Peking Duck.

'No, I don't know,' I had said.

'Well,' he said. 'The taller the man, the bigger the . . .'

'Right.'

'It's simple maths, you see.'

'Of course. And you would know.'

'You're right there, Mr O'Rourke.'

He ate like someone who hadn't seen food in a long time, packing his mouth with rice, bits of fried seaweed, dim sum, anything that was to hand. Then he would sit there and chew, making tiny humming noises like a large child happy to have something to put in his belly. As the evening wore on, he became more and more unravelled, loosening his tie and raising his hand to wipe the beads of moisture that gathered on his forehead. His eyes shone as alcohol came and broke down the frigid reserve that he faced each day with and he began to talk about his wife. I had heard rumours about her. She was dead, I knew that much. She had committed suicide. It was a while ago just before he had moved North. No-one knew the exact story but I do know that a few fingers had been pointed Mr Farrell's way. He told me that she had suffered for years from crippling depression. She found everything difficult, nothing enthused her. It was terrible, he told me, like living with someone who was already dead. That's tough, I said to him, very tough. Yes, he said, he had been teaching in a school just outside Dublin and had returned home one day to find her hanging from the stair rail. It was strange, he said, to open the door and see two shoes that he knew so well just hanging there in mid-air. It was unreal, comical almost. He paused as he told me this as the memory welled up in him to sit glistening in his eyes. Tough, I said again, this time more quietly.

We went back to his house after dinner. By now he was drunk; I was too but I was more practised at it. He stopped many times on the long walk to his home and wagged his finger at me, telling me what a fucker I had been to him. I know, I said, you're right. I don't like you, you're a pain. This made him laugh, a harsh dry laugh that made me think that he hadn't seen love in a long, long time. The more I drank, the stiller I became as if a vast desert had opened up inside me and I stood on its fringe looking at the distance I would have to travel.

As he fumbled for the key to his front door, I remembered that he had a daughter and that one of my colleagues had said that he treated her appallingly. It was no surprise; I saw the way he was with his pupils. He was punishing the world for what had happened to his wife. I knew that rage. I recognised it in myself. I remembered my neighbour May and how we had broken her that night long ago when the moon stuttered in and out of the clouds in the sky above our heads.

His house was immaculate and ordered. There was a large armchair in the living room. In front of it was a pair of slippers, neatly placed. On the arm of the chair was a folded newspaper. On the small dining table was a vase with a single rose in it. He paused and looked at it and said: 'She's a good 'un is my Majella. Come in, come in, O'Rourke.'

He went to a cabinet in the corner of the room and rooted around inside it until he found what he was looking for. It was a half-full lemonade bottle.

'Poteen. Our gift to humanity.'

'Yes,' I said.

'I've had this for fecking ages. Must be you, O'Rourke. Must be you brought it to my mind.'

There was mischief in his eyes as he said this, and also a judgement which brought a kick of anger to my gut.

'How about tea . . . to chase it down with?'

'I'm fine.'

'Oh feck that.'

'Honestly . . .'

He went to the small corridor leading off from the room we were in and shouted up the stairs.

'Majella. We have a guest.'

He swayed slightly as he re-entered the room and put his hand on the back of one of the dining room chairs to steady himself.

'You had me that fecking day you came into my classroom. You had me good, you bastard. Don't think that I've forgotten.'

I smiled and reached over and took the bottle of poteen from him, unscrewed its top and put it to my head.

As soon as his daughter entered the room I saw him point to the kitchen. She stood there for a second in her pyjamas before obeying. I watched as she filled the kettle, insolently wiping the sleep from her eyes. She was thin but well proportioned and I could glimpse the half-moon curve of one of her breasts as she put some cups, saucers and glasses down on the dining table between us. Farrell must have seen me looking because he told her to go and put a dressing gown on. Just before she did she looked at me for the first time.

It wasn't long before the poteen claimed Farrell. He was talking to me about the North, one of his favourite subjects. He told me that we had made the whole fucking thing far too complicated. Look at the South, he said to me, look at the South, busy, prosperous forward-looking.

'We don't fecking want you. Do you follow?'

'What?'

'Us. The Republic. No fecking interest. The lot of yous, Catholic, Protestant. We no more want you than a hole in the head.'

As he said this he burped, it was part food, part air and his eyes glassed over as if someone had just hit him a blow on the head. He looked at me for a moment. I knew that he was trying to remember what he was saying. He raised a glass of poteen to his lips but he only managed to get it halfway before he gingerly put it back on the table. When he fell his large head cracked against the floor and a small bit of food appeared on his lips. I sat on, raising the poteen to my lips. After a few minutes I saw her standing at the bottom of the stairs. I knew that she had been watching me for a while. She was wearing some panties and a light bra; I could see the dark points of her nipples through it. She didn't say anything but just kept her eyes on me with such surety that I thought it wasn't the first time that she had done this. This was her way of tearing him down, of ripping his authority to shreds. He would find out, I knew this; everything done in the dark comes to the light sooner or later. Something flickered in me, a moral flag fluttering on the horizon of my mind, but it didn't last long. I followed her upstairs and watched as she undressed and then turned to face me, the full soft nakedness of her youth on display. I remember smiling. I wanted her purity. I wanted to cram her innocence into my mouth, to devour every piece of unblemished goodness that I saw in her eyes.

Water

'Gabriel?'

'Yes?'

'Do you know where you are?'

'Yes.'

'Tell me.'

'A hospital.'

'Good. Do you know why?'

'Yes.'

'Tell me.'

'Because . . .'

'Go on. There's nothing to be afraid of.'

'Because I've been unwell . . .'

They wake me all the time now. In the hours since I've spoken they keep checking that I am still with them, that I am still connected to the world. I don't mind so much, it's like learning to walk again, familiar but at the same time strange.

'How are you feeling?'

'Terrible.'

'I can believe it. You were in some state when you arrived . . .'

'Yes . . .'

'Do you need anything?'

'I'm thirsty . . .'

'Bring our guest some water.'

I blink as my eyes get accustomed to the light. I was in a

deep sleep and am always groggy from the drugs they are still forcing down my neck.

'You're going to feel very strange for a while. But it's important that you trust us.'

'Yes . . .'

'I need to ask you some questions.'

'Okay.'

'Let's start with your name.'

'Gabriel O'Rourke.'

'Where were you born?'

'Newry . . . County Down . . .'

'When?'

'August 1961 . . .'

'Good man.'

'And do you have any idea why you would be in a place like this?'

'Because I fell . . .'

'You fell.'

'Yes, I fell.'

Wildflowers

Somewhere I knew that I missed him and that I still do, not the man he was but the man I saw glimpses of, the tender broken man who flickered into being sometimes like a ghost shimmering in the corner of a forgotten room. I missed the pact that held us together. I loathed myself for feeling this way. He was not a father, I tell myself, he was a vulture preying on my youth, feeding on the carcasses of my dreams. He took my heart and blackened it on the fires that were consuming him. I think of my mother and the kingdom she built in the dark corners of her life, the shining city filled with the love of God and the smiles and indulgences of dead saints. I think of the look that passed across her face when she spoke of the gift that she had been given, how she could look into other people's hearts and see the heavy cargo of sins that they bore and the secrets they harboured. Yet she was blind to the horror in her own kitchen, oblivious to the devil sitting in her living room, his feet up, a beer in one hand and a betting slip in the other.

I knew that I would fight him all my life even beyond his death. I realised it at a very early age when his eyes found mine and they told me everything I needed to know. So when we buried him he became more alive than he had ever been. My sister never spoke of him after he died, she would smile blankly or deflect the conversation in some way if I ever brought him up.

We never went to the grave, not even my mother. We discovered years later that Petey had gone every Sunday after Mass and placed a bunch of wildflowers on it. Maybe he felt responsible for his death, or maybe guilt for the feelings he had for our mother. Vincey, one of the gravediggers, told us about Petey's visits years later when we laid our mother to rest. He said that Petey would walk the borders of the grave and warily greet my father as if at any moment he might leap out from the dirt and attack him. He would tell my father how everyone was, and eventually on the fourth or fifth visit he told the grave that he loved our mother.

Vincey said that it was quite the weekly event for him and his colleagues, that they would watch from behind a neighbouring gravestone as Petey would wring his hands and bring his handkerchief out from his jacket pocket and dab his balding head. Vincey said the look of fear on his face was comical and they could see the faint shake of his leg through his trousers, like a dog taking a piss, he said.

'What kind of things did he say?' I asked him.

'Oh you know . . . What a bloody disaster, Johnny. Terrible. Terrible. Not what any of us wanted at all. Rest assured I'll look after her. Rest assured that's my promise to you. God bless you, Johnny. God bless you.'

Then he would kneel and bend his head in prayer. Sometimes either Vincey or one of his mates would throw a small piece of gravel, pinging it off another headstone and startle him.

'You would have thought that hell was opening its gates the look of fucking terror on his face.'

I felt sorry for Petey, I always did. He was a child trapped in a builder's body, ill-equipped for the world that had bred men like my father. He loved my mother, of that there was no doubt, and of course Jesus. He told me that he had a heart with room enough for everyone. I know now that when a man says that he is lonely, that life passes through him like the wind through an abandoned bus shelter in the depths of winter. He had never married, it was our mother's fault, he used to joke later, and somewhere it was true, he had saved himself for her. He had followed her to the hem of our Lord's gown; he had worshipped not only God but the God he found in her.

He made a real effort with me when my father passed away, but it was too late, I had already entered late adolescence and I had begun to run with a crowd of boys who wanted to tear down the world that had been built by people like Petey. I began to steal from him, taking money from his wallet whenever he was in our house, usually when he was praying in the front room with my mother and some of the neighbours. I would ask him for money when he came out from his prayers, invariably he would say sure and a smile would crease his large face. I would watch with a quiet satisfaction as he opened his wallet and stared for a moment at his money.

'It's okay, Petey, if you don't have enough . . .'

'No . . . No . . . I was sure there was another . . .'

'What?'

'Fiver in there . . . Strange . . .'

Then he would look at me, and I could see what he was thinking. He would grimace and shake his head. I knew he suspected me, but I didn't care, in a second the thought would leave him. He was too good-natured, too trusting to follow the suspicion through.

'Listen. If it's a problem . . .' I would say.

'No . . . No . . . Here . . . Here . . . I'd be insulted if you didn't . . .'

So he would stand there holding out a fiver and I would make a gesture as if to say you're too generous and then snatch my second note from him.

'Thanks, Petey,' I would say and I'd run from the house ten

pounds richer, laughing at the thick-headed gullibility of the man standing in the doorway behind me. It was no wonder that he believed in God with such a passion, a man like that would believe in anything.

The Kiss that Never Was

One day he left and never came back. He said goodbye as usual after the healing school had held its afternoon session and walked out into the June sunshine telling us that he would be there as usual tomorrow for his Saturday afternoon cup of tea. But he never returned. My mother was frantic with worry for the first few days. She had come to depend on him. After a week of fretting she sent me to his house to find out what had happened to him. I remember knowing that it was pointless. Both my sister and I had talked about it and there was something about the way he walked down the pathway of our house the week before that told us he was done with us as a family. Ciara said that he seemed to take in every single flower with his gaze as he moved towards the gate. When he reached it he stopped and took in the view of the town below and the roll of the hills leading to it. Then he softly shook his head, stood for a second and then continued on his way without looking back. So as I stood on the small lane that led to his small bungalow a week or so later somewhere I knew that he was gone. The shutters and boarded door on his house confirmed it. I knocked for a while on the front door more in hope than anything else but silence was all that greeted me. I walked the short distance across the fields to his neighbour Sam Riley's house and waited as I heard him shuffle his way to the door to greet me.

'Young O'Rourke.'

'Sam.'

'What has you in these parts?'

'I was looking for Petey.'

'Ah. You'll be a long time looking, son.'

'What do you mean?'

'He's gone. Upped and gone.'

'Right. Where?'

'Blowed if I know, son.'

'Mum's worried.'

'Aye. They were tight enough your Mammy and he.'

'Yes.'

'Did he not say anything?'

'No. Not a word, Sam.'

'Well, son. He kept himself to himself did Petey. He had God and that was friend enough for him, I suppose. We were never that close. We'd chew things over now and then but that was it. So one day he was there and the next he wasn't. I didn't pay it no heed. This country's full of people who have left.'

'Right,' I said trying not to laugh.

'Is there something tickling you, son?'

'No, Sam. No.'

'If he didn't say anything to your mammy then I would take a guess that he didn't want any bugger to know what he was doing or where he was going, if you get me?'

'I get you, Sam.'

Sam was a timid man who spent his days hoping that life wouldn't notice him. Sometimes he stayed in his house for weeks at a time peering out of his grubby windows, waiting until the courage to venture out came back to him. It gave him a distracted air as if he was not quite connected to the cut and thrust of the world around him. He had never married, didn't have any pets, he just walked the floors of his house day after day and that was universe enough for him, thank you very much, he would say.

'He could be anywhere, the bugger . . . England . . . the States . . . Scotland . . . He has folks there, I think. Sorry, son, I'm fuck all use to you.'

'Don't worry, Sam . . . I'll tell Mum.'

'Right you be . . .'

When I told my mother about the boarded house and what Sam had said, she just looked at me for a moment and then nodded that she had heard me and that I should go about my business. I left the room thinking that somewhere it had been no big surprise to her. It was only years later when my sister and I were tending to her in the final broken days of her life that we got some inkling as to why he had left.

One night we were both getting her ready for bed, ignoring her childish protests as we tried to get her to swing her legs up and underneath the bedcovers. We had spent minutes at this cajoling her, but she just sat there, her feet planted firmly on the floor, her lips pursed tight. At one point I leaned over her, my face close to hers to implore her to co-operate. As I did she turned her head from me and said: 'We've been through this a hundred times, Petey Macken, a no is no.'

I remember freezing where I was, my body bent, my lips inches from hers.

'What, Mammy?'

'I said we've been through this.'

'Through what?'

'This kissing business.'

'What kissing business?'

'You're a good man. A sweet good man, Peter. But I don't think of you that way. I'm sorry, there was always one man for me. And God made him flawed. I tried when he passed. I tried to get rid of him. You know that. To say that was that. We move on. But you see I married him. In heaven's eyes we were bound and there's no in-between in the matter. So I'm wed and that is something you must respect. So put those lips of yours away.'

I remember looking into her eyes and for a second I thought that I saw the round baldness of Petey's head reflected there. I looked at my sister and smiled. So now we knew. All those years ago he had made one more forlorn attempt to stake a claim in my mother's heart and she had refused him as she had always done. It was one kiss too far for Petey and for him life without her was preferable to life as her companion, aching for something that she couldn't or wouldn't give him. Often after he had left I would look at my mother and see that she had regretted how tough she had been with him. Life was long and for someone like her there were many hours to fill, which from then on she would have to do on her own. We never heard of him again. I missed him, and no longer blamed him for what had happened to my father and I knew that my sister felt the same. He was a kind man and that was in short supply in our house.

Dying Egypt, Dying

I'm talking to them about a poem. I know that some of them couldn't give a toss. I'm telling them how important it is to see life as a series of moments, that they come and go like swifts skirting the gable of a house. I tell them that a great poem can distil a moment, that it can freeze it in its tracks like an ancient mosquito forever caught in amber. I am sweating. It smells of cheap whiskey. I took a few belts this morning to give some kick to my day. It is Wednesday, the worst day of the week, neither the beginning nor the end. I have just read the poem out loud and tried to ignore the snorts of boredom I hear from one or two of my students. It is Louis MacNeice's 'The Sunlight on the Garden'. And it never fails to stir something in me. I think about the scarred ground of my marriage and the loathing that I see rising in my wife's eyes whenever I try to speak to her.

I begin the poem again; I know that one or two of the boys look to each other as I do and snigger. I read it at my wedding many years before; I had been too drunk to do it justice, tripping over its words and its fine sentiments. I remember how my wife had lowered her head with mild embarrassment as I began then stopped and started again. I take a deep breath and wish myself back to that day when I stood beside her, and our families looked our way. I start. I see the food on the tables before us, the cuts of roast lamb and the glint of the fine wines in their glasses. This time I will get it right. I see my mother, how she dabs her eyes with one of the table napkins. I know that she is pleased, content that I have found someone to take care of me. I will no longer have to, she had told me. My sister is beside her, now and then placing her hand reassuringly on her arm.

The musicians are milling around the makeshift bar waiting for the speeches to finish. I had a drink with them earlier, well more than one. They are good guys and joke with me that maybe I should slow down as perhaps I wouldn't be able to get it up that night. Don't you worry yourself about that, I tell them. I remember how the light moved through the grand hall where the reception was being held, how it caught the small pieces of dust in the air. I remember thinking for a moment that maybe there was a God after all, but the thought doesn't last long, it slips away and I know that it will be a while before it surfaces once more. This time I think I will savour each word, I will turn it on my tongue and fashion it into life. The poem will come to life in my mouth and float into the air like the soft beating of angels' wings. I see again the way you looked at me; there was love in your eyes, but also a small fear that had begun to live in the corner of your gaze. This time I will remove that fear, I will crush it in my hand like a small egg. I will reach the highest peak of your heart, I will climb there on the ladder of the fine words that I am about to speak. My finger is shaking as it moves across the lines of the poem.

'Sir, sir . . .'

At first I don't hear him, but when I do, I wonder why he is at the wedding, none of my pupils were invited. I look down at him and see Pettigrew looking at me as if I had taken leave of my senses. I decide to ignore him.

'The sunlight on the garden, Hardens and grows cold . . .'

'Sir, please, sir . . .'

'We cannot cage the minute, Within its nets of gold . . .'

'Sir . . .'

'When all is told, We cannot beg for pardon . . .'

'Sir, sir . . .'

I no longer see the guests, or my wife as her hand sought mine when I began to read. I don't see the fine wines in their crystal glasses. I am back in the shabby classroom. The students are all gathered in the doorway and they are sniggering. In their midst stands Boyle the principal. He is looking at me, there is coldness in his gaze. Pettigrew is tugging at my sleeve. I look at him; there are tears in his eyes.

'Sir, sir, the bell for the end of the class went nearly ten minutes ago.'

Boyle steps forward and comes close to me. He sniffs my breath and then turns on his heel.

'Go home, O'Rourke. I will call you when I want to see you. The rest of you boys go to your next class. Now.'

Snow

We find her in the snow. She is kneeling. Her hands are clasped. She has been there all night. Her body is stiff and angular. Her face is contorted in a final attempt at prayer. She looks like a statue guarding the entrance to a vast white land, one of frost and death. She is no longer the woman I grew up with, the one who steered and prodded us into God's judging face. I think of the last time I saw her when she spoke of angels in the television. In a way she looks beautiful, the last moment of her hard life caught in ice, like a sculpture sent by God's own hand. She must have wandered outside searching the darkness for the truth she always knew lay just beyond her reach. I stifle a cry. The countryside seems reborn; powder-fresh with new snow, as if a wide blank page had been laid across the blackness of our lives, telling us it was time to start anew. In its centre was the kneeling shape of our mother, the only remnant, the last gateway to the long fear-filled hours of our childhood. She died as she lived, prayers rushing from her lips like water streaming around a rock in a river. Two crows skirt the blue of the sky, their wings beating out a mournful pulse, their sharp caws mocking any grief that is beginning in our hearts.

My sister looks at me, neither of us knows what to do except stare at the finality of what is before us. Somewhere I wished that the land around us could stay like this, all its passions and fever held suspended in this architecture of ice and frost, everything hidden and stored in this white cargo of snow. It is too cold to cry; at least that's what I tell myself. I think of the hours I spent at her side, hoping for the word to fall from her mouth, the one that would release me. It never came, and I know now that I was looking in the wrong place. A wind stirs in the branches of the trees that stand like sentries around her body, their skeletal bodies longing for summer.

I see my sister fall to her knees; hear the soft crunch as she hits the snow. She bends her head and stays that way for a moment, stealing glances at our mother's body. The world around us bristles with noise, from the construction work on a new house across the fields to the sound of the wind blowing our hearts wide open.

I make a move towards her body. I don't know what I will do when I get there. I don't want to touch her, to feel her iced flesh beneath my warm fingers.

'Don't,' my sister says.

'We can't just do nothing,' I say.

'Why not, what difference will it make?'

She was thawed out and buried. The expression on her face remained though, the one of dismay, that now she would carry for eternity. She became famous in death for a little while; the undertakers said that it had been a long time since they'd had to collect a frozen one. She was buried beside her husband; even in death she would not be free of him. She wouldn't have wanted it any other way, for all that she had learned about him, for all that she sensed, he was hers, God-given and joined forever. I often thought of her kneeling there in that winter painted landscape where we found her, like an aged and wrinkled Madonna, her hands clasped, her knees rooted in the soil, her eyes half lidded, her soul flown.

References

He smiles as he fires me. Both of his hands are on the desk in front of him, and though he is smiling his eyes are cold and glassy as if was I dead to him. He tells me that he has been patient; he has bitten his tongue as far as I was concerned but that this time it was serious, that the events of the previous few weeks had made his mind up for him. You must realise, he says, that there has been a serious clamouring for your dismissal and I have resisted more than I feel anyone else in my position would have done. I'm not a bad person, he says to me, you must understand this, I am not a bad man, but things cannot go on the way they have done.

I suppose I am relieved, at least that's what I tell myself as I look him directly in the eyes and see a man who is frightened of being disliked. It makes me pity him. It's all about him, about how I will remember him. He's weak, all tyrants are. He explains to me that he had hoped that the little break he had given me after my episode in the theatre, as he puts it, would have sorted me out. We all know that you have been under enormous pressure especially with your mother's illness and death, but the occurrence in the classroom the other day has forced my hand, you see, now the parents of some of the students are involved and once that happens, well . . . He raises his hands off the desk to let them finish the sentence for him. It is the first time he's moved them.

Still I don't speak. I sit there wondering what I will say to my wife, but that quickly fades to be replaced by a bloody-mindedness, fuck what she thinks, fuck what any of them think. Boyle tells me that never in twenty-five years of public service has he known a case like mine. Drunk at the theatre, drunk in class, never has he had a teacher put the welfare and the security of twenty pupils in jeopardy before. I want to say that I think that he's going a bit too far, but I leave it. He's finding the whole firing thing difficult, and the less I speak the more uncomfortable he feels which is fine by me. I think of the first time I arrived at the school over seven years before. I remember how determined I was, how idealistic, now it's nothing more than the last threads of smoke from a dying fire.

He has stopped talking and is looking at me. I know that he has just asked me something but for the life of me I don't know what it is. It's happening to me more and more as if I am slowly removing myself from the world. I decide to wait for him to repeat what he said.

'References,' he says.

I nod. He waits. I nod again.

'You're going to need them.'

I shrug. He waits. I shrug again.

'I've discussed it with the board . . .'

He pauses again as if to say would you like to come in at this point. I don't and won't.

'And one or two of the teachers . . .'

Again he looks to me. This time I neither nod nor shrug.

'This, you understand, is tricky. Because what's not in doubt is that you are a very capable teacher. But we feel – and this was unanimous – that we cannot recommend you to another post until you sort out your problems. Your issues. Drinking, etcetera.'

At this point I stand. I look at him and smile. I feel sorry for him in his plush wing-backed leather chair with his receding hairline and his head full of manners and dos and don'ts. I look through the window at the fields, at the trees moving slowly in the breeze. I pick up my briefcase and on the way out of the room I spit on the floor. As I walk down the corridor leading to the exit I meet Farrell. I can tell that he knows, and as he approaches I can see him debate whether to stop and say something. When I reach him he holds out his hand. I look at it but don't take it. Then I stare him in the eye.

'I fucked your daughter, Mr Farrell. She was sweet. Sweet and willing.'

Memory Down

She stands before me with that look in her eye, the one that I know so well, a hard, tight look that a fighter has before he takes or gives the next blow. I see the way she fills the doorway positioning her body so that I can't squeeze through. I smell the scent of our house, the familiar warmth of breakfast cooked, and coffee brewing. I look for my son, for the bustle of his shape, but he is nowhere to be seen.

'Can I come in?

'No.'

Her voice is hard and pointed like a trowel hitting brick.

'Please.'

'No.'

I hate myself for begging; detest the small boy I hear in my voice. I feel like a whipped dog left in the rain with nothing but the hunger in its stomach for comfort.

'You can't do this.'

'I can and I am.'

She sounds so flat as if she had been programmed, her words are robotic and without feeling.

'I love you.'

Nothing, not even the flicker of her eyes to let me know that she heard me. I pull my hand across my face, and think about lighting a cigarette, but then remember I don't have any. I look at the ground and then at the backs of my hands, for the first time I see the rasp of bruising and drying blood across the knuckles. I stare at them in disbelief, my mind scouring the events of the last twenty-four hours, frantically chasing down what has caused the blush of blood on my hands. She is watching me; there is something in her eyes that makes me stop for a moment.

'You don't remember, do you?'

She makes a gesture at the garden behind me; I turn and see the mounds of earth spewed across the grass and the broken flowers torn from their beds, their heads snapped and limp, barely attached to their stalks. The hedge has a body-shaped hole in it; leaves lie spattered on the pavement like discarded paper.

'What?' I ask.

'Think, Gabriel. Have a long good think.'

'God . . .'

'You haven't a fucking clue, have you?'

'What?'

She gently moves aside so I can see down into the hall; it takes me a while to get used to the darkness, then I see the smashed chair lying on its side, and the coat stand broken in half like it was a matchstick. I move forward to take a closer look, she backs away, there is fear in her eyes. Just behind the door I see two large dents in the plaster of the wall, two fist-sized depressions.

'Fuck.'

She rolls up the long sleeves of her T-shirt and reveals two large bruises on the tops of her arms, two hand-sized grips. I can see the line of the fingers marked in an angry, accusing shade of purple.

'Usually I can manage, you know, when you take it out on me. I tell myself that it will pass like a storm and that you will blow yourself out. You were told the last time, when you were admitted to hospital, that you have to get help. On your own.'

She stops speaking to gather herself, to halt the tears that rise in her. I want to take her in my arms. I gently move towards her.

'Don't. Don't you fucking dare.'

'Please.'

'Your son saw everything. Every bloody thing you did. He saw you for who you really are, Gabriel. He wants nothing to do with you. Do you understand? Nothing.'

'I can't remember. I can't fucking remember. I swear to Christ.'

'It doesn't matter, do you understand? None of it. Not the excuses. Not the promises. It's all gone. You are dead . . . dead. And you don't see it, do you?'

'Oh God.'

'The police were here again, Gabriel. I thought you were going to kill me. You were ranting and raving about . . .'

'About?'

'Being fired.'

'Right.'

'It's not my fault you were fired, is it?'

'No.'

'What sort of a man does this? Tell me. What sort of man does your son see when he looks at you? Do you ever stop to think?'

'What happened?'

'You banged me up against the wall. You had me by the tops of my arms. You were shouting. I swear to God there was foam at the corners of your mouth. You were fucking monstrous. Eventually I got away from you and ran into the bedroom and called the police. They put me on to a lady while they sent someone round. She asked me to tell her where you were in the house. I crept back into the hall and there you were taking lumps out the wall with your fists. Banging as if it was someone's head. And John was standing there watching you, tears in his eyes. Jesus, you should have seen yourself. God. When the police came it took them forever. You had undressed and lain on the bed. They took my statement. And then they tried to wake you up. No chance. One of them started laughing. And two of them lifted you by the ankles. You were buck naked. They told me to leave the house. Although they said you would probably be a different animal when you woke up. That's what they said, a different animal. Buck naked they shook you . . .'

'Jesus.'

'I don't think that even he could help you now.'

'I'm sorry.'

'Please, that's a very overused word as far as you're concerned. Sorry is not going to fix this. I slept with John last night. Sleep, that's a joke. I heard you moving around about two or three hours later and then the door going.'

She lowers her head and stays that way for a minute. I see her hand shake as she moves it through her fallen hair. The next thing she says very softly.

'It's over, Gabriel. It was over anyway. But any chance . . . Well there are no more chances. Stay away.'

I hear her close the door behind me as I walk away. I don't look back because I know that violence still hangs in our doorway like a bird of prey and that it was me who put it there, no-one else but me. I shake my head as I walk down our street. I tell myself to give it time, to get out the way and to stay that way. I will find somewhere to go where I no longer have to think, no longer have to feel. A cold wind blows up.

The first drink tastes of her flesh. It brings her body to the tip of my tongue. I imagine drinking her down, from fingertip to toe, with each sip she is more in me, more completely part of me. I want it to last forever so I take my time.

The second drink tastes of my hatred of her. She is mud and grit; and it slides down my throat like sludge. I want to tear her down, to remove the smug look I saw in her as I stood in my doorway earlier that morning. She's the cause, the beginning and the end of all my pain.

I look to the third drink to remove both women, to stamp them down. I want the thinking to stop, the tearing and the pulling at the fabric of my sanity to cease.

Halfway through the third drink I gag, I sense the barman looking at me but I force the second half of it down and indicate that I want another. I know that I am heading down into the half-light of drunkenness and I welcome it.

Softer than Love

Moira, the doctor with the blue-grey eyes, is back with me. It is a day or so after my session with the young male nurses and my panic in the holding room. She is sitting with me, this time on a small chair beside my bed. I am glad to see her, and I sense that she is too.

'I hear you spoke.'

'Yes.'

'How did that feel?'

'Weird.'

'Yes, I bet it did.'

'How much longer do I have to be here?'

'Do you want me to lie?'

'No.'

'A while, I'm afraid.'

'How long is a while?'

'Think of it in stages. Three or four days ago you wouldn't speak. And you ended up on the floor of the holding room downstairs screaming for your life. Today you are making polite conversation with a lady you hardly know. I would call that progress, wouldn't you?'

'I suppose.'

'You were a teacher?'

'Was . . . was a teacher. I seem to remember I was fired.'

'Why?'

'I think you know as well as I do. I think that it's all written down in that little red file you carry around with you.'

'My, you really are back with us, aren't you?'

'I've never been away. It was the rest of you that went missing.'

Begging for a Fairytale

How often have I stood here, as a child, aching for the future, asking it to come and lift me from the Sunday hours of my young life? Now I want it stopped, this moment forever held. It is in the next second that I know I will decide to get drunk and that I will burn all the promises that I have made. It is two weeks since we buried her and in that time my sister has monitored me, letting me know that the ice I am on is thin and ready at any moment to give way. I have been staying with her and I vowed when our mother died that I would not drink. I have nowhere left to go. My wife didn't even attend the funeral. She sent a wreath and forbade our son from coming, saying that she couldn't trust that I would look after him. My brother-in-law Seamus is not pleased with the arrangement, saying that everyone had tried their best with me and that I would only throw their kindness back in their faces as usual. He's fucked everything up, he said one night as I sat in their living room listening to them both argue in the kitchen.

'We tried to get him help when he went for his wife that time. We had it set up and the fucker said no.'

'Quiet,' my sister said. 'He's in the next room.'

'I don't give a monkey's. He has no job, no marriage and now we're supposed to sit here and wipe his arse for him.'

'Seamus . . . He has no-one. He needs us.'

'So?'

'So give me time with him. Let me work on him. He's not drinking. He's promised us that much.'

'We'll see. We'll bloody well see,' my brother-in-law said.

I am standing in front of my mother's house looking at the spot where we found her. I have walked here from the town. I know I am here for a reason, and maybe it is as simple as to say goodbye, not only to my mother but to the others that consider me theirs, my wife, my son, my sister, and my nieces. I stand at the crossroads of a journey I neither asked for nor wanted, and I know that this small voice of reason I hear, telling me to think not only of myself but of others too, will soon be drowned by the flood of my first pint. I suppose I came here to see if he still walks the hillside, if it was safe to return. I am foolish, I know that he will not show himself in daylight, the night is much more his scene.

My sister takes her work seriously. It is her vocation. It lies down with her at night, and informs her dreams. It hovers over her like an angel in need of peace. I love my sister, I feel inadequate beside her. I always have done.

She works as a nurse in a hospice on the far side of town; she eases the path of terminally ill people so that they can pass through the dark gate that lies at the end of their lives. She woos them and places her heart at their disposal, and they smile at her, thankful for her courage. She tells them that she is there and they have no need to be alone. She prays with them and tells them that God is waiting for them. I see us again as children, our hands entwined. We told ourselves that things would be different. We made a pact as we lay in one of the fields at the front of our house. We placed daisies between our palms and clasped our hands together and told each other that the world would be ours.

'We'll never be like him.'

'Never.'

'We'll never make anyone cry.'

'Never.'

'Promise.'

'Promise.'

We lay there for hours, ignoring the night chill that rose with the moon. We held each other, facing the world that loomed ahead of us, beckoning us. Her head lay across my chest, her hair spilling across my body like seaweed in a rock pool. I remember her breathing on my neck, her hands tugging at my jacket.

Then something rose between us, it had no name but it was clothed in dark colours. It was a feeling, a black pulse of anger, and it smelled of my father. I remember she shifted a little and a moan came to her lips, one of soft protest. I held her more tightly and shuddered as the world grew narrow. It was the last time she spoke of the wound in her heart, when she told me how he waited until she was nearly asleep before his hands began their unholy game. She told me how the world got smaller and smaller. I felt her body tighten as she began to cry. I betrayed her all those years ago. I knew no better. I slipped my hand onto her breast as we lay there together. Her body froze for a moment and then relaxed a little as my hand moved beneath her T-shirt and explored the softness of her stomach. I was doing what had been done to me. I pulled at her jeans buttons and pushed my hand down between her legs. I remember the feeling of warmth and of wetness, and the need rose in me, the hot desire that overwhelmed every decent thought. She turned her head away from me, as I moved to kiss her on the lips and a sound came from her, one of disappointment. I remember how the night fell as I touched her and I knew that darkness bred moments such as these.

I tried to get her to touch me, just like he did and for a moment she co-operated with me, her hand reaching down between my legs.

'Don't,' she said. 'Please don't.'

She withdrew her hand and rolled away from me, her arms wrapped around her body, forming a tight barrier against any further intrusion. I lay on my back looking up at the stars. I could hear her crying, her sobs rising violently from her body.

I didn't know it then but that night my sister fled from me. She cut her body free of mine and she ran. She walled up the rooms in her heart that we used to play in. Never again would we share the same torn ground, or look out on our lives with one pair of eyes.

I think of my job, how it used to thrill my heart to see my students make headway, to grasp the words on the pages of the books in front of them. I think of Boyle's face as he fired me, of the smugness I saw, of the way his hands were joined on the desk in front of him, as if to say this is it, O'Rourke, there is no second chance. I didn't like the pleasure he took in sacking me, but then what did I expect? I was everything he abhorred, a spark in the dry grass of his predictable mind.

I look at the fields surrounding the house and for a moment I think I see my father's shape break the back of the hill and behind him I'm sure I see the scurrying shape of a small boy, his feet trying to make up the distance between them, in his hands the carcasses of two rabbits. I think of my son and the fear I have put in his eyes, of the terror that I slipped to him while he slept. I know I am lost, and the pig in me wants the same for those who follow after me. Yet there is still the child inside me who begs for the fairytale, because on all sides the dark sings to him of the coldness of things.

The Sign of the Cross

I'm trying not to look. I know that it's dangerous and that something has been awakened in me. I am drunk. My sister had made me swear not to drink, she told me that this was my last chance; I said that I understood and made the sign of the cross over my heart. I am babysitting my two nieces while Seamus and my sister have a night on the town. It is at least three bottles of wine ago since they left.

She had crept out of bed and had been watching me for a while.

I didn't notice her until now. She is naked and she is crying. She tells me that monsters are in her bedroom, that she can see them moving the curtains and playing in the dark. She can hear them laughing. Her name is Mary and she is my sister's eldest.

I look at her, at her small body and her hairless sex and something stirs in me. I notice her nipples, how brown and soft they look. She wants me to come to her bedroom with her. There is something in her eyes that draws me; it's a purity that I have long since lost. I want to steal it from her, to have it for myself.

I can't look at her anymore because I am afraid of what is forming in my mind, so I tell her to go back to bed, that there were no such things as monsters. She tells me she can't because she has wet the bed, that's why she has no pyjamas on, she needs some fresh ones and the bed needs to be changed.

'Fuck,' I say.

'Don't say that. It's a bad word,' she says.

'I know it is . . .'

I can't leave her standing there. I ask her where her mother keeps her pyjamas.

'In the press,' she says.

I stand. I can feel her watching me.

'You're drunk,' she says.

'Mind your own business.'

'Shut up,' she says.

It takes me by surprise how grown-up she sounds, then I realise that she's parroting her mother.

'Go and get your jim-jams . . .'

'Pyjamas,' she says very primly.

'Yes, yes, whatever you say.'

I watch as she walks to the hot press in the hall, and notice how white her skin is, like a winter moon. I can see my sister's body in hers, the long back, the small peach-like behind. I go upstairs calling to her to fetch some fresh sheets. When she arrives, she is still naked and is clutching some sheets and a pair of pyjamas to her chest. I tell her to dress herself.

'You have to do it,' she says.

'Why?'

'Because Mummy does it.'

I kneel in front of her. I can smell milk and the sweet breath of her youth. It calls to me, it tells me to taste it. I hold the bottoms out in front of me and have to force myself to look away as she gets into them.

Then I hold the top out and tell her to put her head through, as she does so I feel her hair brush against my face. As her head comes up her eyes meet mine.

'What's wrong?' she asks me.

'Nothing's wrong,' I say.

'You look funny.'

'Do I?'

'Yes, like Spiderman when he's been bitten.'

'Do I?'

'Yes.'

'Are you tired?'

'Bit . . . I'm afraid of the monsters.'

'I know.' I say.

I push the hair back from her forehead and look deeply into her eyes. My fingers are on the down of her cheek, I run them along the line of her jaw. She is so trusting, I think, so open and caring, so new.

'Mummy says you're sad.'

'Does she?'

'Yes.'

My hands have moved to her neck. I am frightened; I can feel the desire stirring in me. This is what he felt, I think, this is what he saw. I remember the bottle of wine downstairs and know that I must get to it, put it to my head and kill the devil that has begun to dance in my brain.

'I'm lonely,' I say to her. 'Do you know how lonely I am?'

Spilled

My sister is looking at me. She has been watching me for a while; I can tell by the way her arms are folded as if she is waiting for a bus that is always late. My eyelids are heavy and my head hurts as if someone had spent the night banging it with a hammer. I try and smile but I can tell from the expression on Ciara's face that it will do no good.

'Get yourself together and meet me in the kitchen. We have to talk.'

I squint into the light that is streaming through the window of the living room. I am lying on the small goatskin rug in front of the fire. Wine has been spilled on it. I curse myself and begin to stand. It takes a moment or two.

'I would love a coffee,' I say but I get no response.

I try and remember the night before but nothing will come, all I feel is the pounding of my head. I am angry at myself for drinking again and I know that my sister is too, but I'll be damned if I'm going to let her know that I am. I see the wine bottles on the coffee table; one of them is half drunk so I reach for it.

'Don't even think about it.'

I look up to see Ciara standing in the doorway that leads to the kitchen.

'Get yourself in here.'

I join her in the small kitchen; she doesn't say anything but makes me a black coffee and dumps it down in front of me. She waits until I have taken a few sips before she speaks again.

'What did I say to you?'

'I don't know, what did you say to me?'

'Don't play bloody games with me, Gabriel.'

'I'm not.'

'I haven't got time for this.'

'Neither have I.'

'Really?'

'Yes.'

'Oh I can see that, Gabriel. You're rushed off your feet. I mean what with having no job to go to anymore. No home, no wife. You're living a packed life, aren't you?'

'Fuck off, Ciara.'

'What did you say to me?'

'You heard.'

'I told you, Gabriel.'

'Told me what exactly?'

'That this was your last chance.'

'Yes, I know.'

'And it was. I want you out of here.'

'You mean Seamus does.'

'Yes, he does.'

'Why?'

'Why do you think? Take a good look at yourself. You had everything . . . everything . . .'

'That's one way of looking at it.'

'I've taken advice. People have been helping me.'

'Good for you.'

'And they say that the best way to help you is to throw you out. Tough love they call it. That it's you and only you who can sort this out when you've gone down far enough.'

'What people?'

'People. Experts.'

I look at her and there is amusement in my eyes because I know that it will annoy her. I don't give a fuck, I feel like saying, but the coffee has made me feel a bit better and I don't want to distress things further.

'What happened last night?'

'What do you mean?'

'With Mary?'

'I don't know what you're talking about.'

'She was in different pyjamas.'

'So?'

'Seamus thinks that . . .'

'What?'

'Nothing.'

'So you want me out?'

For a moment she doesn't say anything but stares down at her hands, when she looks at me again there are tears in her eyes.

'Yes.'

Days Like People

I can't remember how long it is since I stood outside in the air. Days have become like the people I have known, one fading and blending into the other so that I can no longer tell which is which. They have let me sit by the window, so I can see the grounds. It is morning and the world is hung on long curtains of mist. It makes everything look ghostly and half formed. My head feels heavy and I have to prop it up with my hands as I lean on the windowsill. My shaking has stopped; I noticed it this morning when I woke. I was calm as I lay in the bed and looked at the white ceiling above me, something I've not been for a while. They're still drugging me, it has to be this way, or otherwise the demons will begin digging at my flesh again. I was moved to a small ward yesterday. Moira came to say goodbye to me and said that her work was done and that she was handing me over to another part of the hospital. I liked her, she had a sense of humour, tough to sustain in a place like this.

For the first time in a long time I feel safe, and part of me wants to stay here forever, sectioned from life and its pain, dressed in a gown, pumped full of medication and held by these blank, anonymous walls that surround me.

My legs are bare and they stick out beneath me like toothpicks. I see the scars and bruises on them and wonder how they got there. I try to say my name, but it takes me a moment to remember it and when I do it slips away again, like those trout I used to watch in the stream by my house. I look around, a woman shuffles past me and smiles at me, she shows me all her teeth when she does it. It disturbs me for a second, but then I relax and give her a little wave. A man sits by a television set in the corner, his hair is wild and unruly and his shoulders are hunched up around his neck. He is rocking slightly and shouting every time his team gets the ball. He must have felt me watching him because he turns round and gives me a stare as if to say what are you looking at? I shrug, he doesn't scare me; I've been in tighter spots. I can't stop yawning. I see a man across the lawn that lies in front of the building; he is raking leaves, piling them high and then dumping them into black bin bags which he has trouble controlling in the brisk wind. I watch as they flap around his body like big black tongues.

They told me that I will have an assessment this afternoon. A woman nurse came into the ward and sat on the end of my bed and smiled and patted the shape of my feet. She had a small tight smile, well rehearsed, and no bigger than it needed to be.

'How are you feeling?'

'Okay.'

'Good. You look a little better.'

'Right.'

'My name is Bridget.'

I remember looking at her and thinking that I could love her. Her hair is a dirty blonde colour and her eyes have that patience that comes from sitting and watching people in pain, the same look that my sister has.

'I'm . . .'

'I know it's tough. It's a tough time. It seems you went on quite a journey . . .'

'I suppose.'

'Here, take these.'

She holds out three little pills. I look at her for a moment before reaching out for them.

'How long have I been here?'

'Here in this ward?'

I nod.

'Just overnight. We moved you in here yesterday evening. Before that you had your own little room for a while. Do you remember?'

'Yeah.'

'You've been pretty sick . . .'

'Right.'

Yes, I could fall in love with her, with her measured humanity and her tight-uniformed body.

'Anyway, Doctor Garland will go through all that with you as will Doctor Burke. Until then rest. And if you want you can go into the recreation ward and smoke or read. Whatever you want to do.'

'What's your name?'

'I told you – Bridget.'

'Right. You did.'

'Where are my clothes?'

'I'm afraid I can't give you those.'

'Why?'

'It's policy.'

I don't say anything but look away. She leans into me and whispers softly in my ear.

'Have faith, Gabriel.'

I nod. I want to believe her, I really do but there is a fear in me that I'm not sure will ever leave. I look at her as she walks away, just before the ward doors she turns and smiles at me.

The sun is trying to burst free of the clouds. I watch for a moment as the light ignites the sky then I roll a cigarette, leaning my head against the windowpane as I do. I can feel the damp on my forehead. I think of the conversation with Bridget earlier that morning, and wonder about the assessment. I know that

I have been in a strange country peopled with my own fears. What will happen when they stop drugging me, when I no longer have these chemicals in my body soothing me, telling me that everything will be alright.

'Hi.'

I look up and a young woman is standing in front of me. Her hair is unkempt and parts of it lie across her face. Her eyes have a hunger to them; she reminds me of a small animal who hasn't eaten for days.

'Hi.'

'My name is Josey.'

'Josey?'

'Yes, it's short for Josephine.'

'Pleased to meet you, Josephine.'

'Likewise. Mr . . . ?'

'Gabriel. I think.'

'Like the angel.'

'Yes, like the angel. I suppose so . . .'

'Do you have a spare one?'

'What?'

'Cigarette?'

'Yeah of course. Please.'

I give her my tobacco and watch as she rolls her fag. I see her wrists and the long scars on them, thin and ugly and the colour of milk. She notices and turns away slightly, hiding her hands from me. She is painfully thin.

'Thanks.'

'No problem.'

She blushes and looks down. She's dressed in jeans and a T-shirt and white sneakers, they're stained and more grey than white.

'I see they let you have your own clothes.'

'Yeah.'

'They won't give me mine.'

'It takes a while. They have to be sure that you won't make a run for it.'

'Oh I see . . .'

'It took two weeks the last time for me.'

'You've been here before?'

'Yeah, a couple of times. You?'

'No, first time.'

'Lucky you.'

'Well . . . I don't know about that.'

'Yeah, I know what you mean.'

'Anyway I don't know how much use my clothes would be to me. They were pretty fucked, I think. I'd been living in them for a while.'

'Oh they have gear. You know . . . They're used to people coming in, you know, off the streets and stuff.'

'Right.'

'You have very sad eyes.'

'Do I?'

'Yes. Sad and big.'

'So do you.'

'Yeah, I know. I suppose we all do in here. We all have sad eyes.'

No Bounce

'Is there any bounce in the situation?'

'What?'

'Bounce . . . Give . . .'

'No, Gabriel. I'm sorry, there's no bounce.'

'Just a tenner. A fiver . . .'

'No.'

'Come on . . .'

'No. Not anymore. No.'

'Please.'

'Don't beg, Gabriel. Don't beg.'

'What else am I supposed to do?'

'Get help.'

'I don't need help.'

'We have it all set up. There's a place that will take you and you can rest. You can get well.'

'I'm fine.'

'No, you're not. You're far from fine. Gabriel?'

'What?'

'Where are you?'

'It's not important.'

I know that she is on the point of cracking, I can hear it in her voice. I stand there in the phone box hoping that she does before my small change runs out. I try and nudge her, to get her to relent.

'Please, Ciara. Please, Ciara. This is the last time I swear. I swear . . .'

'Gabriel. This is Seamus.'

'How are you?'

'Alright.'

'Right.'

I know now that my chance has gone. I should hang up and keep what dignity I have left intact, but I don't.

'Seamus, I'm stuck for a . . .'

'I know what you're stuck for, Gabriel.'

'Can I trouble you for a . . .'

'No.'

'Is that your final word, Seamus?'

'It's my last and final word, Gabriel. Don't call here again.'

I stand there for a good few minutes after he hangs up, the phone receiver held out from my head as if at any moment I expect the conversation to restart. It begins to rain and I watch as it runs in long lines down the glass of the phone booth. After a while I try the number again but all I get is an engaged tone. I have enough for one more quick call, so I try her number even though I promised myself that I wouldn't. It rings for a while before she answers.

'Hello?'

I can hear the television in the background and our son asks who it is on the phone.

'Hello?'

'Who is it, Mammy?'

'Hello?'

'Mammy?'

'Gabriel . . . Gabriel . . . Is that you?'

I don't say anything but stand there and listen to the fear in her voice, and then I imagine myself beside her watching our child getting ready for bed. I can feel the warmth of our living room, and see the news on the television. I fool myself that it is possible, that I could live that way, happy and mute, never questioning, never raising my voice. I would be content with the boredom that so many people accept. Maybe we would settle down together after John had gone to bed and watch a film, and tell ourselves that storms were things that destroyed other people's lives, not ours. But as I lean there against the phone booth's glass I know that it is nothing more than a myth, that I had my chance and that now I stand where I deserve to, outside of all things.

Dead Man's Hand

I remember a train journey. It was one I had made many times before but this time it was different. I looked at the fields as they loomed into view and then fell away again and I smiled. I was leaving.

Some of the people around me moved places whenever I caught their eyes. I didn't care. The conductor thought about saying something to me, I could see it in his eyes, so I presented the ticket to him with a fuck-you flourish. I think I tried to order a drink from the trolley that passed a half an hour or so into the journey but the young girl ignored me until I stood up and shouted after her. I can't recall what I said but it was enough to bring the ticket collector scurrying back to tell me in no uncertain terms that if I didn't behave I would be asked to leave at the next station. After that I just sat there and muttered to myself. Yes, I was leaving. I was throwing what was left of my life to the wind.

I believe that I see my mother sitting across from me as the train pulls into Drogheda station. I just stare at her for a moment asking my eyes to tell me the truth. I watch as she gets up from her seat and reaches to get her bag from the luggage shelf above her head and I realise that she is getting off. I speak to her; I tell her that I love her. She looks at me and I can see that she doesn't recognise me. I repeat what I said but my tongue must be playing tricks on me because she just looks at me as if I have insulted her. I decide to leave with her and try and reason with her away from the prying eyes of the people around me.

The air when I step down from the train is cold and for a second it snaps my mind into focus, that's when I lose sight of her. I search the platform and just when I am about to give up hope I spot her as she passes beneath the Exit sign. I hurry after her, breaking into a small trot. I collide with someone and think about apologising but if I do I will lose time so I don't bother. I feel as if I am running across a vast desert and my feet slip and sink into the hot white sands. I call her name, but there is no reply and above the vultures circle as they have done so many times in my life. In the end I give up and stand there in the main street. I feel for the bottle in my pocket. I know I am alone and that I am in the place where all things come to die.

Like an Egg

'Hi, Gabriel. I'm Doctor John Garland. And this . . . this is my colleague Doctor Sarah Burke. Please take a seat.'

The office is spartan and bare except for one filing cabinet and a desk, a phone and a few chairs. The window blinds are drawn and the desk lamp is switched on, throwing shadows on the wall behind the two doctors.

'How are you feeling?'

'Like shit.'

'That's to be expected. The mind is a fragile place.'

'Yeah.'

'I have your file here from Doctor Rush. I trust she took care of you?'

'No complaints.'

The woman smiles at me. She is around forty and her hair is swept back into a pony tail, her eyes are brown-black. Garland is maybe four or five years younger and balding which he has fought by shaving his head.

'Yes indeed, the mind is as fragile as an egg. It can't take the damage that you've meted out to it. And that's leaving aside what you've done to your body.'

'I want out.'

'Listen to me, Gabriel. It's normal that you feel this way. You have regained some kind of mental composure and now you're wondering what all the fuss was about,' Garland says.

'I want out of here . . . You can't fucking hold me . . .'

I see them look to each other.

'I'm afraid you're wrong there,' she says.

'What do you mean?'

'We can hold you as long as we see fit.'

'No, you can't . . . Unless . . .'

'Yes?'

'Unless someone signed me in here . . . Who was it?'

'You have people who love you very much,' Dr Burke says.

'Who was it?'

'Your wife signed you in. With the express agreement of your family.'

'You mean my sister.'

'Yes, and your brother-in-law.'

'He's not family.'

'We can understand that this is a shock.'

'Fuck.'

'So. You're here. And our advice is go with it, give it a chance, what have you got to lose? You were in a pretty bad state when you came in . . . This is the best place for you . . . We can help you get back to some sort of normality . . . You have been in an alcohol-induced psychosis. You've damaged your liver. You were a threat not only to yourself but to those around you.'

'My wife and I have been separated for months.'

'Yes, we know but you are still legally married. And it was her wish that you get the help you deserve . . .'

'Bollocks. She just wants me where she can control me.'

'Have you forgotten the events of the past couple of weeks?'

'What do you mean?'

'You believed that you were in danger. Paranoid. About to die.'

'I was . . .'

'Please . . .'

I am shaking. I wish I could stop it, I know that it doesn't look good, but the more I try and control it the more the body refuses to obey.

'I think you should rest,' the woman says. 'I think we should up your dosage. We have you on a combination of Librium and Quetiapine which is an anti-psychotic drug. The best thing you can do is to sleep.'

'I don't want to sleep. All I ever do in this fucking place is sleep.'

'Please, Gabriel, don't make this any harder on yourself.'

'I want out of here.'

This time they don't say anything but look at each other, the woman shrugs and lets out a sigh as if she was dealing with a noisy child.

'I said I want out of here.'

'We heard you, Gabriel,' Garland says.

I can hear a note of frustration in his voice. He shuffles the papers in his lap as if he might find some answers there. So we sit in silence. I can hear the sound of traffic from outside and the low whine of an aircraft.

'This is a fucking joke,' I say.

I get up and try to look as together as I can, but my legs are shaking beneath my gown.

'At least give me my own clothes to wear.'

This time all Garland does is shake his head. He then leans forward, his eyes holding mine.

'We are recommending treatment for you. This will involve a stay in an institution for alcohol abuse, minimum stay four weeks. Now I know this is not what you want to hear. But you were a danger to yourself, Gabriel. You ended up on the streets of Drogheda. Do you not remember? This is no joke. This is a man's life we're talking about. You will be moved from here to a clinic on the other side of the grounds when we feel you are ready.'

'Why not now?'

'I'm sorry?'

'Why not move me now?'

'Because we have to be certain that the psychosis you suffered was alcohol-induced and not something more deep-rooted.'

'But you just said it was.'

'Yes, but we have to be certain. One hundred per cent certain. As I said the mind is a fragile place.'

'I'm sorry, I know that this must be difficult for you,' the woman says.

I hold her gaze and for a second I almost believe her concern is genuine, but then I grunt at her and look away.

'You've been in a war,' she says. 'And it's the worst kind. A war against yourself.'

The Twin

The devil lies here with me sometimes; he smiles a lot because things seem to be going his way. I'm careful not to think too much when he's around because that's meat and drink to him; he gorges himself full to bursting on stuff like that. He takes one thought, builds a nightmare and then hands it back to you with a big Got You grin on his face. I fight him with booze, I build a little island of amnesia in my mind and then drink my way to it and settle down there in peace. She has put me here, in this folded world. She caught me cold and knocked me through the walls that held me upright, and I landed with a smack in this place, in the shadows beneath the sunlight of normal life.

The devil tells me that women are like this, remember the snake, he says to me sometimes at night when I am trying to sleep. His whispering shakes the trees and brings flexing muscles to the dark so that everything seems as if it is on edge. It's bad when I'm broke and can't buy a bottle to pay the fare to the island that I built in my mind. Then I just have to tough it out. I lie by the roadside or in a doorway or wherever I happen to be and quietly sing to myself to drown out the hiss of his words. Once, my defences weren't up in time and before I knew it he had me by the neck and his lizard's eyes looked into mine for a whole hour before he spoke.

'I am your twin,' he said to me. The wind seemed to echo

him beating the words out on the tin roof of a shop nearby. Rain began to fall just as he spoke to me as if in command and I remember the heavy drops falling on my forehead.

Then he became rain, before my eyes his flesh dissolved into water, and for a moment he stayed there looking at me, his eyes now two dark puddles and then he fell away to be washed along the gully that lay at my feet, his words echoing in the air like the swish of a thousand rattlesnakes. I remember I didn't sleep after that, I kept scouring the dark, and the street corners in case he returned. Every passer-by had to be scrutinised in case he had jumped into them and was wearing their skin for a while to fool me. I know that I frightened some of them, but I had no choice, my soul was in danger. I followed one man for a few streets. I tried to be considerate and keep my distance until the chance came to get a good look at his face. At one point he stopped and stood there just ahead of me with his back to me. I waited and then slowly began to inch my way towards him. Still the man stood facing away from me and then he turned to look at me. I could tell immediately from his eyes that he had seen the devil too in his time.

'What do you want?' he asked me. 'Why are you following me?'

He was frightened, his upper lip trembled, and his hands moved in and out of the pockets of his coat as he spoke to me.

'I . . .'

'Well, what the fuck do you want?'

'Have you seen him?' I asked him.

'Who?'

'Him.'

'I don't know what the fuck you're talking about.'

He was lying. I knew that. I could tell from the shifty way he looked around him as if he was expecting someone else to come along. They always lie, the people who have seen him. I knew that. I was different, I wanted to expose the bastard, to pull him out from underneath his stone to drag him into the glare of the world. I needed allies. That's what I wanted to say to this man, I needed an army, I needed it quick.

'Here . . .'

The man threw a bunch of coins on the street by my feet.

'Now fuck off and leave me alone.'

Before I knew it he was gone, his shiny dress shoes clacking their way along the rainy street until the shadows ate him up. I looked at the money around my feet and laughed, because Judas came to my mind: he ended up in the dirt separate and bleeding just like me. I gathered the coins, my hands scraping them from the pavement and the road. I tried to say thank you to the retreating figure but it was too much of an effort so I just thought it instead.

On the Wing

'What happened to you last night?'

'What do you mean?'

'You were jerking about in that bed as if it was on fire.'

'I couldn't sleep.'

'Weird . . . I thought for a minute you were banging one out.'

'Fuck off, Frank. Listen, I'm trying to get another half an hour . . .'

'Okay . . . Okay . . . I was just worried about you, that's all . . .'

'I know, I appreciate it.'

Frank was a porn and sex freak. He was in the bed closest to mine. The orderlies would routinely raid his closet for smutty magazines and erotica of any kind. He was a skinny man, with limbs like a prepubescent and he moved quickly as if he was trying to get to the next moment of his life to see what it held.

He had lost everything, like me. He was a baker, strange for someone so thin. He owned a couple of bakeries in Belfast and had made quite a profitable little business until he started flying first class to Bangkok to get his end away. Drink was in the mix of his life too as it always was where anyone was in pain. He told me he'd met this young Thai girl who was as slender as a bamboo shoot with eyes that made you want to jump in head-first. She could do things, he said, that he didn't think were humanly possible. He set her up in an apartment in Bangkok.

He called her his, she had a family in the mountains to feed, a brother, a niece and a mother and father, so he gave her money for them too.

His wife in Ireland began to get suspicious and asked him why he needed to make so many trips. He told her that golf had become huge in his life and the best holes were in the Far East. He borrowed money from the bank in Belfast using his business and his home as collateral.

He was being bled dry. His wife had him followed at his own expense, and the private detective caught him with his young Thai lover bent over a brand new washing machine that he had just bought her. After that, his debts caught up and the bank took away his business. He told me that he was trying to make a new start and that he would only stick to massage parlours from now on, and that he was trying to save his marriage and reclaim his good name in the community.

I felt sorry for him, but then I wasn't in too good a shape either. I thought of the prostitute I had been to see and I know how easy it is for a man to see salvation in a young girl's eyes, to think that heaven lay between her legs and that angels danced on the tip of her tongue.

'You have a visitor.'

'Who?'

'Your wife.'

'I have no wife.'

'I'm only the messenger, Gabriel. Maybe that's something you should take up with her.'

'Give me a minute.'

'She's in the recreation room. And you realise that I have to note that you are still in bed. It's now 11.30 a.m.'

'I had trouble sleeping.'

I watch as he leaves, his name is Pat; he is one of the nurses on the floor I'm on. I didn't like him from the moment I saw him, mainly because he didn't seem to like the work he was doing and much less the patients entrusted to his care. He was a sweaty individual, his forehead constantly stained with perspiration and his palms when he touched you were clammy and cold.

When I reach the recreation room, I pause before I enter. It is a while since I have seen her and I know that when I look into her eyes I will be seeing a part of my past that I would rather forget.

There is a daytime chat show on the television and a few of the patients are sprawled out on chairs around it. I see her sitting at a small table in the corner. Her head is bent forwards slightly as if she is trying to pretend that she isn't in this hospital, in this ward, where the minds of those around her hang by a thread. As I reach her she looks up and a smile instinctively rises in her eyes, but then almost as quickly a frost passes over them. Her left hand is clasped around a Bic lighter and in her other she holds a packet of cigarettes.

I stand looking at her, telling myself to behave, to keep the dogs in my heart at bay, but I can't forgive her for what she has done to me.

I see Pat hovering in the background checking up on us. I know my wife has probably had a word with him, stressing how volatile I could be, and how it might be better to keep watch in case I blew it.

I sit opposite her and stare at her. I'm owed an explanation and I'm determined not to be the one to speak first.

'Promise me this won't get ugly,' she says.

'Why on earth would it get ugly?'

'Come on, we're not children. You're angry with me and I understand that.'

'That's a fucking understatement.'

'Don't, Gabriel. You're not the only one who feels the world owes them.'

'Why did you do it?'

'I had to.'

'There was no had to it. You just wanted to fucking control me . . . Like you always fucking did.'

'Jesus, Gabriel. Have you no notion of the state you were in? Of the danger you posed not only to me or John but to yourself as well.'

'I would have been okay. I just needed to get it out of my system . . .'

'Get what out of your system? Normal people don't spend nights sleeping on the street to get things out of their system. Normal people don't terrorise those close to them to get things out of their fucking system. They talk, Gabriel. They sit down and face each other and talk. That's what normal bloody people do. Jesus, I'm with you five minutes and I'm back to square bloody one, shaking and bloody crying. This is no good, it's just no good . . .'

I lean forward and put my hand on hers; she withdraws it and tightens her grip on the lighter she's holding. I know this woman so well, I think to myself, better than anyone else and yet there is a gulf between us that I can't help feeling that I spent the length of our marriage putting in place.

'How's John?'

'Why?'

'What do you mean why? How is he?'

'Oh all of a sudden you care. You sit here and you care. Where were you when he was crying for you? Did you care when he saw you punch holes the size of tennis balls in the walls of our house? No, I doubt you did. Jesus, I promised myself I wouldn't do this. I wouldn't cry or fight with you. I just wanted to come and see if you were okay and then get on with my life . . .'

'Cathy?'

'Yes?'

'Is he alright?'

'Yes.'

'Does he miss me?'

'Yes.'

'Thank you.'

We sit in silence. I think about getting up and leaving but something keeps me there. I know that we are both taking stock of where we have ended up, of the shattered mirror of our marriage. I see her shake her head, I want to take her in my arms and tell her that I feel strength returning to my bones, that my eyes are clearing and that my heart is hers for the taking. But I know better than to disturb the quiet that has settled over us. Besides I built our lives together on the fragile ground of hollow promises. I reach over for one of her cigarettes. As I do she seizes my hand, I feel her fingers tighten on my knuckles. I look at her and see her eyes fill with tears. The ferocity of her grip surprises me.

'Gabriel, I'm sorry but this doesn't change anything.'

'It's okay,' I say.

'You know?'

'It's alright. Please, it's alright.'

'My parents want me to go ahead with the divorce.'

'Okay. That's not really a surprise. I mean they wanted you to divorce me even before we got married.'

'It's not funny.'

'I know it's not funny.'

'I told them that it was between you and me.'

'You got that right.'

'Right.'

'What do you want me to say, Cathy? What do you want me to say?'

'Nothing. There's nothing to say. We've worn out every word we've ever said to each other.'

When she leaves I ask the nurse to give me something to knock me out, something strong to burn the sentences my wife spoke to me from the lining of my brain. I'm told that medication wasn't a room service menu to be dialled up and sampled whenever I felt like it, and that I will have to sit with whatever is bothering me. I tell her to stuff her fucking tablets which doesn't go down too well. I am given a warning, it doesn't make any difference. I tell her to fuck off again, and that I want my clothes, that I am going home. She tells me that isn't possible. I then march to the security door and start yelling to be let out. Pat appears. I can tell he wants me to keep shouting because then he can have his way with me. I remember the figures that had hovered about me all those nights before, the glint of the syringe and the faces that floated in the air around me like satellites ringing the earth. I tell myself to calm down; I won't give Pat the pleasure of getting his hands on me. I take deep breaths forcing cool air into my hot and fiery lungs. I turn to see Josey looking at me; her eyes are warm and full of understanding. She raises her hand and holds two fingers out to me, giving me the victory sign. I nod and look at Pat; his eyes are narrow and dark like a predator's, waiting to pounce. I smile at the fucker, a big toothy grin even though my heart is breaking.

Raw

I am with Dr Burke. She is sitting opposite me. I have been called back. It is because I told the nurse to fuck off and caused a bit of a scene in the visiting area. I don't mind, it's not as if my day is brimming with activity. My head hurts, maybe it's the drugs they're giving me, maybe it's the journey I've been on.

'You were very angry earlier on apparently.'

'That's one way of putting it.'

'Your wife visited you.'

'Yes.'

'We thought long and hard about whether it was a good idea or not.'

'Well you obviously got it right. I mean it all went swimmingly, didn't it?'

'Well, it was to be expected. You're upset. You're raw.'

'You're the doctor, doctor.'

'Yes. Being flippant won't help anything.'

'But it sure as fuck makes me feel better.'

I watch as she grimaces and looks down at her notes. She thumbs through them and then says: 'The longer you are contrary, Mr O'Rourke, the longer you will stay here.'

'Fine.'

'It doesn't seem to bother you but I know only too well that it does.'

'As I said, you're the doctor, doctor.'

'Tell me about the time you spent on the street,' she says.

'Why?'

'Why do you think?' she asks.

'I don't know, that's why I'm asking you.'

'You can be a bloody-minded so and so, Mr O'Rourke.'

'So can you.'

'That's my job.'

'I'd rather not . . .'

'What?'

'Remember . . .'

'You will eventually whether you like it or not.'

'What?'

'Remember.'

'It wasn't something that I set out to do . . .'

'I'm sure.'

'It just . . .'

'Yes?'

'Seemed to be part of the story . . . Part of the fall . . .'

'You see it as a fall?'

'Yes, don't you?' I ask.

'Yes . . . Yes, I do.'

The Cave

I am on my knees looking up into the confused gaze of a stranger. Someone I plucked from the stream of his life, an ordinary man who one moment was travelling to the warm predictability of his job and now stands embarrassed as another human being clutches at the hem of his coat. It was arbitrary, there was no design in my choosing of him. I suppose it was a little like fishing; I just cast out the line of my desperation and caught this young man, with his two-tone collar and bright 'I'm alive' tie. For a moment we just look at each other, no words separating us, no fumbling to get away, just for a second we connect and see two versions of the one soul. I see him gulp and a bead of fear prick his brow, and I know that I have him, that he will throw something my way just to be free of me, because he has seen a part of himself in my eyes. People step around us, refusing to look at the tableau that sits before their eyes. I don't care, I'll hold on to the one I've got, please, my eyes say, please, I'll protect you, as long as there is me down here then it cannot be you. He pushes a couple of coins at me, I see they are golden, that they will buy me a small plot of land in that country where the dead roam and sing you to sleep.

I let him go and grab the coins from the pavement. In an instant he has gone, swept into the business of his day. I know that the thought of me will stay with him. He will probably make a joke of it, telling his workmates how I smelled, how I had him by the coat as if I was going to propose to him, and how he hurled the coins at me to get shot of me. What's the city coming to, he will say, adjusting his collar, toying with his cuffs, it's ridiculous, dangerous to have these wretches in people's faces.

The off-licence is open when I arrive. The walk there is difficult, my heart is sore and lonely in my chest and my head throbs from the noise of cars and buses, and people jostling. The owner doesn't look at me; he asks me what I want and then gets it without raising his eyes to mine. He is fat from sitting behind his counter day after day, year after year. I think about saying something but I decide against it, all I want is what's in the bottle he sells me. As I leave I try and smile at him but it hurts my face.

I hide the sherry in my coat and walk back out into the glare of the day. I search for somewhere to drink it and eventually find an alleyway and sit down behind one of the bins that dot it. I don't want anyone to see me when I'm taken away by the booze. I tear at the cap of the bottle, throwing it away as soon as I tear it off; I cut myself on the serrated seal that runs along its neck. I put it to my head and close my eyes; I feel the rush of the liquid, the sweet punch of its taste. I rise to meet it, my soul, my heart, my will, every tired and hungry piece of my being. I feel myself being put back together.

I ache for the moment to last. I drink again, head back, throat open, taking it down, but already it's fading, and my body is rebelling, my stomach churning. I gag some of the liquid back into the bottle but keep it tilted so that it comes back immediately. I drink through the retching, through the nausea, getting it into my system as quickly as possible. Eventually I take it from my head and lie back against the wall. The world quickens around me, melting into itself, the alleyway becomes a warm cave lit by the glow the alcohol has put in my stomach, and children play at the mouth of it, their shadows leaping joyfully onto the wall behind them.

Within minutes I am swimming in the deep waters I have been looking for all day. I am in a stupor where everything goes through me like a light breeze leaving no stain, no worry, and no pain. My eyelids are hooded, my mouth slightly open, and my hands lie by my side as if they belonged to someone else.

For a while I didn't see them, the strangers that came to take from me. I thought that they were just ghosts from my mind thrown up onto the wall of the alleyway. I didn't even feel frightened when one of them grabbed me by the hair and shook my head from side to side, I think I even smiled. One of them put his face up close to mine; I could smell his breath, it smelled like mine. He grinned at me for a long time and his mouth made little chewing noises like a mouse that's come across some cheese.

I tried to say hello but the words wouldn't come; they rattled around my brain and never made it to my mouth. It wasn't until I could feel their hands rummaging in my pockets that I realised what they were at. I put my arms up and kind of waved at them to say no, to say stop it but I think one of them thought that I was trying to hit him so he smacked me in the mouth. The pain arrived a short time after the blow, like when I was a kid watching a farmer in the distance hammering fence posts, the noise of it reaching my ears a moment after he struck them. I could taste the blood in my mouth and then he hit me again in the same place, his grin getting wider.

The smacks to my mouth immediately put flesh on my

attackers and I tried desperately to get to my feet, but they were on me in an instant, kicking and punching, tearing and pulling. Then it went black just like in the films and all the sound and madness stopped and I was left fading into the dark.

Shilling Hill

The nurse on night duty has given me a sleeping tablet. I had to ask her three times. It is difficult to sleep now that they have lowered the dosage of my medication. I lie in bed waiting for the pill to take effect. For a while nothing seems to be happening, but then slowly but surely I feel a numbness invade my brain stilling all the squibs of thinking that have held me prisoner for the past few hours. My heart settles into a calm rhythm. My body is warm and relaxed and I picture myself standing by the ocean at Shilling Hill just south of Dundalk, watching the trawlers fighting the swells of the water, hounded by a smattering of feeding gulls waiting to steal scraps of fish from their decks.

It is a summer's day, the kind that tells you there is hope; you can see it in the swirl of the birds as they play in the rising wind. My father is there. He had come to my bed a few nights before for the first time, and this day was his apology, I know that now, his present to replace what he had taken from me.

My mother too was there, opening the packets of fish and chips that we had bought on the way, laying them out on the tartan car rug as if they were the food of kings. My sister was running along the shoreline, taunting the surf that ran hissing onto the beach. I don't see any of them, I claim that day as my own. I was the only person alive, the only one with eyes to see.

'Are you alright, son?' my father asked me.

'Yes.'

'You sure?'

'Yes.'

I see him standing beside me, smaller, diminished by memory and the deed he had done. There was guilt in his voice, I heard as surely as the call of the seagulls that wheeled above us. He shifted his weight from one foot to the other and raised his hand to his forehead and gazed out at the horizon. The skin on his face looked grey and bloodless.

'What a day.'

'Yes.'

'You sure you're okay?'

'Yes, Dad.'

Then he put his arm across my shoulder, lightly pulling me to him as we stood and faced the sea. I know now that it was as close as he ever came to saying that he was sorry. I could feel it in the way he held me, even though my skin was crawling. It was gentle and tender as if he was trying to make up for what he had done to me. I remember the way my mother looked at me that day as we ate huddled together on the car rug. It was different, like she was seeing something in me for the first time. She held my eyes a little longer than usual, as if she was trying to solve a riddle I had presented her with. It unsettled me and I found myself looking away and finding refuge in the horizon beyond.

As always, we had prayed before we ate, my mother leading the way. I remember how the words stung my mouth and refused to be born. I clasped my hands together and bent my head, willing myself to give thanks for what I was about to receive but nothing would come.

It is the look on my father's face though that haunts me as he stood beside me and we faced the vastness of the world together that day all those years ago. He had the look of a man staring into the abyss, knowing that what was left of him lay in pieces at its bottom. He no longer had the playfulness in him, a shadow had moved across his heart and he now walked hand in hand with the broken of this world and he had given me the same privilege.

I am drifting into sleep; I feel my mind give in to its gentle call. I like the feeling as if a burden has been lifted from me. I try to say my father's name but it sticks in my throat, I try to forgive him, but the thought of it lights a fire in the centre of my being, so I push the image of him from me. I see my wife and the hope she carried in her eyes when we first met. Even then as we held each other, an army of two, ready for what the world would throw at us, something in me told me that I would lose, that I wasn't made for happiness.

I am nearly asleep now. I can no longer feel my body, I am moving beyond it. I am falling and the walls around me are dark and as soft as a woman's inner thigh. Nothing is holding me anymore; I am free and moving towards sleep and its strange blank pastures.

The Warriors of Winter

'What's your name?'

'Huh . . . ?'

'What's your name?'

He is young, but his eyes look older than his face, they are clouded with impatience and a seriousness that I know that I must be careful around.

'My name?'

'Come on. Sit up when you're talking to me. Come on.'

I can feel his hands on me. I can see how he turns his head from me as he touches me, as if he was disgusted by me.

'Come on now. Do what you're told.'

'Wait . . . Wait . . .'

I raise my hands in front of my face to let him know I'm no threat, but he doesn't understand. I had a bottle, I'm sure I did, I kept a bit to help me through the morning, I know I did. Fuck. I know I have to be quick as he's getting really impatient now; his grip has tightened on me. My eyes hold his, there is a plea in them; maybe it will buy me a little more time, and my hands begin to hunt along the spaces around my body.

'Come on. I haven't got all day.'

He begins to hoist me, I feel my body slipping and sliding inside my clothes.

'You don't understand?' I say.

'I understand very well. Now up on your feet when you're told.'

He raises me to my feet and rests me against the wall. His radio crackles and hisses like a nest of snakes and he looks me in the eye.

'How are you feeling?'

I shrug. His change of tone surprises me and for a moment I forget the thumping in my brain and the need in my fingers to raise my bottle to my head.

'Tell me your name.'

'I haven't got one . . . I sold it to a passing stranger.'

'Smart arse.'

'Yes, you're right, I am . . .'

'You can't sleep here.'

'But I did . . .'

'I know that you did. But you won't in the future. Understood?'

I look at the neat line of his uniform, the way the peak of his cap cuts across his gaze giving him an air of mystery and authority, and I wonder what he sees when he looks at me. How many men and women has he lifted up from the gutter of their nightmares and asked them over and over again for their name, their address, their next of kin. I can feel the quaking beginning in me. It starts in my gut and moves quickly to my heart and then along my limbs. I know what my body is asking for and I must get free of this young policeman. Perhaps I hid my bottle so that it wouldn't be stolen from me as I slept, the trouble is I can't remember, I can never remember.

'Please,' I say.

'Yes?'

He looks at me with a mixture of pity and impatience, his eyes holding mine.

'I need to . . .'

'Yes, I know. I know what you need. This will only take a moment. Until then you will do as you're told. Okay?'

I nod, but even that is becoming an effort.

'Let's go back to the beginning. Name?'

'Gabriel . . .'

'Well that's one half of a good answer.'

'O'Rourke . . .'

'Good man.'

'Address?'

'Well . . . ?'

'Address?'

'It used to be Temple Drive just off the Dublin Road.'

'Used to be?'

'Yes.'

'Number?'

'17.'

'Where's that?'

'North . . . Yes, the North . . .'

'You're a long way from home. I'd advise you to go back there.'

'I can't.'

'Get off the street. Okay?'

'Okay.'

I look up the alleyway and I see one of his colleagues standing there. He is smaller than the one that is dealing with me and has a dangerous look in his eyes as if at any moment he could be at your throat. I'm glad he's not dealing with me.

'We have to log everyone we see in situations like yours. We have to take their names and their addresses and if they are not in imminent danger to either themselves or others we let them go on their way. Where you slept last night, if you can call it that, is the trade entrance for quite a well-known restaurant. Their manager rang us and asked that we come and remove you.'

'Okay, I understand.'

'I don't think that you do.'

'What do you mean?'

'I've seen you now. And once I've seen you you're mine. So if I see you again I will run a check on you and if I so much as smell trouble in your past you will regret it. Okay?'

'Okay.'

'Good. Go home. Winter is on its way.'

For a moment I watch as he walks away to join his colleague. They give me a brief look before moving into the tablet of sunlight at the end of the alleyway. Yes, winter is coming, I can feel it in the air. I look up at the sky, storm clouds move across it like dark monsters in a children's fable. My whole being is begging me to feed it what it needs. I look around at the discarded cans and newspapers and the smudged dog shit. I get on my knees and begin to root around, throwing over bins, my fingers slipping in and out of the squelch of decaying food. I try not to panic, I know that I hid it somewhere; like a dog with a choice bone terrified that another will be drawn by its scent.

I feel as if my mind is twisting and spiralling in my head like that kite I watched all those years ago, fluttering and dipping across the inside of my skull. I close my eyes and tell myself that when I open them I will see what I'm looking for. I know that I must look stupid kneeling in front of an upturned bin. I don't care; I know that the war is beginning in me as it does every morning, and that only one thing will quell the forces that are rising in me to take me apart. Yes, winter is coming and I tell myself that I am ready for its army of frost and steel.

Among the Bridges

They are moving me. I knew it was coming. Every day I have felt the storm in my mind ease a little until I began to wonder if it had happened at all. I had a brief meeting with Dr Sarah Burke and Dr Garland this morning; she began by asking me if I still believed that I was in danger. I tried to make a joke and said, no more than anyone else. She smiled when I did this and then asked me again. No, I said, and then repeated it, no. She nodded and said that now my real work must begin. She told me that they were pleased with me, with the progress that I have made. My episodes, as she called them, have gone. When you first came here you had to be restrained regularly. It's normal, she said, for someone who was in your state. Your dosage of drugs is being lowered day by day and soon hopefully you will be drug-free.

She told me that I will no longer be in lock-up and that I will be joining a treatment programme in the main building, that I will continue in some form or other for the rest of my life. You are lucky, Sarah said to me, very lucky. God has shown you in the most violent way possible that you cannot drink anymore. Some people spend their lives shuffling from one moment to the next wondering why they hurt. You, she said, pointing at me, have been told in no uncertain terms what is wrong with you. God is asking you a question that most people are never lucky enough to hear. At the mention of the word

God I shifted in my seat and my face darkened. I saw Dr Garland reach over and put his hand on her arm to get her to change the subject. Anyway, she said, there's time enough for all of that. Yes, I said. They told me to wait in the ward and that I would be moved in about an hour or so. As I got up I asked about my son, if I will be allowed to see him, that it feels like a long time since I held him. My eyes clouded with tears as I said this. I felt stupid and unmanly sitting there, fighting back the sadness that suddenly had me by the throat. I saw them look to each other. That's up to your wife, Sarah said to me, there was a softness in her voice as she spoke to me. Give it time, her colleague said. Then Sarah said something about trust and rebuilding bridges that have been torn down. But I was no longer listening.

There are two of them. They stand beside my bed and tell me it's time. One of them I recognise, the other I've never seen before. I gather my things together and follow them out of the ward. They walk either side of me; sunlight bleeds across the long hallway making the faces of my escorts look pale and bloodless. They stay close to me, indicating now and then with the gesture of an arm or the nod of a head if we should turn left or right. I know that I am still dangerous to them, that they are not taking any chances. I try and remember the night that I arrived, but all I can see is a man screaming, it isn't my face, but it is my scream. We walk through a series of doors with coded locks on them and take a flight of stairs. As we descend I try and joke with one of my new friends, telling him how important I feel, like the Pope or a president being ushered from one important affair of state to another. The one to my left looks at me and says: 'Don't kid yourself.'

We reach a small reception area and I'm told to stop. The receptionist holds out a clipboard with a form on it and I'm told to read it and sign it. I look at it, it's a release form. I sign and one of my guards signs as a witness. I nod to the receptionist but she has already drifted back into the daydream that we woke her from. I look at the big glass doors and see the world beyond them. For a moment fear rises in me as I remember how alone I had felt out there in the world of men. One of the nurses moves ahead of me and opens one of the doors and indicates that I should pass through it. As I do I feel the sting of the November wind on my face and it seems to bring a sudden onslaught of memories with it. I shake my head and try and stay positive, ignoring the gnawing in my mind.

'Let's go.'

'Right.'

We move across the grounds, our feet kicking up dying leaves. I hear the squelch of the wet grass beneath my feet. I don't know what awaits me, but something in me is telling me to trust it, to go with it, it can't be any worse than where you've been. We reach a large building. It looks Victorian and paint is peeling from its large grand walls. A few people are standing outside it; one or two are smoking and look at me as I am led past into the large lobby area. A man comes up to us as we cross the threshold of the large doors.

'Welcome, Gabriel,' he says. 'Welcome to St Patrick's.'

They take me to a small holding room. My hospital coat is removed as are my gown and my shoes and I stand there naked as hands run up and down my body. I feel like saying that it was highly impossible that I had smuggled anything in the short distance between the two buildings, but I don't, I am as docile as an overfed dog, the drugs in my veins are seeing to that. I think I even smile.

'Good man,' one of them says. 'Good man.'

Planet Earth

My first night is difficult. I am starting to remember things more clearly and I realise that I have been very unwell. It scares me. I am in the room that they have given me. It has a small single bed in it. There are many bedrooms on the landing that I am on, full of people like me. There is a small nurse's station, manned constantly by one or two nurses. One of them escorted me to my room earlier in the afternoon and laid down the law, the dos and don'ts of what I would have to follow while I was there. Breakfast was mandatory, as was the programme that I was about to embark on. No shirking, she had said to me. She was a few years younger than me and not yet old enough to be cynical about the job she was doing.

'Lights out at 10.30 p.m. sharp.'

'Okay,' I said.

'No guests or fellow patients in your room at any time without express permission from either me Alex or my colleague Jan.'

'Okay.'

'No reading material. No radios. No TVs. No food of your own, only that provided by the institute. You're lucky, some have to share with another person, you have a room to yourself.'

'Lucky?'

'Yes, Mr O'Rourke. Lucky.'

'Right.'

'We have given you some clothes. The ones you were in when

you arrived . . . well, they were . . . You won't be allowed visitors until the second week of your stay here. So maybe then you can request that a loved one can bring you some of your own things as I'm not sure that the ones that we have given you will fit.'

'I'm sure that . . .'

'No phone calls until the second week. No reading material. Oh I've said that already . . .'

'Yes. Can I take a dump?'

'Sorry, a what?'

'A shit. Or do I have to ask for permission?'

'Well, I think that I've covered pretty much everything. Don't forget to come to the station later to get your medicine.'

'Right.'

I watched as she walked to the door of the room then she looked back at me and said: 'We've had worse than you in here. Don't think that I'm as shockable as I look. Good day to you.'

I smiled. I liked her. I was glad to be alone, to have my own space where I could try and rebuild what was left of my life and my mind. The daytime I know that I can just about cope with. It is the night that I fear when the mind turns inwards. I think about what they told me about my psychosis, about how I had been divorced from reality, believed that I was moving through cloud, hurtling earthwards towards an unnameable fear. There is a fog in my memory where that time should sit. It baffles me as it isn't that long ago, a matter of days, weeks at most. I feel like I've woken up from a strange dream or maybe this is the dream that I've woken into, this small room with its white walls and hard single bed.

Alf

He is English, but don't hold that against me, he says, as he stoops and offers me his hand. He has warm eyes and there is mischief in them. I look at his hand for a moment before taking it. His flesh is warm and the palm of his hand is dry, mine isn't, it has a seam of sweat that I can't seem to shift. He gently wipes his hand on the side of his trousers after we've greeted each other. He tries to hide it but I see it all the same. He has a large belly that spills over his belt and now and then he pats it as if it's an old friend he hasn't seen in a while. He sits beside me. He makes a small gesture with his hands as if to say is it okay? I don't respond but keep looking straight ahead. We sit there in silence. We are on the small bench in front of the main building. There is a large garden leading to small buildings and offices where I know that most of our classes will take place, we were told at breakfast this morning. I came out here to smoke before going to see one of the counsellors for an induction talk, as they put it. I hear the Englishman beside me sigh and know that he is about to speak.

'When did you get here?' he asks me.

'Yesterday.'

'Yesterday? I thought that they had you in lock-up.'

'They did.'

'Then you couldn't have arrived here yesterday.'

'No, I meant . . .'

'Oh you meant here to the recovery unit. To the alcohol programme.'

'Yes.'

'I see.'

'How long were you in lock-up?'

'Dunno.'

'It's rough.'

'Yes.'

'I'm a counsellor here, my name's Alf. I'll be taking you for group therapy and one thing and another.'

'Right.'

'Are you always this accepting?'

'No.'

'Where are you from?'

'The North.'

'Never been there. Stupid, isn't it? I've been in this country for five years or so and I have never been there. I hear it's beautiful.'

'It was.'

I am bored now. I want him to go away. This is what I'm facing for the foreseeable future, smug men in cashmere and jeans digging and probing into my life, whether I like it or not. I light a cigarette and watch as the smoke climbs into the winter air.

'Mind if I trouble you for one?'

I give him the packet without looking at him, followed by the lighter.

'Must stop these. But as the man said, I'll deal with my addictions in the order that they're killing me.'

I can feel his eyes on me looking for a response. I don't give him one.

'You must find all this very strange. Like being on a different planet. They were worried about you when you were brought in. You were . . .'

He doesn't complete the sentence but lets it trail off. In my mind I see a man crawling around on all fours. I hear the cry that comes from his lips.

'This is the best place for you.'

I see his body falling in and out of light, his arms outstretched, and his mouth open. I hear his screams and feel the tremor of fear in his soul.

'We'll start gently. Get you acquainted with our methods.'

I see insanity and sanity lying side by side. I see him walking across the bridge that connects the two. I am afraid. What if he never comes back? I turn and look at this large man sitting beside me.

'It's cold where I am . . .' I say. 'It's cold . . .'

'I know it is, son . . . I know it is . . .'

The Beast with Two Backs

I am playing along with him. Maybe he can sense that. I don't know, I don't care, I doubt it. I think he is too in love with the fineness of his words, with his high and mighty take on life. He is a small man immaculately dressed in a dark grey suit, starched white shirt and crisp black tie. His hair is finely coiffed and is steely silver in colour. I am sitting opposite him, nodding when I feel I ought to, my hands laced in my lap as if I was at an important business lunch poised to close a deal. I know that presentation is important to people like him, he has eyes that can see beyond the obvious, he has eyes like mine, that much I will give him. He has been talking to me for a while now, his voice droning on, blending with the sounds outside, the faint whine of a workman's drill or the throaty punch of a motorbike as it passes on the road nearby.

I resent him. I hate him for his newness, his brightness of spirit. I can't stand his prim attention to what he's wearing, it smacks of self-celebration, arrogance. He loves his hands; he keeps examining them, flexing his fingers, holding them to look at them as he speaks as if he's a concert pianist about to give the recital of his life.

I don't say anything even when he looks to me and pauses, offering me some space to contribute. Fuck him, I think, you carry on, I'll just sit here and let you waffle on about your life, philosophy and all things you.

He is saying that he was like me. He is telling me I have a disease, an illness, just like him. He says it's our curse and our blessing. Bollocks. He says that life is out there waiting for me, that it is an adventure, a gift, that there is no need to sleepwalk through it anymore, befuddled and be-fucked by booze. He says that this is a programme that uses Alcoholics Anonymous and that it espouses total abstinence from our drug of choice, in my case alcohol. I would begin going to meetings in the next day or so and that I had no say in the matter, that they were compulsory.

He asks me if I believe in God. I don't reply. He says he does, that it was a long journey but that he had to otherwise he would have drunk again. Big fucking deal, I feel like saying, God left the building a long time ago, all that's left is a shadow, and that's what I believe in, the dark where we all end up, in the cold arms of Nothing.

I suppose he can see the scepticism cross my eyes. Think about it, he urges, you don't have to decide now, let it sit, he says. His name is Thaddeus; it suits him, it goes with his 'I'm so special' way of dressing, and his 'I love the sound of my voice' way of speaking. He then starts talking about how all of the heavens and all the hells are inside people like us, and that we spend our lives trying to return to where we came from. As he says this he points upwards. We use booze, drugs, sex, anything to forget ourselves and the pain and injustice of this existence. But I stop listening. I take my mind and walk it past his shoulder and through the window behind him into the park, onto the grey concrete path that cuts through the lines of stark trees. I wish myself from the room, and ache to feel the cold bite of the wind on my skin, to stand alone in the November cold. I know myself there, in the aloneness of the landscape I see beyond this room.

He has stopped talking, it takes me a second to realise it, and when I look at him I can see the glint of one of his contact lenses as the weak winter sun hits it.

'Where did you go?' he asks me.

'Nowhere.'

'Have you heard anything I've been saying?'

'Some of it.'

'Some of it?' he asks. 'Well repeat it to me.'

'What?'

'Repeat it to me.'

'I'm not a fucking child.'

'Do you want to get well?'

I stare at him.

'Do you want to get well? Stop sulking.'

'I'm not sulking.'

'Then answer me.'

He waits. I lower my head and gaze at the black spirals on the nylon carpet. I drop my head because I'm afraid I'll lose it and take this perfumed man in front of me apart, pull his pampered head from his shoulders and shove it up his sweet-smelling arse.

'Is that your answer . . . to run away?'

Still I say nothing.

'I'll sit here for as long as it takes,' I hear him say.

His words are like someone thumping a pillow, muffled and soft. I can feel my hands begin to shake and I hate myself, my body and my mind forever at war, forever pushing and pulling in different directions. I think of my heart, I see it labouring in a vat of feeling like a drowning man throwing a few last desperate swimming strokes.

'I'm still here,' he says.

'Fuck,' I say. 'Fuck.'

Then he touches me gently on the point of my knee, I feel his fingers through the cloth of my jeans. I can feel what they're saying, it's alright you can trust us, they say, you're tired. Suddenly I want to talk to this man in front of me, to spill every word I've ever thought in his direction; I want them to scuttle from my brain like a horde of beetles. I want to be free of the tangle and braids of my darkest thoughts.

'Please . . .' I mutter.

He takes his hand away and just looks at me.

'Make it stop,' I say.

'Make what stop?'

'This.'

I point at my head and then begin to rap it gently with my knuckles.

'Please help me to stop it.'

'It will take time,' he says. 'And time is something that I'm prepared to give you.'

I think of my sister and myself when we were young. I see us scurrying like frightened mice, eager to escape the house behind us. I see the fear in our eyes, and I glimpse the secret that we have woven into the workings of our hearts, it peeps at me across the fallen days. I wonder at these two children, their faces blank with pain, the world stretching out before them. I ask God where he was when the sky lowered, when the birds fell silent, and the moon stuttered in the sky as the night clouds claimed it? Where was he when the world shifted and the deadness poured in? Did he cry? Did he smile, did he stand like a warrior in our persecutor's dreams, promising him hell and fury when his time on this earth was done?

I thought that my father was dead but he is only asleep and he lives in a box deep in the black ground and waits so that he can cross the dark water to feed on us once more.

Words of Flame

I'm sitting here by the side of the road, outside a town the name of which I used to know, but so much has happened, so much blood has been spilled that I can no longer remember the things that used to hold me together, like the names of towns, days, people's faces. Even the earth looks different to me now, sometimes it whispers to me as if it had a personality. Trees have a soul, I hear them sometimes in the night moaning, calling out to one another across the darkness.

I wish you were here to tell me who I am, Mother. I think of you in the dirt of your grave, your bones melting into the soil. Was He there when you died, did He hold you as if the world was being born in your smile? Did He thank you for believing in Him all this time, in spite of your husband and in spite of me? Did He ask after me? Did He? Or am I beyond even God's love?

I know that He sometimes sends spies. They give themselves away because they all have the same look and a grin that crosses their faces, one that never exposes their teeth. They stand and stare at me. They ask me questions, like 'where are you sleeping?' or 'you know it doesn't have to be like this?'

'Please,' I say. 'I need to catch the next train to heaven and I have no change.'

They don't know how to answer that. They look at me for a moment and then back off as if I carried an infection or a disease. I smile and shrug because I have them. I have seen things that they can only begin to wonder at.

Mother, my hands are not my own, the ones I have are someone else's, they are useless to me. My old ones have been removed and these old man's hands have been grafted on in their place. I took a flower the other day and rolled its stem between these lumps I now have for fingers, trying to woo some sensation into them but it was hopeless. My feet too are different; I'm convinced they are not my old ones. It must happen while I'm asleep, when the shadows deepen and the forces of the in-between come alive. I walk a lot, I have covered many lonely miles, and I know every blister and crack that lurks between my toes. They are not mine, I am sure of it. My other ones were my two soldiers, battle-hardened, as tough as a leather purse. Now they are like accountants' feet, milky and fine, more used to snuggling beneath a hardwood desk and they scream in pain when I put any weight on them.

Maybe the armies that spy on men's and women's hearts when they are asleep are irritated at me, annoyed that I can sense them, that I challenge them in the black long hours before dawn. So a plan has been formed to cut me a new body limb by limb. My old body is hacked from me when I do chance to sleep and the new part sewn on. I know that it is hurried because I can trace the fine stitching across my joints, it is like a cobweb line from a spider's web, you have to really look or you will miss it. They are working at me, changing me, piece by piece. It will end with my eyes, because when they replace them, they will have my soul.

The Tough Guy

The day after my induction meeting with Thaddeus I join the rest of the new patients in one of the small buildings at the bottom of the large garden. There are about fifteen of us and we all sit in silence, waiting. One or two of the women speak but the men mainly look at each other and nod. Alf the Englishman is the first to arrive and he enters the room bristling with energy, greeting us all with a loud 'Hello'. Some mutter a reply, others like me don't bother. He tells us to bring our chairs forward and to make a circle. For a moment I think about leaving but in the end like everyone else I comply. To my right is a young man who I later find out is called Greg. He keeps staring at his hands and shaking his head as if he has just made some major decision that he regrets. I gently nudge him and ask him if he is alright. He doesn't reply but hides his face in his hands until I stop looking at him.

Then Thaddeus makes his entrance, opening the door with a sudden snap as if he is trying to catch us in some unseemly act. The theatricality of it makes me blurt out a laugh. He greets Alf with a short nod of the head and takes up position in the centre of room, one hand in the trouser pocket of his green tweed suit, the other holding a large black folder across his chest.

'Thank you, Alf. I'll take it from here.'

'Thaddeus . . . Good morning, everyone.'

Alf left, closing the door softly behind him.

Thaddeus looks at each one of us and then nods slowly to himself. He pulls one of the chairs away from the wall and joins the circle. He places the black folder on the ground and then says: 'Welcome, everyone. This is the most important day of your lives. You may not know it. But then again I do.' He grins at us as he says this.

'My name is Thaddeus and I'm an alcoholic,' he says. 'There's no trick, no dirty deed, no fucked-up immoral act that I haven't done. I am a card-carrying alcoholic of the first kind. I've been to hell. I've been sectioned, I've been beaten with sticks, and I've held a knife to a man's throat and asked him to love me. I've cried, and I've made those who love me cry. There's nothing you can say to me that I haven't said, there's nothing you can do that I haven't done. This is an illness that delights in telling you that you haven't got it. This is a disease that will bide its time, that will fuck you as surely as God made little green apples. It will take your wife or your husband; it will take your child, your home, your nice gleaming car. It will take your dignity, your pride, your love of all things, most importantly your love of self. Let's go round the room and introduce ourselves so we all know what we're dealing with. We'll start here.'

He points at Greg. He shifts in his seat and eyes Thaddeus distrustfully, flicking a glance to the rest of us, appealing for help.

'Excuse me.'

'Why are you here?'

'Well . . .'

'Yes. What's your name?'

'Greg . . . I'm a lawyer.'

'So?'

'Sorry?'

'It doesn't interest me what you do. Only why you are here. Now let's start again. Why are you here?'

'I don't really know to be honest . . . My wife set it up . . .'

'Your wife?'

'Yes, my new wife.'

'Your new wife . . . And why would she do that?'

'I don't know . . . I think she felt I could do with a break.'

'So let me get this straight, one day your wife just decided that maybe a spell in a psychiatric hospital might be just what you need by way of a holiday, or a bit of fun.'

'I didn't say that.'

'What?'

'Holiday . . . Bit of fun.'

'That's the impression I'm getting.'

'I . . .'

'Where are you?'

'In St Patrick's.'

'And what does St Patrick's . . . ?'

'Deal with?'

'Yes.'

'Depression.'

'Try again.' Thaddeus leans forward in his seat and places the flat of his hand up to his ear.

'Drink. Alcohol.'

'Well done, Greg the lawyer.'

He looks around at the rest of us, slowly taking in our faces; it's self-conscious and designed to intimidate.

'Let's get one thing straight before we go any further, it's not by chance that you good people have ended up in here, something deep inside of you all is begging you to listen for the first time in your lives. Something is crying out for you stop otherwise you would still be in your bars, or crack houses or dinner parties, doing whatever it is you did to anaesthetise yourselves. These chances don't come often, sometimes they never come at all so gather your lives in your hands and do whatever it takes.'

He points at me. I stare back deep into his green eyes. I feel my fists clench. I remember our meeting and am angry at myself for giving in to him, for being weak and mealy-mouthed. I feel something harden in me. I look at his neat suit and his crisp neat shirt and wonder if this is what is waiting for me.

'You know my name,' I say.

'Yes, that's true. But it's not for my benefit. It's for everyone else's.'

'I don't give a fuck about that.'

I can hear one or two of the women snort their disapproval.

'Does it give you comfort to curse?'

'Not especially.'

'Then why do it?'

'Because it gives me something to hang on to.'

'Right. Does it make you feel tough . . . just like your father?'

'Don't push it.'

'Is that a threat?'

'Maybe.'

'You lost everything, didn't you? You ended up in an alleyway pissing yourself. Begging for money . . .'

'So?'

'Where's your dignity? Your self-respect?'

'None of your business.'

'Not only did you lose everything. But you lost your mind too.'

'Whatever you say.'

'And now you want to get violent, don't you?'

'Fuck off.'

Greg told me later that he thought that I was going to get up and punch him. He said he had never seen someone so angry. Instead I left the room and stood outside and tried to calm myself down. Then I looked at the sky and saw myself there. I saw myself as I was only a short time before when the world bristled with threat and there was nowhere for me to lay my head.

Mrs Johnson

I watch her as she sits beside me, her heavy body causing the wooden spars of the bench to sag. She doesn't look at me but brings a hand up to her face and slowly passes it across her mouth as if she was a farmer looking out across a freshly mown field. I think about moving but something stops me, I am fascinated by her, she has the same watchfulness to her that I know in myself. She seems tired, weary. I know that she has been in the fire just as I have. For a while we watch the sky and the people moving about the grounds. I have often seen her in the recreation room seated in front of the television, the volume up loud, watching some turgid soap opera, her hand playing with the wisps of her short blonde hair. After a moment she takes out a packet of cigarettes and puts one in her mouth and then offers me one. She does this without looking at me. I take it and nod thanks and put it to my lips. As she lights my cigarette she looks at me for the first time. We smoke and return to silence. Out of the corner of my eye I can see her head gently nodding. As she stubs out her butt I see that her toenails are painted different colours, red, pink, green and violet. I smile, it is deep winter and she is wearing flip-flops.

'Mrs Johnson.'

She holds out a hand. I take it and shake it.

'Pleased to meet you,' I say.

'I have been watching you. Mrs Johnson has been watching you.'

'Yes?'

'Yes, Mrs Johnson likes you. I had to wait . . .'

'Wait for what?'

'Until I was Mrs Johnson so that I could say hello.'

'Right.'

'The others are not so sure . . .'

'The others?'

'Yes.'

'Not so sure of what?' I ask.

'Of you.'

'Oh okay.'

She looks at me and smiles. She seems pleased with herself as if she has just completed some arduous task.

'Gabriel,' I say.

'I know. Mrs Johnson asked around . . .'

'Do you enjoy being Mrs . . . ?'

'Yes. She is very correct, very clean. I sorted my room out today. Washed every surface. Dusted every nook. Mrs Johnson likes order.'

'Right.'

Then she leans in close to me so that her face is inches from mine. I can smell the rich odour of face cream.

'It's the others who drink. Not me. No, not Mrs Johnson.'

'Who are they, the others?'

'Well there's Cassie. She's a dirty stop-out. Would sleep with anyone in pants. And then there's Angelina. She's a princess.'

'A princess?'

'Of the heart.'

'I see.'

'But they both have terrible problems.'

'Yes.'

'Needs that never can be met. Drink, drugs, gambling . . . desperate needs.'

She turns away from me to gather herself; there is a long streak of black in her hair at the back which she had missed with the dye bottle.

'I have tried to tell them,' she says, her head still turned away from me.

'Tell them what?'

'Leave it to Mrs Johnson. She doesn't drink. Doesn't smoke. Doesn't open her legs. She will keep the others in check. She will make them behave.'

'And what did they say?'

'They just laughed at me. I know that I have to learn. I have to be able . . .'

'What?'

'I have to be Mrs Johnson. I get so frightened when she goes. So lonely.'

'I know what you mean.'

She turns to face me. Her cheeks are streaked with tears. She looks deep into my eyes, it makes me feel uncomfortable. I break it and look down at my hands.

'Will you have a word with them?'

'I don't think that they will listen to me.'

'Why not?'

'Because . . .'

'Cassie tried to kill herself the last time. It was terrible. Awful. I tried to call Mrs Johnson but I couldn't reach her. She booked herself into a hotel.'

'Cassie?'

'Yes. And ordered a large bottle of Middleton whiskey and took some pills. But she was caught out.'

'How?'

'I found Mrs Johnson just in time and she called reception. And they called an ambulance. You see . . .'

'Yes . . .'

'So you must talk to them.'

'I'll try . . .'

I say it to deflect her. I smile to reinforce it.

'Good. Good. Mrs Johnson will hold you to that.'

'Okay.'

'Laundry,' she suddenly says and stands.

Fucking Around with Love

'A penny for them.'

I turn to see Alf standing there. I am outside, standing on the gravel that runs along the steps of the main building.

'It's all coming back to you, isn't it?'

'What?'

'The pain. The booze. The mess.'

'I don't know what you mean.'

'Oh I think you do.'

I don't answer but stub out the cigarette I'm smoking and begin to make my way inside.

'That's it. That's it.'

'That's what?' I say turning back and spitting the question back at him.

'That's your answer for everything, isn't it, it always has been.'

'What?'

'Walk away, fuck this, and fuck that.'

'You said it.'

'Isn't it time to stop, isn't it time to come home from the war?'

An aeroplane moans above us, beginning its descent into Dublin airport. He walks towards me.

'I've been in your head. I've looked out through eyes like yours and seen the grey shit of my life in front of me.'

He's close now. His breath is sweet and wholesome. Like a

farmer's wife who has spent her life elbow-high in butter and cream.

'Give in, Gabriel. Stop fighting. I'm only trying to help. Life is simpler than you think it is. You are loved. You may not believe it but you are. We all are.'

I look at this big man, at the purity of his gaze. For a moment I ache to see the God who soothes his life. But I stamp it out, I kill it.

'I've tried it your way,' I say.

'Really?'

'Yeah I've fucked around with love.'

'You've fucked around with love?'

'Yeah.'

'That's an interesting way of putting it.'

'Don't patronise me.'

'I'm not patronising you. You're doing a good enough job of that yourself.'

Clive

He was an American. He had tried everything, he told me. This was his eighth attempt. It was his last chance. He had just arrived. His wife had made him sign a piece of paper saying that if he failed this time all assets would be hers. Very American, I remember thinking.

There was nothing he didn't know about getting sober, except the one thing that it was all about, staying that way. He was a big man in his forties. He had long grey-blond hair, like a fading rock star. He worked with computers. He had a successful business repairing them and reconditioning old ones to be re-sold. He told me that we were lucky to have the chance to take stock, to rebuild our shattered lives. Especially you, he would say to me, this is your first time, and it's always magical, always special. His name was Clive and his eyes were dark as if thunder lay across their gaze. He had tried many places, ones in America where they treat you like a king and bring you tea and medication in bed, to places where you had to clean toilets and prepare your own meals. It was always the same, he said, his rage would subside and his body would begin to repair itself. He would greet each day with the vigour of the converted. He would devour all the literature he was given to read, and be full of love for everyone and everything. But it never lasted, it couldn't, you see, I'm too extreme, he said to me, we're too extreme all of us. Usually he would get a month or so, once he even made it to a year, but that was tough, he said. It was always something stupid and small that tipped him over the edge, a car that wouldn't start, or a virus in one of his computers, you know, something that other people would shrug off as the luck of the draw. Not him, no, sir, before he knew it he was in a bar and halfway through a bottle of Bourbon. Then the ugliness would come back, that pig-headed fucker who would begin a fight in a monastery. This time had been the worst. He had shat on his sofa. He didn't remember doing it but his wife lost it completely, he told me, when she saw this big turd sitting in the middle of her prize chaise longue. I laughed, it felt strange to do so, but it was funny. We don't half fuck ourselves up, don't we? he said. I nodded. I'm sure you have stories, he said, we all do, that's all we have are our stories. I said yes. He looked at me as if to say and . . . ? But I said nothing, I just stared back, holding his gaze.

We were waiting to see our counsellors. He told me that he had always found women difficult; they brought out the worst in him. He blamed his father, he said. He had stayed with his mother even though she had affair after affair. It was a bad example. As a child the first woman he knew was conniving and duplicitous and it coloured the rest of his life. It was something that he had spent years trying to come to terms with. It was one of the reasons that he drank, he told me. He also said that he didn't know an alcoholic who didn't have rage in his soul, he was no different, and you're no different, he said, looking at me. It's in your eyes, he said, they are the window to everything after all. I look at the side of his face and wonder at what it is that drives men like us to destroy the beauty of the world around us. I think about where I've been, about the dangerous places that my mind took me to, of the terror and the pain. I know that insanity stalked men like us, that it was the coat that we had been given to wear.

'Don't make the mistakes I've made, my friend,' Clive said.

'What do you mean?'

'Find out what it is. Find that fucker deep inside you that breaks everything you touch and drag him into the light and kill him dead.'

Christopher, Clive's counsellor, was standing in front of us; neither of us heard him arrive. He had a smile on his face.

'I couldn't have put it better myself, Clive.'

Almost Time

She doesn't look at me as she takes her seat. She is late and we have been waiting for her. I want to be anywhere but here, in this modern room with its large panes of glass, surrounded by people who have pain carved into their faces and misery in their gaze. I don't want to be counted with them, I am different. I resent the glances of comfort I get from one or two of them; I want to tell them to concentrate on their own hearts. I need nothing or no-one, I want to tell them. I'm sweating, it is not fear, I tell myself, pull yourself together, look the world straight in the eye and tell it to fuck off like you've always done. Thaddeus comes over to me and kneels in front of me. For a moment I don't look at him, but he waits until I do, I have the feeling that he will wait all day if necessary.

'You okay?'

'Yeah.'

'You don't look it.'

'I'm okay.'

'Don't shut down.'

'What?'

'You heard me. I know that this is tough.'

I look around at the faces, at the other drunks and their wives, at their clasped hands.

'You have to give this a chance,' Thaddeus says.

I look back at him. I try and tell myself that he cares, that the concern I see in his eyes is real.

'This is your first time and you're bound to want to fight it. Family programme is an important part of recovery. You must try and trust the process. Your wife understands this. We've talked to her.'

It is then that she arrives. It is over a week since I've seen her. I was so drugged that I'm not sure if it wasn't something that my imagination had dreamed up. One or two of the couples sigh impatiently as she makes her apologies. Thaddeus gets up and goes to the centre of the room to meet her and indicates with his arm that she should seat herself next to me. He smiles as she takes a chair and positions herself at the end of the far row of people as far away from me as possible. All this time she hasn't looked at me. Thaddeus walks over to her and leans down to speak quietly in her ear. I see him look in my direction. For a moment she doesn't say anything and then looks at me. I can see she is deciding whether to come and sit beside me or not. Then with a sigh and a murmured 'Excuse me' to the couple next to her she picks up her chair and comes and places it next to mine. Instinctively I reach out to take her hand that's resting on her lap. She pulls it away without looking at me. I look at the side of her face, I can see the tendons in her jaw tensing and relaxing as the anger pulses through her body.

'Okay,' Thaddeus says.

'I'm sorry I'm late,' my wife says before he can continue. 'I nearly didn't come at all.'

'That's fine, Mrs O'Rourke. We all understand that this is a difficult situation. Everyone in this room is not a stranger to this . . .'

'I still don't know why I'm here . . .'

'But the fact is you are.' he says.

'I'm so sick of this . . .' she says.

'I know. It's normal that you should feel like this.'

'Give it some time, love,' one of the other wives says.

'That's all I've fucking done. Excuse me for my language. That's all I've ever done is give it time. Time only makes it worse.'

I stare at the floor. Clive leans into my ear and tells me not to worry. I don't look at him. I think of the mess, and the terror that I laid at her door. I think of my son and the question in his eyes whenever he looked at me, as if to say which father will you be today, the good one or the bad. It's a moment before I realise that Thaddeus is talking to me. I look up to meet his gaze.

'I'm going to start with you. Both of you. Bring your seats out here into the middle of the room and place them facing each other. I want you, Mrs O'Rourke, to . . .'

'Cathy,' my wife says.

'Fine. Excuse me, Cathy. Place the chair at a distance that you feel sums up how close or how far apart your relationship is at the moment. Do you follow?'

'No,' my wife says.

'Okay bring your chairs. I'll show you.'

We both walk to the centre of the room and he takes the chairs from us, placing them one opposite the other so that the front of their seats are almost touching.

'Very close,' he says. 'Maybe too close. A marriage that is intimate to the point of suffocation . . .'

He then takes one of the chairs and puts it down far away from the other near the outer ring of the circle of people. He points to it and says: 'Divorce territory. No hopesville. You see?'

We both nod. He goes to move the chair back to the centre of the room when my wife says: 'Leave it there.'

Someone laughs. I look to Thaddeus, he shrugs.

'So be it. Please, both of you sit. Now all I want you to do, Cathy, is have a think for a second and then address Gabriel. Talk to him. Tell him the things that you have wanted to tell him. Explain what it was like to be with him when he was using, how it affected your life. Please remember this is confidential. And that everyone in this room will be in these hot seats . . . Sooner rather than later . . .'

'I can't do this,' she says.

I see her look to me as she says this as if to say I won't betray you. I know that this won't do, that Thaddeus is sharper than that.

'With all respect, Cathy, it's not important what he thinks, this is about you. You owe it to yourself . . . to your child . . . to stop this. To reclaim the time that his illness has taken from you. And that begins by defining it . . . by telling it. Do you understand?'

She nods. I see her take a deep breath. The room is waiting. I am waiting. I have nowhere left to run to.

'And Gabriel?'

'Yes?'

'Listen. Just listen,' he says.

'I don't love you anymore. That's what I came here to say today. I don't know you. Not the man you've become. I want out. Normality, that's what I want. Boring, boring normality . . . for me and for our son. I don't want the jealousy, the worry and the pain, the violence. It wasn't a life what we had. It was just one crisis after the other. People don't live like that. I'm sorry, but for a while I thought that I could . . . help. But I think you're beyond help. Even a place like this is no use to someone like you. What saddens me even more is I think that you don't remember half the things that you did . . . the dirty sordid things. The way you spoke to my friends, my family. You're just an animal. And you still blame me for everything: for your sickness, for putting you in here. Do you realise that you ended up with the winos lying in the street, like a dog that was dying. Do you? You don't see, do you. You never have.'

She takes the tissue that Thaddeus offers her and nods her

thanks. I look around the room. One or two of the women are crying, some of the men are staring at the floor. I know that they see themselves in what they have just heard.

Thaddeus looks at me. For a minute or two I don't return his gaze. When I do I see that he is smiling. I know that he is trying to reassure me, but I don't want his concern, or his professional empathy.

'Do you want to say anything?'

'He won't say anything. He never does,' my wife says.

'With all respect . . .' Thaddeus says, raising his arm as if to say you've had your moment.

'Gabriel?'

I don't reply. All I see is the dark dance of my body falling, flailing into the end of things. I feel the vastness of space holding my body as I tumble, like a large black blanket unfolding into infinity. I see the shape of my despair as I flit between the clouds; I feel its hungry breath on my skin. I see the ground lying below me like a bride eagerly waiting in her marriage bed. I think of the faces I have worn in my time, ones of deceit, ones of pain. I hear the whistle of the wind in my ears and the roar of my old life splintering like an oak tree hit by lightning. It won't be long now, I tell myself. No, it won't be long.

Walking Backwards

'You are my special project,' Thaddeus says.

'I don't know whether that's a good or a bad thing.'

'Believe me it's good. It's very good. I asked for you. Made my pitch at the weekly meeting of the counsellors. I see me in you. And I think that I am in a good position to help you.'

I watch as he tightens the knot on his tie and then smoothes it with the palm of his hand. I know that means he is ready to begin. I ask him if I can smoke. He shakes his head and smiles.

'No, afraid not.'

'Why not?'

'Good thing to hide behind, a smokescreen. I prefer that you are present and not hidden by clouds of cigarette fumes. I'll give you a few minutes at some point and you can nip out. Deal?'

'Deal.'

The first time I had met him, I wanted to shove his smugness where the sun didn't go but I have mellowed towards him, in spite of myself. There are still moments though when I want to strike out at him. I'd like to take the coffee I'm holding and dribble it down the front of his immaculate blue suit.

'The other day was difficult for you, wasn't it?'

'What do you think?'

'Yes. Stupid question, I suppose . . . Family meetings are always barbed with resentments and anger. Still we all have to go through it . . . to bring those secrets out into the light . . .'

'I hated the way she looked at me.'

'Like you were an animal?'

'Yes.'

'How is your head?'

'It's okay.'

'No strange beliefs or . . . ?'

'No.'

'Well we are at the point in your treatment where things get a little more serious. A little more grown-up. You are someone who needs to be force-fed reality sometimes. Now it gives me no pleasure to say that. But I was the same. My mind was a tinderbox looking for a match. And alcohol was that spark that made me, well, insane.'

'I wasn't insane.'

'No.'

'No.'

'Why do you say that?'

'Just . . .'

'I have your file here . . .'

'So?'

'So. The black and white of these pages tell me something very different to what you're saying.'

'Is that a fact?'

'Yes. On the street. Cautioned for violence. Sleeping in doorways. Begging for money. Harassment of your wife and child. Hospital stays. Lock-up ward . . .'

'Alright. Alright.'

'Now I know that in the light of day and with a bit of distance and some food in your belly these things can seem outrageous, as if they happened to someone else. But the fact is, Gabriel, they happened to you. That's the truth.'

'Yes.'

'The only way to stop them happening again is to arm you. To give you a recovery programme that is watertight.

That involves going to meetings and staying dry. It's going to be difficult.'

'How did I know that you were going to say that?'

'Nothing that's worth anything is easy.'

'How did I know that you were going to say that too?'

He leans forward and holds me with his eyes.

'Let's get one thing straight before we start, Gabriel. I have a very thick skin. And you . . . You have yet to grow one.'

Missing

There are about twelve of us. We are crammed into a white minibus. I'm sitting between Greg the young lawyer and Clive. There is another one behind us that holds the rest of my group. We are on our way to our first AA meeting. Two people are missing so we are waiting, the engines of the buses idling as one of the counsellors scours the rooms of the institute for them. Mrs Johnson hasn't turned up, which is no surprise to any of us. She had spent the previous few days saying that everything was a big mistake, that she knew who she was now, that she was indeed Mrs Johnson and that the others had left her for good and since it was they who had the problem, she was free and demanded that she be allowed to go home. At first she had made her request politely, but the more she was ignored by the therapists the more her voice rose. At one point Thaddeus had turned round and told her to be quiet, that she had been assessed, and that no-one believed her stories of Cassie and Angelina, that it was a trick to cover the fact that she was just a dirty drunk like the rest of us. That had shut her up for a while. Thaddeus had that effect on people with his no-nonsense voice and his unrelenting stare. But her protests continued and eventually one of the other therapists, a woman called Ursula, had asked her to step outside one of the classes so that she could have a word with her in private. We all sat and listened as we heard Mrs Johnson's voice rise, saying that they had got her wrong, all wrong. 'I'm fine, it's just me, just Mrs Johnson now.'

The other person who is missing is Josey, the girl I met in the secure unit. She has been skipping more and more sessions, sometimes arriving late, her thin face drawn and haggard, her eyes moist and red. As I sit in the minibus waiting for the news on our two missing people I think of how within the space of a couple of weeks my soul had righted itself, and how the other man I had become had begun to recede like the shadows in a dark room as daylight invaded it. But for all my sudden optimism I knew that he would always lurk within me, waiting to pounce like a cheetah bringing down its lunch.

'Right. Let's go.'

The counsellor is back. He climbs into the passenger seat of the minibus and whispers something to the driver.

'Any luck?' Clive asks.

'Sorry?'

'Any luck with the others?'

'No. They won't be joining us tonight.'

Alf had taken me aside earlier in the day and told me to keep up the good work, that I had been doing really well, and that I was unrecognisable as the angry spiteful man who had arrived ten days before. He told me to have faith and that the powers that be had made a decision to allow me out to go to my first meeting as they felt that I was ready for what I would hear. He then leaned into me and said that this would be the single most important moment of my life and that I should make sure that I stayed open and receptive. He told me to listen for the similarities in what I would hear, to be positive. Identify, he said, identify with the people in the room. So as we pull out the drive of the hospital, I try and quell the desire to run that rises in me. I realise that it's because I am suddenly travelling in the outside world again, that it's been a while since I've seen its streets and felt its hot energy in my veins. I look through the van window at the rain-black streets and the lights as they bend and twist across the night. I see myself as I was only a few weeks before, a figure shorn of love, spinning in the terrors of his mind. Every building we pass seems to house a bar, and I imagine myself there cocooned in their warmth, lifting a beer to my lips. I wonder at the hold it still has on my heart, this thought, this substance that all my life I have looked to, asking it to solve me, to hide me from the world. I shake my head and wipe away the condensation that has formed on the glass. I see the ghostly reflection of my eyes as I do. I see the hunger and the need in them.

'Attractive, aren't they?'

I look around to see Clive looking at me.

'Yeah.'

'It's just bullshit propaganda, brother. Like the rest of our stupid world. Just bullshit propaganda designed to make us pay with our souls.'

A Land of Paper

Today I won't drink. I'll ignore the rage that starts in me, ordering me to obey. I'll sit here on this pavement and shake until I crack down the middle before I succumb. I know that things will be sent my way to bend my arm, to force me into raising a bottle to my head. I must soothe my body today, talk to it, tell it that everything will be alright. My mind is racing. I have become used to the dark land where drink takes me, where the sun is blotted out by shame, and the trees have withered limbs from lack of water. I have spent so long there that I can no longer tell when I am there and when I'm not. There is a woman standing in front of me staring at me as if I was less than human. If I blink maybe she will evaporate, dwindle into nothing, melt down into the shit and debris that litters the footpath. I would hold out my hand if it wasn't shaking so much, just to annoy her, just to see the curl of disdain begin at the edge of her mouth. I could say something to her, bite her through the heart with some choice words but I think better of it. After a moment she moves off, she grunts as she does, fuck her, and fuck the look she gave me, fuck the ground she walks on.

Glass glints all around me as the morning sun moves into view. The shaking has moved to my heart, maybe it began there, I don't know. I think of my old life, how it seems so remote now, separated by distance and the fever of my thinking. It seems like a land of paper delicately swaying in the black winds of my memory. I know now that all my life I was only one lit match away from burning it down. Even the people I knew and tried to love were too flimsy for my hard heart. Each day that passes another piece of my past is blown away, lifted and tossed into the distance, a huge swatch of paper dipping and fluttering in the breeze like a wounded white bird.

I think of the girl I fucked while her father, my friend, lay passed out downstairs. I see again the look on her face as I was having her, the way she lifted her head to mine, her fingers grabbing at the flesh on my back as if she was falling away. I remember her breath, as hot as hell burning into my conscience, her lips wet with passion. I was a man fucking back, hanging his soul from a meat hook, taking the fist of his sex and nailing anything that moved. She was as giving as a young girl can be, taking my rage, taking my fear, taking my humpbacked heart. I remember his face later when I told him that I'd had my way with his daughter, as if he had just been punched. It was revenge, it was sweet then but now I wonder why it tastes so bitter. I fucked her to fuck him. Simple as that.

I look around me at the street I'm on. I don't remember arriving here. The days and thoughts come and go now, one bleeds into the other, folding and twisting in my mind. I am derailed, I know this, and I am looking out on a world bloated with its own importance. I was someone once, I think. I am fucking sure of it. Yes, I was someone. And now . . . Tomorrow I won't drink.

The First Meeting

I am sitting beside a woman. She is older than me. She is smiling and looking at me as if she knows me. I want to tell her to stop. It's uncomfortable, but she just keeps grinning at me as if I am the answer to all her problems. I shift my body slightly so that I am angled away from her, but I can still feel her eyes on me. Eventually I look back at her, anger flaring in my eyes.

'This is your first time, isn't it?' she says.

I don't say anything and I feel my anger slip away as quickly as it rose in me. There is something about the softness in her eyes that unnerves me, that makes me think again.

'Yes,' I say. 'Is it that obvious?'

'No . . . Well . . . Yes . . .'

I smile and I nod and realise how nervous I have been ever since we had all arrived, our counsellors telling us to find seats near the front of the meeting and to take them with the minimum of fuss.

'Don't worry, everyone has a first time . . .' the woman says.

'Excuse me, I don't know your name.'

'Pauline M. I'm an alcoholic. And you?'

'Gabriel.'

'Pleased to meet you, Gabriel. This is a big moment for you.'

'So I'm told.'

'Are you up the road at the treatment centre?'

'Yes.'

'Good. It's a good place. You're in good hands.'

The room we are in is small and it is filling by the second, smoke hangs in the air and men hand chairs across seated bodies, nodding to one another. Everyone seems to be smiling and it irritates me. I want to leave to stand outside, to be swallowed by the darkness and smoke one cigarette after another.

'You're a very brave man,' Pauline says to me.

'So everyone keeps telling me.'

'Well that's maybe because you are. We're not as weak as other people think. In fact if anything it's the opposite.'

There is a small hatch at the far end of the room opposite the entrance. A young man is handing teas and coffees out through it. His scalp is shaved and his nose looks like it's been broken a few times. He is wearing a grey V-necked sweater and politely nods as people come and collect their drinks from him. On the walls are posters with sayings written on them in large bold type. A lot of them contain the word God and for a moment I think about using that as an excuse to leave but I know that won't hold sway with my counsellors. In fact it was one of the final things that Alf said to me when he had pulled me aside earlier that day.

'Tonight you're going to see and hear a lot of "God" business. It will be difficult. It was difficult for me. I thought that I had landed in a bloody cult or something. Ignore it. Focus on the stories you hear. Leave the God thing for those who are comfortable with it. All you have to do is say that I am beaten and only you can save me. By that I mean the solidarity of the room or the power of people's experiences. The God issue is for another time.'

'Hi.'

I look up to see an older man standing over me. He nods at Pauline and she smiles back.

'My name's Frank the Book.'

'Frank the Book?'

'I own a wee bookshop in the city centre. It's called Books in Nooks.'

'Right.'

'First-timer?'

'Yes.'

'Pleased to meet you, son. Mind if I sit next to you?'

'No.'

I watch as he lowers himself into the seat next to me. He is a big man and he smells of biscuits and coffee. He winks at me and shouts a large hello to every person that passes him. One or two people stop to talk with him. He asks them how they're doing, I hear him tell a small ratty-looking youth to take the second thought, dismiss the first and go with the second. The youth nods at him and tells him it's difficult. Of course it's fucking difficult, he roars, we're not the same as others. We're built differently, and he looks to me as he says this to make sure that I'm listening. It's the first thought that does the damage if we obey it. It tells us to pick up the drink, to shag the girl, to tell the driver who's just cut us up exactly what we think of him. The second thought is the normal thought, he says, looking at me, his eyes full of humour and mischief.

'I bet that your first thought has got you into some scrapes in your time,' he says to me.

I don't reply but look away at a large poster that says 'Let Go and Let God' in large black type. It is hanging on the wall behind a desk at the front of the room. I think of my mother and what she would say if she saw me in a place like this. For the first time in a very long while, her memory doesn't slice me up inside, or bring the sour taste of anger to my mouth.

'You want this,' Frank says to me.

'What?'

'Your soul wants this. It's begging you to open up your ears and listen.'

A man is hovering around the desk at the top of the room.

He has a folder in his hands and he is gesturing to a woman to come and join him, which she does. They both sit down and the man picks up a small hand bell that is sitting in front of him and rings it. He has to do it a second time as the first one fails to stop the hubbub of people talking and laughing. Gradually the room falls quiet and he clears his throat and says: 'Hello, everyone. My name is Fergal and I'm an alcoholic.'

'Hello, Fergal,' the room says en masse as if it suddenly had one throat.

'Is there anyone else here who is an alcoholic?'

People snigger as he says this and then a forest of hands is raised high. I don't, my stubborness is still alive and well. Frank and Pauline raise their hands, smiling as they do so.

'At least I am not alone,' Fergal says. Again people laugh. 'I think that we've all spent more than enough time alone in our lives, don't you agree?'

'Yes,' the room says.

Fergal then gets someone to read out the twelve steps of AA. It sounds like the manifesto for a cult and all I can hear over and over again is the word God, until I almost believe that I am back in my living room as a child with my mother holding me down by the neck, breathing the hot passion of her belief into my young brain.

My head starts to swim. I stand and begin to make my way out of the meeting, avoiding everyone's eyes as I do so. Once outside I lean against the wall of the building, taking in deep gulps of the night air. It takes a few moments to calm my body down. I fumble in my pockets for a cigarette and quickly light it. I don't see Frank the Book. I don't even hear him arriving.

'If you want to think this one out on your own, just let me know and I'll piss off,' he says. 'But if you're built in any way like me thinking will only make it worse.'

'Then what do you suggest?' I ask, looking at him.

'Do . . . Don't think, do . . . Action is character . . .'

'Right . . . Do . . .'

'Yes, do . . . Or at least be willing . . .'

'Willing?'

'To change. Because God knows and tell me if I'm stepping over the line here. The old you landed you in this place at the end of a long night where everything you touched broke into pieces, where every step you took was a fall. Now if you're anything like me, that is . . . And I have a suspicion that you might be . . .'

I look away. I see a man trying to cross the road opposite us. He is drunk. I watch as he staggers out into the glare of the headlights from the oncoming traffic and then wince as I see him lurch back again to avoid being hit. I hear the high drone of the car horns as they sound their disapproval at him.

'Now,' Frank says. 'We look at that poor fucker over there. Us . . . people like you and me. And we don't see what other men see. Sure he looks pathetic. He looks fucking hopeless. But you know what the fucked-up point of it all is. Somewhere fuckers like us . . . We find it attractive. No worries. No cares. Like him. Just bobbing along like a float cut loose from a fishing line. That's what we want. That's what we fucking crave.'

'I ended up sleeping in fucking bins,' I say.

'I know.'

'How do you know?'

'Because I did too. That's how I know. Your story is my story. That's all that room in there is about.'

Killing Two Birds

The next day Clive has a fit. Three orderlies try to restrain him. They called me because they said he liked me. I asked why he had lost it, he was doing so well. Someone had moved the Bible he was reading. They had taken it from his bedside table, looked through it and then left it on the bed instead of putting it back where they found it. He went crazy and challenged his roommate who told him to fuck off, that he didn't read pornography. That only made things worse. He grabbed the guy by the throat and shook him until his nose bled and then he butted him in the face. He was gone, he was history, I knew that much. His ninth treatment was over almost as soon as it began.

When I reach him he is on the ground screaming his head off as nurses swarm all over him, pinning him down. I stand there not knowing what to say or do. I look at my friend's face bulging with rage and I see myself there. He is fighting himself; he is trying to break the bars that hold his spirit. He wants out, like I do.

One of the nurses lying across him sees me standing there and motions with his head that I should try and talk to him. But I am frozen by the fear in my friend's eyes. He is a big man and suddenly he decides to get to his feet.

'Fucking bastards, I'll take every one of you with me.'

I watch as they try and stop him but he succeeds in shaking

one of them free and finds his feet, grunting as he hauls himself to a standing position. He manages to get one of his arms loose and starts using it, swotting one or two of the nurses across the face.

'How do you like that, you fuckers. How do you like them fucking apples.'

One of the nurses falls backwards into a large rose bush. I can't help smiling. It is then that he sees me for the first time. He stops and nods at me. I say nothing but nod back. I knew that this was goodbye, that he wouldn't come back from this one. I see the sweat on his brow, and the wildness in his eyes. He was going to lose everything; he knew it and I did too. I hear the sound of feet thumping on the pavement behind me. I turn and look and see four more orderlies hurrying to help their colleagues. I step out of the way to let them past. Clive gets one of them with a sweet left hook just as he arrives.

Then he begins running; he takes off across the large garden. As he does he yells 'Fuck it' at the top of his voice. One or two passing inmates begin applauding him. It looks like a crazy silent film, Clive tearing across the grass with seven men in white chasing him. When they catch him, they don't fuck around this time; I see one or two of them put a dig in as he crashes to the ground. One of the orderlies sits on his head while the others hold his arms and legs down. They then turn him over onto his front and pull his arms across his back.

He is led away. I stand there looking at the marks in the grass. I think of the madness I saw in him, and how attractive it was to someone like me. His roommate is led past me, a handkerchief pressed up against his nose, his head held back. His name is Stuart, and he works in a bank. Clive had never liked him. He said that he was one of those high-flying fuckers, who think everything was expenses this and expenses that. His bank was paying for his treatment which riled him even more. So I suppose it was coming. He had been waiting, biding his time, until he couldn't bear it anymore and had to get out. So he used Stuart to do it, killing two birds with one stone.

Being Kissed by Angels

Josey is crying although she tries to hide it when she sees me approaching, running the palms of her hands quickly across her face and forcing a smile to her lips. I stand for a moment before I sit. The day is bright and the sunlight makes the frost on the branches of the trees glitter and sparkle like the treasure in a pirate's cave. She is sitting on one of the benches in the grounds. I think about leaving her to her thoughts, but she makes a small gesture with her hand, patting the space beside her, indicating that I should join her. As I do I offer her a cigarette, she takes it. I light it and watch as she inhales deeply, sucking her cheeks in and blowing out fiercely as if she was trying to expel every bad thought she ever had. I ask her if she needs anything, she shakes her head and looks at me, we hold the gaze for a second and then break it. It seems a lifetime ago since we both met in the lock-up ward. We are different now, our time here has seen to that. We no longer view the world with the same disgust or cynicism, but in its place is an emptiness that we will spend the rest of our lives fighting. I gently place my hand on hers. She lets it stay there for a moment before moving it back to my lap, smiling as she does so.

'That's the last thing we need, Gabriel.'

I nod. I feel foolish but it quickly fades. I laugh quietly, my breath forming small speech bubbles in the frosty air.

'What's funny?'

'Nothing . . . I was thinking about how absurd this is . . .'

'What?'

'All this . . . Being here . . .'

'Yes . . . It's funny . . .'

'And scary . . .'

'Yes and scary . . . Very scary . . .'

I remember the previous week in group therapy when she had talked about her mother and the words had stuck in her throat and tears had risen to sit in her eyes. We had waited, each one of us in that room knew those tears, we had tasted them in our time in this place. Alf had been the facilitator. He was gentle with her. He had steered her to the point where she was facing what she had spent her life fleeing. He had walked her down the corridors of her youth, his voice calmly telling her that she had nothing to fear. Her body grew more and more still until she sat rock solid in the face of his questions, her eyes wide and unblinking. She had reached the point where there was nowhere else to go, no-one else to see except her mother. Her voice grew younger and younger as she described how she was beaten every time she had tried to assert herself, how she had to wear dresses that completely covered her skinny body, how make-up was forbidden, how any potential boyfriend had been scared off and threatened. She described waking in the middle of the night with the demonic shape of her mother bent over her, cursing her and the husband who had fled many years before.

'It's your fault,' she would say.

She described the first time she used. She had smoked a couple of joints with some friends. One of them, a man, was older than the others. She talked about the freedom she had felt as she got stoned and left her mind behind. She said it was like being kissed by angels. She stayed the night with her friends and the older man came to her bed, ignoring her whimpers of protest, forcing himself on her. She knew then that she could trust no-one and vowed from then on to take before she was taken. She moved on to heavier drugs and more destructive men. She spoke about leaving home, just packing her things and going without a word of goodbye. She said that her illness had made her do things that she wasn't proud of, horrible depraved things. Why not? she said, looking around the room at the rest of us. I was worth less than nothing so . . . why not be less than nothing? Men had abused her; one or two had kept her imprisoned in her own apartment, ripping the phone out of the wall, locking her in, fucking her when they felt like it, and beating her when they didn't. Eventually she had returned to her mother, she had crawled back, she said. It was humiliating, her mother had won, she always won.

As I look at her now a week later I know that the session is still with her, that it will take days for her soul to settle. She smiles at me and knows that I'm concerned.

'I had a dream last night, Gabriel.'

'Yes?'

'I dreamt that I used again . . . And I loved it . . . I really loved it . . .'

State

'We've just had a phone call from your sister.'

'Right.'

'Yes. She wants to come in and talk to us. More specifically you.'

'Okay.'

I am in the grounds of the hospital, between the main building and the series of small huts that make up the alcohol recovery programme. Thaddeus had stopped me with a shout as I was making my way to my next class, a talk on spirituality, something I wasn't looking forward to. It is around 9 a.m. and my mind is closed to the soft morning that has sprung up around me. I want to be anywhere but here. I resent everything I see from the delicate swooping of the birds to the smile I see in my counsellor's eyes.

'This is a chance to lay everything down.'

'What do you mean?'

'To get it out into the open so it loses its power. Your sister grew up in the same house as you did. You've been through a lot together.'

'Yes.'

'Come on. Don't forget I'm just the same as you. I know how frightening this is.'

'When?'

'Today.'

'Today?'

'At 4.30. I spoke with her last night. She was in a terrible state. It seems that you being here has brought up a lot of stuff in her. It always does in family members. It is to be expected.'

'It's not like her.'

'What isn't?'

'To be in a state.'

'Let me tell you something. Everyone is whether they let on or not. And the bigger the act the bigger the crisis.'

I look away. I don't want to look in his eyes. I know that he will be pleased with what he's just said.

'I thought that she didn't care,' I say almost to myself.

'You know better than that, Gabriel.'

'Yeah.'

I look at him and he smiles.

'And it's okay to be apprehensive.'

I nod and then I smile.

'And it's okay to do that too.'

'What?'

'Smile.'

My Brother, My Killer

It is a long time since I've seen her. I am nervous, not of her but of what seeing her will do to me. I am sitting with Thaddeus. He hasn't spoken to me except to tell me to find a seat. I know what he's doing, he's letting me know that he must be neutral, a blank page for what my sister and I are about to write together. When she arrives she stands for a moment in the doorway and smiles at me, her familiar eyes lighting up with warmth. Thaddeus stands to greet her and indicates with a nod of his head that I should too. I think how only a short time ago if a man had done that to me, I would have called him on it, told him to fuck off. When she reaches me, she puts her arms around me. She holds on like a drowning man who has found a piece of driftwood. Eventually she lets me go and takes a small step backwards; she stumbles slightly and for a moment looks almost comical. Thaddeus walks up to her and gently placing his hand in the small of her back, steers her to the empty chair. I watch as she sits and gathers herself. She apologises for crying.

'Please . . . Please . . . If you can't cry here where can you cry?' Thaddeus says.

'Yes,' she says.

'Now.'

I watch as Thaddeus straightens his tie and looks us both in the eye.

'Let me first of all say . . .'

'Ciara. That's right.'

'Ciara. Thank you for having the courage to come here. And rest assured that anything that is said in this room will stay in this room. So please be brave and be honest with each other.'

'Thank you,' Ciara says and raises her head to look at me.

A silence settles between us. I think of that summer long ago when she tore herself from me, when my hands did what his had done to me. I taste the pain of that evening again as we regard each other. I know that she is here to lay that moment at my feet. I think of her child and the night that I babysat for her and her husband. I see the accusation in her eyes and wish I was somewhere else, anywhere but here. It is she who breaks our look, turning her head to stare at Thaddeus as if to say, what now? He looks at her and smiles, gently nodding his head as if to say, go on, speak. It is then that I know they have spoken in depth. I feel trapped. A panic rises in me. I put my hands to my face, and hide there for a second, I know that it is only a temporary respite and that I will have to look them both in the eye again.

'Well. We could sit here all day . . .' Thaddeus says. 'In this very uncomfortable silence. Doing exactly what you have both have done all your lives, ignoring the pain that lies across you both. Or you can engage with each other. I can help you both. Get you started. But that would defeat the purpose of this, don't you think?'

I remember what Clive had told me, get the fuckers out, he had said, those little bastards that keep us sick, those monsters that break our goodness and lurk in the corners of a man's soul, waiting to bring him down. I don't remember beginning to speak and my voice when it comes sounds like someone else's. I begin by telling her that I am sorry, that I wish I could step back into the dark hallways of our childhood and change everything. She stares at me impassively as I say this as if she is watching a sports match that doesn't particularly interest her.

I knew that it wouldn't be good enough. I was fudging, as Thaddeus would say, skirting the meat of what ailed us both, but I continue talking about fear and our father's drinking and how difficult it was for us as children, how our mother didn't protect us, that we had no chance. Eventually Thaddeus raises his hand. I stop and look at him.

'We're all victims.'

'Yes,' I say.

'But we are perpetrators too.'

'Yes.'

'You've talked about how tough everything was for you both. How alcohol shaped your world and your perception of it.'

'Yes.'

'But with respect it could be anyone's childhood. I can think of a hundred, a thousand childhoods that have been like yours. I didn't hear you in it. I didn't see you or your sister. We need to be specific. And that takes guts . . . balls. But it's a start. Ciara?'

I see her shift in her seat as he addresses her, it's the same adjustment of weight that she made whenever our father entered a room, and it spoke of readiness, of wariness.

'I don't know where to begin. I mean I know where to begin. But I don't know if I can . . .'

'It's alright. It's alright. You're safe here,' Thaddeus says.

She looks at me and her eyes harden.

'I hated you . . . So much of my life . . . I've loathed you . . . To me you were just the same as him . . . You looked the same . . . You even smelled the same . . . I know now that he did the same things to you . . . I know that now . . . But . . .'

'Go on.'

'But you . . . You did it to me too . . . Didn't you . . . Didn't you?'

I feel Thaddeus turn his head in my direction, but I ignore

him, my eyes are locked on my sister and I am looking down the twin barrels of my past.

'When I think of you . . . I see him . . . When I think of him . . . I see you . . . You were my older brother, you were supposed to look after me . . . To protect me . . . I know now that you were sick . . . That we both were . . . That we had no chance . . . But for a long time I wanted to kill you . . . When I was small . . . I thought that if one of you were dead the other would disappear . . . It's stupid . . . For a long time . . . For a long time I wished you dead, Gabriel . . .'

As she says this there is a catch in her voice and she closes her eyes for a second and nods to herself, as if she was listening to a voice that only she could hear.

'All my life it has been Gabriel this and Gabriel that. Always you. What about me? Where did I go? Do you know what it's like to be invisible, do you?'

'I'm sorry,' I mumble, but I know that it is pathetic and half-hearted.

'I tried to get her to love me . . . Our mother . . . I thought that would be enough . . . That it would see me through . . . I became like her . . . I stole her prayers and made them my own . . . I said to myself she knows God and maybe if I can be like her He will forgive me . . . He will tell me that I wasn't dirty . . . That I wasn't full of shame . . . But . . . But all she could talk about was you . . . Oh how is my boy? He is so unhappy . . . He won't let God into his heart . . . He is so unhappy . . . How can we make him happy? How can we place him in God's grace, Ciara? What about me? What about me?'

Her voice rises as she says this until she is shouting. Thaddeus leans forward and pulls a couple of tissues from the box on the table in front of him, and as he hands them to her he says: 'Do you want to stop?'

She shakes her head and looks at me once more.

'All my life I've tried to make God see me . . . To tell Him that I was there . . . I've prayed so much . . . Do you know how much I've prayed? I've tried to live a good life . . . To be good. But how can someone be good when they hate so much? How?'

'Is this the first time you've talked about this?' Thaddeus asks her.

She shakes her head and looks down at the floor.

'My husband . . . Seamus . . . I've told him . . .'

'When?'

'On our wedding night . . .'

'That must have been difficult.'

'I had to say something. I wouldn't let him touch me. I froze . . .'

'Of course you did.'

Then she looks at me, I see the years of hurt in her gaze, I see the loneliness and the pain.

'Seamus believes that you abused our daughter. Did you?'

I don't say anything but look at her. I know what I'm doing; I'm buying myself some time by putting a hurt look on my face. The truth is that I can't remember. I see her young body standing before me; I see the openness in her eyes as she looks at me. I hear my mind telling me to claim her, to make her mine.

'What makes you say that?' Thaddeus asks her.

She doesn't look at him as he asks this but keeps her eyes on me.

'You babysat for us. Do you remember? Do you remember?'

'Yes.'

'And?'

'Go on,' Thaddeus says.

'When we came home . . . When we came home . . . You were out of it . . . Gone . . . And . . .'

'Yes . . . Go on . . .'

'Mary was asleep upstairs in her bed . . . She had different pyjamas on . . . Not the ones I'd put on . . . and . . . she was wet as if she had been sweating and there was an empty bottle of wine beside her bed . . . Did you? Did you?'

'She had wet herself . . . I changed her . . . She asked me to . . .'

'Did you . . . ?' she asks again.

'I can't remember . . . I swear to God I can't remember.'

'That's very convenient . . .'

'I would never . . .'

'What, Gabriel? It was done to you. It was done to me. And you tried to do it to me. Until I stopped you.'

'God help me, I would never ever . . .'

'Seamus wants to kill you . . . I'll tell you that straight . . .'

'Have you asked her . . . Mary?' Thaddeus says.

'Yes of course.'

'And?'

'She said that he changed her and put her to bed . . . That's all . . .'

'Okay . . .'

'But maybe she's lying . . . We lied, didn't we? We've lied our whole lives until now . . .'

'I didn't.'

'How can I believe you?'

Thaddeus then says that time unearths everything, that I have been very sick and that if I did abuse her it will come to light and then appropriate steps would be taken. He looks at me as he says this. I shake my head and look down at the floor. My sister leans forward in her chair.

'I was glad when you fell, Gabriel. Do you hear me? I was glad when you fell.'

'Gabriel?'

'Yes.' My voice sounds feeble and weak.

'Take a deep breath,' Thaddeus says.

'Yes.'

I look at them both. I think of the ground that is moving towards me and of all the lives that have passed through mine.

I feel the sting of her words, they echo across the clouds of my past. I feel moisture bathe my face. I can taste it on my tongue. Then I realise that I am crying and that my aloneness is almost at an end. I think of the room next to my heart where a small boy sits holding a butterfly, waiting for the light that will set him free. I think of every prisoner that I took, chaining them to my greed and my selfish heart. I see the little girl who for a while was the second part of me, the good part. I look at the woman she has become, the one who now faces me, asking me for the key to her childhood. She has her own fall.

A Whisper Away

I'm standing with Thaddeus. We are in the reception area. I have just said goodbye to my sister. Strangely she turned her head towards me as I went to kiss her on the cheek, so that our lips almost met. I paused, my mouth a whisper away from hers. I saw the look in her eyes, the fuck-you defiance and I pulled back and murmured goodbye to her and watched as she made her way to the waiting taxi outside. She didn't look back at us, but lowered her head as the taxi reversed and pulled out of the driveway. I realise Thaddeus has been staring at me, watching every flicker of sadness on my face.

'She sees him in you. At the moment for her there is no difference.'

'I know.'

'You were a child, Gabriel. She understands that. In the deep part of her she realises that you are not responsible. She wants someone to blame. He's not here . . . So . . .'

'Yes.'

'Look at me.'

I turn and see that he is closer to me than I thought he was, his green eyes searching mine.

'Her child . . .'

'Mary . . .'

'Yes . . . That's another story . . .'

'I didn't touch her . . . I remember wanting to . . . God forgive me . . . But I didn't . . . I'm sure I didn't . . . God . . .'

'It's tough, isn't it . . . hanging on . . . Living life as if it's a battle . . . Always in armour . . .'

I nod. My body is trembling. People are moving past us on their way to their next session.

'I believe you. I don't think you did what your sister and your brother-in-law said you did. But you realise that I have to log it. And if . . . if – and I think that it's a big if – something did go on that night, then you and I are going to have a very different conversation.'

'Yes, I know. But . . .'

'It is closed. This subject is closed. Your sister has spent her life hiding behind your illness. You're an alcoholic. We're obvious. We drink too much. We fall over. We wreck something. Other people are not so fortunate. They have their own fucked-up minds and hearts. But then they see someone like us and they think, he'll do, he'll take the heat from us. I can hide and point at this fella and say, my God look at him. He's fucked. Thank God everyone's looking at him and not me. I can just carry on fooling everyone. You see? As I said, the issue with your niece is closed. We must concentrate on you. This is a gift, Gabriel. This is the moment your whole life has been moving towards. Getting well is infectious. First you, then your sister. It moves like that. I will recommend Ciara talks to a colleague of mine and you and I will break this bastard that has held you back all your life.'

He walks away out into the grounds of the hospital. I remember the first time I met him and I resented his fine clothes and what I thought was his self-regard. I know now that it was vigilance, that here was a man who knew the world for what it was, and that in order to get through the minefield of day-to-day life you had to be watchful, but at the same time lace everything you did with love. It takes me by surprise that I'm thinking about him like this, only days ago I wanted to stuff his fine words back into his mouth. I realise that for the first time in my life another man has got through to me and I haven't wondered what he wanted or whether at some point I would have to fight him for the little piece of ground that we both stood on.

Cassie

Her voice is hard and sharp like metal scraping a marble floor. Her eyes, though I recognise them, are wilder than before, and they have more white in them. Her hair is arranged differently, held up from her wide forehead with pins and ties. One of them has a large ladybird on it. I smile at her as she sits beside me, her large bulk once again causing the spars of the wooden bench to sag. This time her energy is more aggressive, more on the front foot than before and it makes me pull my head away from her.

'Don't be afraid,' she says.

'I'm not,' I say.

'You're a pretty one,' she continues. 'A little worn out around the eyes and there's nothing that a good feed wouldn't fix. But a sexy wee fucker nonetheless.'

'Right. Er . . .?'

'Cassie.'

'But I thought . . .'

'Cassie.'

This time she emphasises it by shoving her hand out and gestures that I should take it. I do, it's warm and snug like the inside of a church at Christmas.

'Gabriel. You know we've met,' I say.

'I don't think so.'

'Yes, last week . . .'

'No, son . . . Mistaken, son . . . Mistaken . . . I've just arrived in this Godforsaken hole . . .'

'Come on . . .' I say.

'Come on where?'

'You're . . . Mrs . . .'

'You calling me a liar?'

'No.'

'Good, because there's nothing like a disagreement to dull a romance.'

As she says this she places her hand on my thigh and lets her fingers do a little dance there.

'I'm lonely, son. So lonely. Sometimes I can't breathe . . . I'm that on my own. Do you know what I mean?'

'Yes . . .'

'I know you do. It's in your eyes just like it's in mine. They don't fucking understand us. There's fuck-all talent in this dump . . . Well nearly fuck-all . . .'

As she says this she looks at me and she licks her lips, just like the femmes fatales in those black-and-white films that I watched as a child.

'A little bird told me that you've been talking to that fat slob Mrs Johnson.'

'Yeah?'

'She's a liar.' She leans in as she says this, her head coming in close to mine; again I smell the heavy odour of cheap face cream.

'She spreads rumours about me. None of them are true.'

I watch as she tilts her head away from me and looks up at the sky. She whistles the piece of a tune that I can't quite place. It takes a moment, at first my brain doesn't want to believe it, but there is no mistaking the strong scent of alcohol. It seeps into my nostrils, into my thinking. I realise that she has hit the bottle. Instinctively I pull away from her, moving to stand to put some distance between her and me.

'Where are you going?' As she asks me she puts her arm across me, as if I was a distracted child about to cross a busy street.

'Listen . . .' I say.

'You know something?' Her eyes are wide as they look into mine and her breath comes in slow heavy bursts. 'I could fuck you dry.'

They found her two hours later in the small wood beside the treatment centre. She was singing, a soft song, the kind that you sing to a child who is afraid of the dark. She was topless and her hair had lost its pins and its ties. She tried to run from them but she was too heavy and too drunk. Someone had sneaked in the booze for her, one of her friends who didn't believe her problem was alcohol. She left two days later as Mrs Johnson, back to her prim and organised self. I was sorry. I had never got to meet Angelina the princess. Three days after that she was dead. Sleeping pills and vodka came and took her loneliness from her.

Light and Stone

I am with Thaddeus. I have softened towards him. Sitting beside him in the grey overcoat of a November day I feel warm despite the cold. He has been keeping his eye on me more and more, especially since our talk with my sister. He knows it can't have been easy for me to sit there and take what she had to say. He is as immaculately dressed as ever and now and then leans forward to straighten the crease in his suit trousers, smiling at me as he does.

'How long are you sober now?' he asks me.

'I don't know . . . A couple of weeks . . .'

'Right. You know it's important that you remember . . . We spend so much of our lives trying to forget.'

'I suppose . . .'

'What's the longest you were ever sober?'

'A few days . . . maybe a week . . . Something like that . . .'

'So this is by far the longest you've been without a drink.'

'Yes . . . Yes, I suppose you're right . . .'

'You know, you're still hedging.'

'What?'

'Your bets. Hedging your bets.'

'What do you mean?'

He sits up and begins to mimic me, hunching his shoulders and saying, 'I don't know.' And, 'I suppose so.' I look at him and nod.

'You know we could sit here forever letting each other off... Shrugging our fucking shoulders and saying maybe and perhaps until the world goes up in flames. It's time to think about being strong.'

'Right...'

'We had someone leave here the other day. And three days later she was found in a cold bath, dead... This illness lives off I don't knows and supposes...'

I don't reply but look away across the garden we are sitting in and see the bench that Cassie and I sat on only days before. It was hard to believe she was dead. It didn't make any sense. I know what he's trying to do; he wants to put the fear of God into me, and I no longer have the same cynicism. I know that it has begun to shatter. I look at the mist that lies in pockets in the wood beside us and imagine Cassie in there, her naked torso stained with sweat and dew, her eyes focused on a faraway land where all her pain would fade. I think of how insanity had conquered my thinking too, how I ended up crawling around in the filth of what the rest of humanity threw away.

'My wife did exactly what your wife did to you.'

'What do you mean?'

'She sectioned me. Just like yours.'

'I didn't know that.'

'Nineteen years and five months ago... Well, let me see, five months on Saturday... Not a day doesn't go by but I don't think about it... but that I don't taste it... You know, here...'

He gestures to his heart and then places his hand over mine.

'And that's where you need to taste it too...'

He gets up gently pulling the back of his jacket down, and then runs his hand across his face and glances up at the sky.

'You never know, there might be sunlight yet.'

Buried Alive

'Describe him for me.'

'I can't.'

'There's no such thing.'

'I can't.'

'Take a breath and describe him . . . Tell me what he's doing . . . Go on . . .'

'Please . . . Please . . .'

'Come on . . . You're doing really well . . .'

'It's too difficult . . .'

'If it wasn't difficult . . . it wouldn't be rewarding . . .'

Everyone is looking at me. It seems as if I have been sitting in this chair in the centre of the room for a day, but I know that it's only been minutes. The session is called Trauma, and one by one we are being asked to come up and sit in front of our peers and relive a moment from our childhood. Our facilitator is called Tanya. She has biceps almost as big as mine and a short spiky hairstyle. She is tough, that's what she wants us to think at least. She has seen many things and been many people, just like you, she said, pointing at all of us as she arrived to take the class. It is a week since Clive left and I have only a couple of weeks to go. I am apprehensive about what will happen to me when I leave, about the first days without the walls of this treatment centre to hide me from the world.

'What is trauma?' Tanya had asked as she stood in the centre of the room when she first arrived. 'Does anyone know?'

'It's pain . . . isn't it? Someone said.'

'Yes . . . Yes . . . But more than that . . . Something else . . .'

She then pointed at me, singling me out. She looked at me as if to say, any ideas? I shrugged and quickly looked away. I could feel her eyes stay on me for a moment and then she turned her attention back to the matter in hand.

'Trauma is pain which has been buried alive.'

As she said this she began to pace up and down in front of us, letting the weight of her words sink in, a small smile playing on her lips.

'It's good, isn't it?' she said. 'So imagine . . . In the heart of every one of you is this alive . . . screaming pain . . . And it has brought every single one of you here to my door. It has fed your addiction. It has made you so angry that you burned everyone who reached out to you. It has lain down with you at night and brought terror to your dreams. Now you might think that this is a little strong . . . A little rich . . . But look around you. Peer into the lives that you have, the relationships that you have tried to foster . . . And you will see trauma lurking there . . .'

She then looked over to me again and told me that she needed a volunteer. I know that she was reacting to the look I gave her a few minutes before. It was when I shrugged and looked away. I wasn't in the mood for the day that was happening around me. My sister was on my mind. I could still see the look of disgust she gave me as she sat in front of me. I look at Tanya.

'What about the trauma we give to others,' I said.

'Very good. We certainly do that . . . please . . . ?'

'Gabriel.'

'Gabriel. Take your seat and come and sit here in front of us.'

For a moment I thought about saying no, but I knew that

this was no longer the way, neither was anger, or rage, these things have been taken from me, they have to be.

As I sit I look at her. Her eyes are hard and seem to glitter like pebbles on a winter beach.

'Don't be afraid,' she says.

'I'm not.'

'Well we'll see . . .'

She moves away from me past the rest of the patients, now and then looking back, as if at any moment she expects me to bolt. When she reaches the back of the room she asks if I feel comfortable.

'I'm okay,' I say.

'Don't you think your life deserves a better response than that?'

'Maybe.'

'Right . . . Okay . . . Maybe . . . Perhaps . . . You can't build much on words like these.'

'Who says I want to build?'

'Who did you give trauma to, Gabriel? Who is walking around with pain inside them that you put there?'

It shocks me how quickly she changes subject. I think of my wife, my child. I look away.

'Well . . .'

'Please.'

'Who are you thinking of?'

'My son.'

'Describe him.'

I see the look on his face that time long ago when the world poured unfiltered into my mind. He is standing in the hallway of our house watching as I hurl his mother against the wall.

'I can't,' I say.

I hear again the scream that came from me that night. I see my wife move away and I continue screaming at the blank wall she had stood against only moments before. I feel my breath bouncing back into my face and all the while my son watching, his face a mask, his small fists clenched.

'Tell me. There's nothing to fear, Gabriel.'

Tanya is now kneeling in front of me. She is looking up into my face. Her eyes are softer and she is smiling as if to say it's alright, everything is alright.

'This stuff will kill you, Gabriel. If you don't let it out.'

'I can't.'

'Yes, you can.'

'I'm ashamed.'

'I know you are, I know.'

'I hurt her. I broke everything she ever gave me.'

'I know.'

'And my son . . . My son . . .'

'Yes.'

'He saw . . .'

'Yes.'

'He saw my hands around her throat . . . He saw my fists on . . . On the wall . . . Beating . . . Beating . . . Oh God . . .'

'But you were sick . . . So sick . . . You knew no better . . .'

'Fuck.'

'It's alright . . . It's brave . . . Brave what you're doing . . .'

'Yes . . . No . . . I'm bad . . . I've always been bad . . .'

'No . . . Do you hear me, no . . .'

I look at her. I see the urgency in her eyes. I wonder at this woman who only minutes ago I had dismissed, and now is closer to me, to my pain, than anyone has ever been.

'You're no different to me . . . To a lot of people in this room . . .'

Afterwards a few of the men come up to me and stand with me. One or two place their hands on me, touching me on the arm or the shoulder before moving on. A couple stay with me, one of them is Greg. He asks me if I need anything but I shake my head. I smoke one cigarette after the other. Every nerve in me feels shredded. One or two of the women avoid me, I expected nothing less, it must have been difficult for them to listen to what I said. I think of Clive and wonder what he's doing, if he's drunk, if he's on his back. I know now that he was right, that we have to get rid of the shit inside us, offer it up to the heavens, to the world around us. I look at the sky above me and watch as a bird tumbles in and out of cloud, its small body twisting and falling.

I smile as I look at it; I feel the beginning of something inside me, like the small push of a daffodil through frosty ground. I watch the bird again and realise that it's me I'm looking at, and that maybe I'm not falling after all.

Buying Beauty

It is Sunday. Visitors' day and I am sitting in the grounds of the hospital wrapped up against the cold, smoking and sipping from a lukewarm coffee. I tried to call my wife last night to see if she was coming but I couldn't find her. I left a message asking her to think about it as it would mean a lot to me, especially if she brought John with her. It seems like an eternity since I saw him. I am angry that she hasn't let me know one way or the other if she is coming or not, but then I suppose I can't expect too much after what she said in the family counselling session. I try not to dwell on it. More and more in the last days I have begun to see my recent past with some kind of clarity. The noise and fear in me seems to be abating and for the first time in my life I am not looking to the next moment to save me, but seem to be content to sit where I am. I look at the couples dotted about the large gardens. I see Greg with his young wife who replaced his older wife. He told me the other day just after the session with Tanya that's why the wheels came off. The older wife had him worked out. She could cope with the binges and madness. She would let him have his way, watch as he wrecked this, that and the other and then pick him up, dust him down and send him off to his nice big law office so the money kept coming in big weekly chunks.

The younger one freaked out, he told me. She got drunk with him, and the two of them ended up in bits, house fucked, job on the line and eventually no weekly chunks of money, just a suspension pending assessment. So she got him a bed here at St Pat's hoping that the cheques would reappear once he had been cleaned up. From what I can tell, she might need a dose of what Greg and I are getting, but it's none of my business. She is pretty, but it has all been bought, from her cupid bow lips to her pert bouncy front.

Josey is with her mother and I can tell that she is finding it difficult. Every now and then she takes a step backwards as her mother never seems to be less than six inches from her daughter's face, as if she was trying to read her very thoughts.

A car is pulling up in front of the main building. A woman is driving, beside her sits a small child. It is Cathy and John. I stand and begin to walk towards them. I watch as the child struggles to open the car door. When he gets out I can see that he has grown and my walk turns into a run. When he sees me he smiles and then drops his head. My wife gets out and comes round to the passenger side of the car so that she is standing with John when I reach them, her arms criss-crossed across his shoulders. Her act of protectiveness angers me but I push it back down into my gut. I stand there for a second, unsure what to do. I look at my son and then at my wife. I feel stupid as if I'm asking for permission to bend down and greet him. But after everything that's happened I don't blame either of them. Cathy nods and then gives me a wistful smile.

His hands are cold when I touch them, so are his cheeks, and only when I say his name does he lift his head to look at me.

'How are you, John?'

'Fine, Daddy.'

'Good . . . You've grown, son. You're putting on the pounds . . .'

'Have I?'

'Yes.'

'Maybe we could play football later on. I think that one of my friends has a ball that we can borrow.'

'Okay . . .'

I'm allowed to take them to the room I'm staying in. I apologise for the mess, hurriedly clearing dirty clothes and AA books from the bed.

'I didn't know if you were coming or not . . . So . . .'

'It's alright, Gabriel . . . Don't worry . . .' Cathy says.

'I left messages . . .'

'I know . . .'

'So?'

'So?

'So why didn't you let me know? You know, one way or the other.'

'Does it matter. We're here now.'

'Right.'

'And we can't stay long. I promised my dad that I would take John up to see him.'

I don't say anything. They were here, I suppose that was something. I sit on the bed and ask John to come and join me. He looks to his mother who nods.

'Do you want a cup of coffee? Or tea? Or something?'

'No. We're fine,' my wife says, answering for both of them. 'You look better,' she says.

'Well they tell me that I'll never be better. That I have to be vigilant.'

'No, I didn't mean that. The drinking. I meant you. Your skin, complexion. You . . .'

'I'm eating.'

'It's just you look better.'

'Cathy . . .'

'You don't remember, do you?' she says.

'What?'

'How you got here?'

'Bits and pieces, that's all.'

'Jeffrey found you.'

'Who?'

'The teacher. You brought him to the school open day. He called the ambulance service and then called me. You don't remember?'

'Jesus. No. Jeffrey?'

'Yes, he said you were in an awful state. He was in Drogheda. He has an aunt there on his wife's side. He said you were babbling about a sign or something . . . Half naked . . . I can't believe you have no memory of it?'

'I've thought of a lot of things since I've been here . . . In the lock-up . . . In the programme . . . Mum . . . Dad . . . You . . . But no . . .'

'You owe him, Gabriel . . . You owe him a lot. He found you. You were lost and he found you . . .'

'My God.'

'People care for you, Gabriel. In spite of everything people care.'

'Jeffrey?'

'Yes . . . He was amazing. He waited until I got to the hospital . . . He sat with me. We could hear you screaming . . . It was awful . . . Awful . . . He doesn't drink . . . He said that he knew why he was sober that day so that he could be there to lift you up from the gutter.'

'I didn't know.'

'How could you? You were . . . You were like an animal.'

'I'm sorry. I'll make it right.'

'If I've heard that once from you, Gabriel.'

'I am . . .'

'Well, don't tell me, show me, show him . . .'

She looks away as she points at our son. I can see that she is trying not to cry. When she looks back the screen has come down again in front of her eyes, the one that tells me she is back to her disengaged self, at least where I am concerned.

They leave shortly after that. John holds on to me until his mother has to come and ease him away from my arms. I realise that I don't know my own son, how could I when I don't even know myself? I watch as the car drives away. I can see her adjust the rear-view mirror and lean over to whisper into our son's ear and then gently pat him on the head. I think of Jeffrey, I imagine him bending over me. I hear him call my name. I see my face as I respond, it is ugly and it fears the chance that a fellow human being is offering me.

The Sign

They pass me as I stand there, my arms outstretched, my mouth forming the warnings I know they must hear. One or two stop for a moment and ask if I'm alright. I look into their faces and see the sorrow of their lives on their grey skin. One, a woman of about fifty, asks me if I want her to phone for an ambulance. I tell her that man cannot hold me or fix me. She goes about her business, throwing little glances of concern back at me.

I look at the heavy sky above me and watch for the sign that I know is coming, the sign that only I will comprehend. I lift my hands to heaven as I see the tear begin. I smile as the sky peels back on itself and the window to eternity appears. It is slight at first, a small peep of glory in the black sky. Then the gash widens and a cascade of light and love enters my upturned eyes. I stand transfixed. I feel it touch every tired and broken hope, every fallen dream, every molecule of anger and hate, such light, such tumult, such violent love. The voices begin, whispers carried from God's own lips and they enter my brain and begin their work. They re-programme me, undoing all the damaged circuitry, all the cynical yearning of my heart. I am filled with gratitude and tears, they fall from my eyes. I know that the poison of this life is leaving me, bursting from me. I can taste its saltiness. I can taste its horror. I know I must undress. I must leave the old shape of me behind. I begin to pull at my coat and hurl it from my back.

My shirt is next. For a moment I hold it aloft before throwing it onto the pavement. I move with the ecstatic purpose of a saint. St Francis, I am thee.

Sing, a voice says, *sing of Babylon, sing of the fall.*

Soon I am naked. It doesn't bother me, it is His decree not mine. The light above me has become a prism and I realise with joy that I am the final colour.

The unholy made holy, a voice says, *the fractured made whole.*

I see things for what they are, for the first time I truly see. My heart is open; staggered at the freedom it suddenly feels. I see the street before me full of people hurrying, blinkered and closed to their greater selves. I see into their spirits. I see their burning hearts. I hear the cry of the child in the cave of their souls.

You are special, the voice says, *you are free, clothe yourself with me.*

I drink deeply from the bottle in my hand, when it is empty I throw it from me as I know that I no longer need it. I fall to my knees and lift my arms to heaven in thanks. A man is standing above me. There is a look of fear on his face.

'Gabriel . . . Gabriel?' he says. 'Is that you?'

I use my hands to tell him to leave me be. I am no longer who he takes me for. I have become one with the engine that runs his world and mine.

'Gabriel . . . Gabriel . . . It's Jeffrey . . . Stay where you are . . . I'm going to get help.'

I think of the woman who gave birth to me. I no longer call her my mother because I am moving beyond my own blood and hers.

Hallelujah, the voice says, *say it, my son, say it.*

'Yes,' I say. 'Yes, Hallelujah . . . Hallelujah . . .'

The man who was there only moments before is back, there are two other men with him, and they wear uniforms. I know the face of this man who looks at me with such concern but

I can't place it. I decide to move away but they shadow me, asking me to stay where I am. The man keeps speaking to me, telling me to trust him, that there is a way out. I know that he is lying, that he has been sent to trick me. Other men arrive and a small group has gathered. I tell them to fuck off, that I have grown wings, that I no longer need the earth beneath my feet. This puzzles them, one of them laughs and I wag my finger at him. I'll show you, I say, I'll fucking show you, none of you understand.

'Gabriel . . . Gabriel . . . Look at me . . .'

Where do I know him from, this man who is talking to me? 'Fuck . . . Fuck . . .' I say it very quickly. 'Fuck . . . Fuck . . .' This worries them, I can tell, because they look at each other with frowns on their faces.

'Calm down, Gabriel.'

'Fuck . . .'

'Calm down . . . We'll look after you . . . I promise . . . Look at me . . . I promise.'

I smile at him, this man who thinks he knows me. As they grab me I laugh because I am no longer in the body that they grip so tightly, no, I am falling in the moist beauty of the air and my spirit is free.

Spirit Against Spirit

'A man named Frank called this morning. We know him. He's a former inmate and he was wondering if he could come and talk to you.'

'Frank?'

'Yes, he said that he met you at the meeting the other night. That you shared a cigarette together . . .'

'Yes, I remember . . . How did he know to ask for me?'

'Well we only have one Gabriel . . .'

'Right.'

'Listen, you don't have to meet him. He's a good guy. Been through a lot like the rest of us and he helps out here from time to time.'

Alf smiles and waits for me to reply, his eyes gentle and warm.

'You're still bloody debating, aren't you?'

'What?'

'Oh come on.'

'I don't understand.'

'You still can't give in to it . . . To the fact that you're one of us. If you want to survive in this fucked-up world it's your only option.'

'I . . .'

'It can't hurt, Gabriel. He only wants to talk to you not chop your dick off . . .'

'Okay.'

'Good man.'

It is later that afternoon and I am waiting for him. I have been excused from Trauma which makes me smile, there's not many people in this world can say that. I have just started a cigarette when I see him walking up the long drive. He is smaller than I remember him. In the room the other night he seemed larger than life, like a big bear in a tiny wood. I also notice that he walks with a slight limp. He is whistling. For some reason I am nervous as if I was about to sit a very difficult job interview. I start down the drive towards him and meet him on its final curve.

'My good man.'

'Hi, Frank.'

'Let me look at you. Man, you look well.'

'Thanks.'

'This is great. You are standing here with me on a beautiful winter's afternoon. You are clean. You are sober. The old you is dead. Smashed to pieces. And the new you is standing here doing things for the first time. Like saying good afternoon to an old bollocks like me. Don't forget this magic. Because I tell you something, we're lucky fuckers we've been given a second grace. There's not many can say that.'

He smiles at me. I laugh and take his hand, shaking my head as I do. As we walk towards the reception area he says: 'One thing you must get about me from the very beginning, my man, is that I don't give two sweet fucks about anything. Except staying sober. The rest is just noise and half-arsedness.'

We find a seat in a quiet corner of the lobby area. He tells me that he had been born wrong but had spent his life thinking he was right until it had been beaten out of him, had to be, he says, something had to give. I am two drinks short of normal, he says, but the trouble is that I can't stop at one or two, my illness kicks in when I take the first drink, first fucking sip never mind drink. Every now and then he stops and asks me how I am doing. Good, I say, I'm doing good, and somewhere I almost believe it.

'I'm rambling on like this just so that you can get to know me. It's not because I like the sound of my own voice. Well, no, that's a lie,' he says, smiling at me.

He tells me that he has been in prison twice, married once and now lives alone with a small dog called Finn, less hassle that way. His first wife left him for the coal man. She liked diamonds, he says, and that was the closest she could get to them round our way. That's how he got his limp; he went for the coal man, waited for him one night and battered the fuck out of him but kicked him so long and so hard that it left him with a limp.

There's nothing you could tell him about rage that he didn't already know, he came out of his mother's womb with his fists raised. Drink eased that, took the bite out of his thinking, at first, he says, looking at me, his eyes widening slightly to emphasise what he had said. Then it became an enemy of the worst kind because it not only wanted his body but his fucking soul too. I wonder at him, at this mild calm man I see in front of me and try and put him together with the lunatic he is describing to me. But then I only have to think about my recent past to see that madness can come and go as quickly as a spring shower.

'You know the fucking Romans had a saying about alcoholism?'

'Did they?'

'Yes. They said it was *Spiritus contra Spiritum*. Spirit against Spirit, my man.'

I look at him. I admire him; in spite of myself I am attracted to his sheer fuck-you love of living.

'I went pretty far down, Frank,' I say.

'I know, son.'

'A man called Jeffrey found me on the street. From what I

can remember he doesn't drink . . . I think so . . . For some reason it has stuck in my mind that he doesn't.'

'You owe him your life.'

'Yes, I do.'

'You see. All we have is each other. Keep going to the meetings and don't worry about the God thing. It drove me nuts in the beginning. God is the best person you can be, someone said to me once . . . And I said that'll do me . . . Whether you believe it or not God was in that man the day he found you. Don't blow this, Gabriel. You may not think it . . . But there's always farther to fall . . .'

When he says goodbye, he tells me that it's really hello. He gives me his number and tells me to call him when I get out, that he will be at my disposal. I watch as he walks away. I like him, he is warm and his heart is open to someone like me which means he has more courage than I gave him credit for.

Not for Diamonds

He is a new arrival. His name is Michael. He is in the room next to mine. The fingers on one of his hands have no tips and the ones on his other hand are all but gone, so that all he's left with is a fleshy stump. He had lost them trying to save his taxi. It had been hijacked many years before when the Troubles were at their height. He had been made redundant from the factory he had been working in and he had used some of the lay-off money to set himself up with a brand new Nissan and a taxi licence. He joined a local firm in the town and began to ferry drunks to and fro late at night when the bars no longer wanted them. He kept to himself; he had learned that the hard way. It comes from living in this poky little country, he said, someone's always fucking earwigging you. The ones that tipped the best were the old ladies, he said, they liked the company and the chance to jaw with someone. The others, he said, forget it, the boozers were more tight-fisted the more they poured down their necks.

For a while all was working well, no complaints, at least there was food on the table. Then one night it went sour. It had been one of those days where you felt like there was a fucking devil sitting on your shoulder, pulling at you, not letting you get at things right. He was on his way back into the town. He had just done a drop-off in the sticks somewhere and was about a mile from the office when somebody stepped out into the middle of the road and flagged him down. It was a woman, young and quite fit, he said. It was past midnight and he remembered thinking that it was dodgy for a young lass to be out on her own, the times that were in it. If it had been a guy no way would he have stopped, not for diamonds, but a girl, that was different. So he pulls up beside her and winds down his window. Sweet she was, he told me, like sunlight cracking a grey sky. She asked to be run into an estate on the outskirts of the town. As she got in he heard the other door open at the same time, and as he turned his head to see who it was he felt the muzzle of the gun meet his cheek. He was told to get out by a man who had a voice that would have frozen your blood. What could I do? he said to me. What the fuck could I do? He watched as the man climbed into the driver's seat and put the boot down and he and the bit of stuff and his brand new Nissan disappeared into the night.

He walked home and opened a bottle of Bacardi. He ignored his wife's questions. First things first, blind drunk and then he would deal with the hysterics he knew were coming his way when he finally told her what happened. About three hours later he got a phone call from a mate of his who was a cop, nice fella given what he did for a living. His brother played on the same pool team as him. His car had been found abandoned on some wasteland about two miles from the town. It was intact and nothing appeared damaged, but there was a large black bin bag in the back, and they had to make sure that it wasn't a device. What does that mean? he asked. We have to check it out, his mate told him. I'm coming down, he said. He got his neighbour out of bed and got him to run him to the place where his car was. When he got there they had it cordoned off and they were about to send in one of those fucking robot things, he said, to do a controlled explosion. They didn't give two monkeys about me or my taxi; they just wanted the job done and home. The insurance would take a lifetime and a half to come through and he would be back to square bloody one, no, square bloody minus one.

Maybe it was the Bacardi, he said, but one second he was standing there thinking this and the next his legs were carrying him at speed towards the car. He had no idea what he was going to do when he got there but past the cordon he went, past the surprised faces of the security forces and straight to the back door of his taxi. He whipped it open, he said, and reached in and pulled out the black bin bag and ran like fuck back the way he came. This time the police and the army dived for cover as he passed them. All he wanted to do was get the fucking thing as far away from his one source of income as possible. Out into the centre of the wasteland he headed, his heart jumping around like a whore. The blast when it came sounded more like a pop gun, he said. They told him later that it had been a small device and that he was lucky that he had already let go of it when it went off, because it would not only have had his fingers but his head too. He said that they had trouble getting him into the ambulance as he insisted on crawling around in the dirt trying to gather up his missing fingers with what was left of his hands.

It's funny, he said, you know, what life does to you. After that when they had grafted this and that bit of skin onto his knuckles and the stumps that now had to pass for fingers, he couldn't give a fuck about his taxi, or making a living. He sold the Nissan, he took a beating on the sale, he didn't care. He drank every bit of that motor, he said to me, raising the gnarled lump he now had for a left hand so that it sat in the air between us, and he drank his house and his wife and his child until they no longer existed. He erased them; just like these have been, he said, indicating his hands with a nod of his head. I learnt a fucking lesson that night. Don't break the cordon, son, never ever break the fucking cordon.

Sanctuary

It's Josey's last day. Her mother is collecting her at 4 p.m. and she has spent the day in final counselling sessions and saying goodbye to the rest of us. I will miss her. She was the first friendly face I saw as I was coming out of my nightmare. I have grown attached to her in the three short weeks that I have known her. I tell her that I will call her when I get out.

'Why?' she asks me.

'Well . . . I don't know.'

'You won't. We seldom do, us lot. We don't keep in touch with anyone . . .'

'I'm different . . .'

'So am I but that doesn't mean anything. It still won't make us pick up the phone.'

'I'll see you at meetings.'

'No, you won't . . .'

Then she walks away, her suede handbag hanging down from one of her arms. After a short while she stops, looks back at me and comes back, her eyes holding mine as she does so. When she reaches me she puts her lips to my cheek, kisses me and then says: 'You're a good man, Mr Gabriel, no matter what they say.'

It takes me by surprise and I grin back at her unsure what to say or do. As I look into her eyes I know that her stay in this place has failed. There's deadness in them, like someone had just switched off a light in a bare room. She would use again and if she was lucky she would end up in the only place that brought her any comfort, here. If she was unlucky she would never again look at someone with the same warmth that she is looking at me now.

A few of us stand outside and wave her off and watch as her mother barks instructions at her from how to pack her belongings in the car to how to sit in it. She has no chance, I think to myself. After she's gone I walk for a while with Greg. I have grown to like him. He means well, if anything too well and it has caused him a lot of pain in his time. No-one can be all things to all people, I remember my father saying, then again he wasn't anything to anyone. Greg tells me that his young wife has refused to take part in any more sessions, and that she is talking divorce; join the club, I tell him. He tells me that she thought he was stinking rich and when she found out he wasn't, well . . .

'Yes, I know,' I say. 'And fresh body parts cost a fortune nowadays.'

He stops and looks at me and for a moment I think he's going to get angry with me, but then he laughs and nods his head.

'You're a hundred per cent right. You know I think that I could make a good case out of this. Misrepresentation. I married one woman and ended with a totally different one. I could savage her in the divorce proceedings.'

'I don't think that would wash,' I tell him.

He tells me that since he's been here he has felt himself changing, hour by hour, day by day. At first he had wanted to leave. That's normal, I say, so did I.

'You know something?'

'What?'

'I looked at you when you first came in and I would shake my fucking head. No way, I would say to myself.'

'No way what?'

'No way was I like you. I mean you gave me hope . . . I'd look at you and think, well he's had it pretty rough . . . You know, going missing . . . On the street . . . Excuse me for saying this . . . Mad . . .'

'Don't worry. We're all mad in our own ways,' I say.

'I know. I suppose you're right. Look at Mrs Johnson. Or Clive.'

'Yes.'

'Well I hadn't lost everything . . . You know, like you . . . Nowhere to go . . . Pissing in your pants . . . Well I suppose by the end . . .'

'You were close to losing everything.'

'Yeah you're right.'

'It doesn't matter how we got here, Greg. The fact is we're here. I remember you in our first therapy session how you couldn't look anyone in the eye.'

'Yes . . . It's true . . . Fear is a fucker. You know I'd like to continue this conversation when we get out of here,' he adds.

'Me too,' I reply and I smile.

I offer him a cigarette. He shakes his head and pats me on the shoulder and walks back to the institute. I stand there and think about what he said. He was right, I had gone pretty far down and as the winter light begins to fade I stand there hoping that there isn't much farther to fall.

Tea with the Vicar

'Tell me. Tell me. What are you afraid of?'

'I'm not interested in this . . . Not fucking interested . . .'

'I'm still asking the question, Gabriel. I'm still here.'

'You can ask all you want.'

'So you're just going to sit there and stonewall.'

'If that's the way you want to put it.'

'Say it.'

'No.'

'So you think that you can drink normally?'

'No. I don't know. Yes.'

'Which is it? Which is it?'

'No.'

'I didn't hear you.'

'No.'

'So?'

'So?'

'If you can't drink normally?'

'I can't drink at all.'

'And . . .'

'I'm not going to fucking say it, Thaddeus. So you can stop digging.'

'Say what?'

'That I am an . . .'

'An alcoholic?'

'Yes.'

'Leave him alone,' Greg says.

The rest of the room looks at him. I can see the surprise on one or two of their faces.

We are thirty minutes into our group therapy session, and Thaddeus has spent the last ten of them hunting me down. Every time I shifted position in my seat his eyes seemed to be on me, taking me in, weighing me up. So I knew it was coming. Perhaps he felt I was ready to be broken. For now though Greg has taken the heat off me and I watch as the counsellor gives him his full attention.

'He's not a child.'

'Excuse me . . .'

'He's old enough and big enough to look after himself. He doesn't need you bleeding all over him.'

'I just thought that you were being a little tough on him, that's all.'

'Did you?'

'Yes, I did.'

'Maybe you should concentrate on solving yourself before you leap to the defence of others.'

'Maybe, but I don't think it's right,' Greg says.

Thaddeus looks at him and I can see that in spite of his dismissal of him he is pleased that Greg has found some kind of voice. Then he gets back to the matter in hand.

'This is not afternoon tea with the local vicar. Do you understand? This room is maybe the only shot we have. And it begins with honesty – the first step that we will take. Now my name as you know is Thaddeus and I am an alcoholic. No hiding. No dissembling. Oh maybe I drank a little too much when things got on top of me. No, I had to be broken. I had to be dragged from my fucking cave and forced to look at the reality of what I was. And it hurt. Christ, it hurt. Yes, I am an alcoholic, that's the first and the last thing that you need to know about me.'

He pulls out a handkerchief and dabs his forehead and then wipes away the little clusters of saliva that have gathered in the corners of his mouth. He looks at me and for a second I think that I can see into the very depths of his passion, into its fiery core. I catch a glimpse of the man he was before he rebuilt himself from the ashes of what he had destroyed. It frightens me because I know that the same is expected of me, and that this man sitting in front of me will hound me until I am smashed wide open. No-one speaks, but we all sit and watch as he regains his composure. After a moment he clears his throat and fixes me with his eyes.

'So, Gabriel. Where were we?'

A Second Face

My sister is back. This time her husband is with her. She has asked for another session with me. Thaddeus thinks that it's a good idea. I'm not so sure. I know that Seamus is angry with me and that it may turn ugly. I try to tell Thaddeus this as we walk one of the institute's many corridors. He tells me that it's not going to be that kind of meeting and to have faith. That's easy for you to say, I reply. He stops dead and turns to look at me.

'No, it's not. It's not easy for me to say. Faith is something I have to beg for every day of my life.'

I agree to be there in the counsellors' staff room at 3 p.m. I feel strange, as if someone else was staring out of my eyes, and that the man I was before had fled as the house he lived in went up in flames. I try and explain it to Thaddeus.

'That's pretty normal,' he says to me.

'It's unsettling.'

'Of course it is. You haven't a clue who you are. You've taken away the thing that masked that. No, that's gone and the real you has to come into focus. The best thing to do is not to panic.'

'Right. I'll try.'

'Good man. Don't close down. Let this new guy you've become take his seat at the head of the table where he's supposed to be.'

'Right.'

'You're a good man, Gabriel. It's the disease that's bad not you. And by the way . . .'

'Yes?'

'Yesterday . . . group therapy,' he says.

'I was angry.'

'So was I. But one thing I can assure you. One day you will say it. You will be sitting there and you will suddenly own up to what you are. And what a day that will be.'

I spend the next couple of hours thinking about the last time I spoke to Seamus I asked him for money. I threw what was left of my dignity at his feet and said, go ahead, stamp on it, grind it into nothing. I think of his daughter Mary and the night I babysat for them when something ugly moved across my heart.

When he sees me later that day he walks over to me and looks me directly in the eyes.

'Alright?'

I nod and hold his gaze.

'Good. There were many times I wanted to rip your head off, you know that . . .'

'Yes . . .'

'And I only stopped . . . well, because of what I feel for your sister.'

'I know . . .'

'It's not easy what you're doing . . . This place . . . Counsellors, all that shit . . .'

'No . . .'

'Well maybe at last you've found your balls.'

'Maybe . . .'

'We've talked and talked about this. Just so you know. We've asked wee Mary a hundred times . . .'

'I didn't touch her, Seamus.'

'I know.'

'I wanted to.'

'I know. But you didn't.'

'No . . . Jesus, I couldn't . . .'

'That's what the therapist said . . . The one we sent her to . . . She said the scars would be obvious in the way she spoke, the way she thought. So . . .'

'So?'

'Let it go. That's all. That's it.'

And with that he takes his seat beside my sister.

'Sit down, Gabriel,' Thaddeus says.

My sister looks to Seamus as if to say I'm going to speak now. He nods and takes a deep breath.

'Gabriel, I'm sorry for the other day. I said things . . .'

'It's alright . . .' I say.

'Don't be nice to her,' Thaddeus says. 'Let her say what she came to say. It's difficult but it would be of no value if it wasn't.'

'Okay . . .'

'I will try and forgive you, Gabriel. That's what I came to tell you. It will take time. There are so many things that I remember . . . that hurt me.'

'I know.'

'I need time.'

'Yes.'

'Give me that.'

I see her husband's hand move to cover hers. He looks at her. There are tears in his eyes.

I say nothing but wait. Thaddeus looks at me and nods as if to say let her be, let her struggle with this.

'This is not what I saw. You know?'

'What do you mean by that?' Thaddeus asks.

'When we were little. This is not what . . .'

She doesn't finish but moves her hand across her face and then looks at me.

'That morning when he hit Mum . . . Do you remember?'

'Yes.'

'And I wet myself.'

'Yes,' I say.

'I pissed on the floor . . . like a dog . . . I think of it every day . . . every single bloody day . . . But I'm not like you, Gabriel . . . I don't wear it like a bloody medal for the world to see . . . Maybe I'm more like her . . . Our mother, I mean. Sometimes when I was a child I thought that I was her, you know . . . That's how I could escape . . . Maybe that's why you are here and I am not . . . I don't know . . . I don't know anything anymore . . . I thought I could manage . . . You know . . . get by . . . But then when you got sick . . .'

'I've always been sick,' I reply.

'I know. So have I. So have I.'

'And now I'm trying to get well.'

'Yes and I love you for that, Gabriel . . . I love you for that.'

A Mouthful of Rain

I am standing in the rain. My head is turned towards the heavens. It is something I did a lot in the world outside. Tonight I am doing it one last time. Why? I'm not sure. It is about six hours since my sister and her husband have left and I am alone in the large garden at the front of the treatment centre. I should be in my room getting ready for lights out at 10.30 p.m., but something called me out here into the dark. I didn't question it but just left everything I was doing and wandered out here, and stood here until my clothes were soaked through and my hair lay in plastered lines about my face. I am not worried. I don't see it as a backward step, that my madness is returning. I am enjoying it. I like the sensation of the water running across the contours of my body and into my eyes and my ears. I can feel the hot passions that have steered my life for so long crying out to be cooled and I am happy to oblige. I am well; I know that I have never felt this good in my life. I think of what my sister said to me. I see all the times when the two of us stood alone until she crossed to join my mother and left me to face the monster. I don't blame her. She re-invented herself, she had to. Me, I wasn't equipped, I had only one face until now. I know now that no-one chooses to be in pain. It is sometimes given to them when they're born and it can take a whole lifetime to shake free of it. I know that I stand at a point in my life where all these broken things lie at my feet and ask me to look on them. Some I will repair, others I will bury with my father's bones. The one thing I ask as I stand here on the border between the past and the future is that my son will accept the second man that I am trying to build. My mother died in the strange country where reality wears a mask, one that I have visited too. I feel the rain gathering in my mouth, settling in the well beneath my tongue as I think these things. I am comforted by it. I like its harsh sting. It is telling me that the world is around me and that it is there to be savoured. I know that I have spent my life questioning every thought that I ever had, taking it apart as it broke like a wave across the shoreline of my mind. There is no need to do that anymore, I tell myself. Open, be open. As I sneak back into my room I meet the night nurse making her rounds. For a moment she just stands there and looks at me. I know that she is weighing me up, wondering if I've lapsed as I stand there in my soaking jeans and sweatshirt. I tell her not to worry, that I've never felt better. She shakes her head and tells me to get to bed. As I feel the crisp sheets welcome my cold body, I think of my sister and how she had walked back to me today across the burning ground of our past. As I drift off to sleep I think that if she can try and forgive me, maybe I can too.

The Child

I am looking at an empty chair. Thaddeus has placed it in front of me. For a moment he stands behind it, his hands resting on its back before moving away and sitting down beside me so that we are now both facing it. We say nothing but stare at it. For a second I think that he has invited someone else from my past to confront me and that we are waiting for them to arrive. I wouldn't put it past him.

'Now I want you to take your time. And I mean that . . . Take your time, we have all day if necessary. This is important . . .'

'Right . . .' I say, not sure where he is going.

He points at the chair in front of us.

'You have two choices.'

'Two choices?'

'Yes. You can either put yourself or your father in that chair. If you decide it's yourself then I want you to take care. I want you to choose an age . . . preferably in the range of your childhood years . . . Seven . . . Eight . . . Something like that . . . Because if I'm right that's when the abuse began. And I want you to tell the child that you put in front of us exactly what happened to you . . . To you both . . . I want you to tell the child that now you're an adult you are working on looking after him. It's important that you put a name to what was done to you . . . That you bring it out of the dark . . . Okay?'

'Okay.'

'So which will it be?'

'The child . . . I want to talk to the child . . .'

'Right . . . Take your time. Gather your thoughts and remember that anything you say here will be treated in the strictest confidence.'

'I know . . . I know . . .'

I tell myself to be kind. My mouth has dried. I am afraid that when I speak no words will come out, only a long whine, like a dog that has been kicked once too often. I can feel Thaddeus's eyes on me. I know he is waiting. I think of my life and how much of it I have spent running and now here I am in a room facing an empty chair more alone and more fearful than I have ever been. A part of me seeks refuge in how ludicrous this situation must seem, a grown man talking to an absent boy, but I know that won't wash. I remember the times when I felt him trying to reach me, this young kid that I'm now trying to summon. His blood is mine, his truth is mine, but as I begin to speak to him I find rage and not empathy giving me eloquence like it has done so many times in my life.

There is another four-letter word apart from love, listen to me, child. There is no land of dreams, no Nirvana. Can you hear me, little one? He made me hold his cock. He made me move my hand up and down.

'Slowly,' he would grunt. 'Slower.'

This is a bedtime story, little one, one that you will never forget. You mustn't tell anyone though; it has to be our little secret, our pact. You see, that's how stories like this get to be told, in the dark, away from the light. Then he put his big hand on my tiny cock and fiddled with it. I would feel something underneath the shame. I would feel pleasure, a little tick of joy in the bottom of my stomach, and I hated myself for it, I still do, child. Shall I tell you what else he did? What? You don't think that I should tell you? Why not? It's only words, only stories.

Then he put his hand on his own cock, and started moving it up and down and a sound came from him, deep inside him like the rumbling of a bear waking from a deep sleep.

No, please don't struggle, you need to know this, this is a cruel world full of people who will take the dreams from children as they sleep, and replace them with nightmares. He would then pull my small hand and put it under his and guide me. That was the worst moment, because that was when I felt trapped as if a mountain lay across my chest. Then he moved his hand faster as if he was milking a large cow, and mine underneath moved faster too.

Do you know what it is to have the light go out in your small life, child, to feel the devil rear at the end of your fingertips? That's what I felt, that's what I saw. All the playgrounds and meadows were closing as he pushed my hand up and down; each jerk brought the curtain down on another dream. There goes God and the holy host of angels, there goes trust, there goes goodness. His fingers are now a blur on mine, pushing and pulling, skin on skin, father on son, sin on sin. Everything is suspended and all of time is pouring into this one act of filth. My breath has stopped and my throat aches from the rage building in it. I don't pray anymore, I've given that up because it doesn't work otherwise it wouldn't be happening, would it? God wouldn't have allowed it. You see, that's when I knew for sure that we had invented God because we were afraid of the dark, and he was just a thought to keep us warm, to pull us through the long winter of our lives. Don't struggle, little one, no, please don't give me that look, I'm not like him, I couldn't be, I'm only arming you with the truth.

Then the stuff would come, the substance that lived deep inside him, it would spill all over our joined hands, sticky and warm like glue. A grunt told me it was finished and his hand loosened its grip on mine. I slowly pulled it away; my fingers were beginning to stick together. A smell filled the bed, a rich yeasty stench; it made me want to gag. It came from the deep lake inside him where everything begins, where we both began. He pushed me away from him, he seemed defeated, broken.

I would slowly pull my pyjama bottoms up. I would feel ashamed of my erection, it was hard and needy, I was disgusted at what had been awakened in me. It was evil and so was I. I'll let you go in a minute, child; I just want to tell you about the long dark night that followed, when he slept beside me. I felt his milk dry on me, cake my hand, some had got onto my belly and made it itch. I spent the next little while scraping him off me, using the sheet and the corner of my pyjama top. Then I concentrated, little one, I used every ounce of my thinking to wish him dead. I imagined all possible scenarios and I bent my will into making them happen. I saw him being beheaded. I saw him lose his guts in one go with the quick shiny swish of a large sword. I imagined him falling under a train and heard the wheels mash his bones into powder, and saw his blood flowing across the tracks like a red river.

Yes, I know, it's too much for you to take in, but one more thought to take with you, sweetheart, for all that, for all the pain I wished him, and myself, I still wondered how I could make him love me.

Breaking Free

'How are you feeling?'

'Tender.'

'That's a good word for it.'

'I suppose.'

'I don't want to diminish what you've just done by crawling up your backside and saying . . . Oh you know . . . That was marvellous . . . Such bravery . . . This isn't an American TV show . . . But . . .'

'But . . . ?'

'But it took a lot of guts to do what you just did.'

'Thanks.'

'I mean it.'

'Right . . .'

I can't look at him, I am afraid to in case I crack wide open like a rotten tree trunk, so I gaze at the floor or out the window.

'There are people who spend their lives skirting what ails them. I can think of one or two not a million miles from here . . .'

'I feel like someone has had their hands at my throat for the last hour,' I say.

'That's normal. You've held that shit inside you for years and it's caused you no end of pain. From here on in it can only get better.'

For the first time since I've spoken about my father I look

at him. He smiles at me as if to say, believe, all you have to do is believe me.

'You're still very angry and that's understandable. When you spoke to the child you were bitter and resentful but that will change in time. It has to. There are things to do. People to talk to. Your sister. Your wife. But there's time for that. Today I want you to look after yourself. Right?'

'Right . . .'

'Have a walk. Smoke your head off. Anything that will help you come down from this height that I've taken you to. Okay?'

'Okay.'

'This isn't like taking a drink, Gabriel. It's not an instant fix. It will take time. Although I'm guessing that by the end even the booze no longer did what it used to.'

'Yes.'

'This is a long-term thing. This is about healing.'

I look at him and smile. He nods. Outside in the cold November sky the sun has broken free of a cloud, I watch as the light bleeds across the garden, igniting the branches of the trees with colour, and just for a moment everything seems possible.

Touched

In the days that follow we are taken to meeting after meeting in various parts of the city. Each time we are asked to open our ears and listen, give in, give in, our counsellors urge us. I try and sometimes I am sure that I can feel something like peace steal across my heart. Other times I am not so certain and I sit there fidgeting, eager to be free, and I take refuge outside in the cold air chain-smoking until the meeting is at an end. Frank told me that if I wanted to I could go on experimenting and fall even further, maybe into the arms of death this time. I met him again at a meeting off George's Street in the centre of the city and smiled when I saw him. Again he followed me outside when I'd had enough and stood a polite distance from me until I turned round and greeted him.

'You're no different to me, son. No different.'

'What do you mean?'

'I spent most of my first year in the cold outside at meetings. Half in, half out. You know?'

'It's just . . .'

'What?'

'The God business.'

'Right. The higher power stuff?'

'Yes. The higher power stuff.'

'You have trouble with it. It's normal.'

'My mother . . . She believed, Frank. She believed so much

it hurt her, it caused her pain. She had a gift. She thought she had. And . . .'

'It sickened you.'

'Yes, it sickened me. Because . . .'

'Go on.'

'She spoke in tongues. She said it was the voice of the Holy Spirit moving through her. She would make me pray . . . Force-feed me . . . And fuck, I don't know, Frank . . . I don't know . . .'

'And your old fella?'

'What about him?'

'How was he with all this?'

'He touched me, Frank . . . He touched me where he shouldn't have . . .'

I didn't mean to say it, but out it sneaked like a thief leaving a house that he's just burgled. We both looked at each other. I broke it and looked away tugging hungrily on my cigarette. I stamped my feet as if to shatter the quiet that had settled between us.

'That's a bastard,' Frank said after a moment.

'Yes . . .'

'A right fucking bastard . . .'

'Yes . . .'

'Who's your counsellor?'

'What do you mean?'

'Who's treating you at the place up the road?'

'Thaddeus.'

'Have you worked on it with him?'

'Yes . . . Yesterday, no, the day before . . . It was tough . . .'

'I'm sure it was, son.'

'So when I'm sitting in there . . . You know . . . I look around and all I see, all I hear is God this and that. It fucks me off.'

'Ignore it.'

'Right, ignore it. The whole thing in there is built on it. It's the fucking foundation of the programme.'

At this point someone came outside. It was the small man who had greeted people as they had arrived, nodding and smiling, indicating where there were spare seats. He had irritated me. I remember thinking that no-one could be that happy, that it was a biological impossibility.

'Please, gentlemen, please can you keep your voices down.'

I thought about having a go at him, but I knew that it would only make the situation worse. Frank could see it in my eyes and spoke quickly before I had a chance to reconsider.

'Apologies, Harry. Point taken.'

'Right.'

For a moment neither of us said anything. We listened to the soft murmur coming from the room behind us as the meeting greeted another speaker. I lit a second cigarette and offered Frank one. He shook his head.

'You know,' he said. 'I'm fucked sometimes if I believe there is a God. But if it's of any help, there is a hell. I should know because I've been there. And from what you've just said so have you.'

'But heaven, Frank . . . Heaven . . . When does that kick in?'

Shotgun

I don't trust the memory that is rising in me. I can feel it moving up through the dark of my mind like an alligator moving in on its kill. It is of my father and he is crying. I am young and I cannot sleep. I have come downstairs to get a drink of milk and I see him there in the white snow light of the TV screen. The programmes have ended for the night and he is sitting staring at the fuzz a dead channel makes and tears are running down his cheeks. I freeze where I'm standing, my hand poised above the stair rail, my eyes widened with concern. I watch as he puts a can of beer to his lips and then hear the forlorn gasp that comes from him as he drinks. He looks older, broken and his head is deep in thought. Where has it come from this picture, this image? I have no recollection of it, and my first impulse is to dismiss it. But it is begging for admittance, it is crying to be given life in my heart.

I am frightened. I don't want him to see me and yet at the same time something in me wants to reach out to him to tell him it's alright. It baffles me. He is not the father I remember; he is smaller and more beaten by life. His clothes seem loose about his body. He begins muttering, half words, drunken language of fever and wistfulness. He shakes his head and then forms a fist and holds it up in the ghostly light of the television and stares at it for what seems an eternity. If I turn and go back upstairs he will hear me, if I continue down he will see me. In my memory I can feel the hard patter of my breath. I feel sorry for him; I want to tell him that I know the dark too, that I know the demons that lurk in the hallways of a man's soul. But that boy who is watching him has yet to drink from the deep water where anger lurks like cholera. All he sees is a man on the edge of terror. It is not a memory I remember being made. I don't feel it the same way as I do many of the others. It doesn't live in the redness of my blood. I'm imagining it, I tell myself, it is nothing more than whimsy but when I see him reach down and pull his shotgun up from the floor I realise that what I'm being asked to remember occurred. I know because of the stab of pain I suddenly feel across my gut. I also know because I can taste the steel of the gun barrel as he puts it to his lips as if they were my own. I think of all the times that I had wished him dead, for him to dissolve like last night's snow on a busy main road and now here I was looking at a man one step from giving me what I had always wanted. It puzzles me why I have never been visited by this ghost from my past before. I can feel my small boy's hand form a fist. I see my father's jaw close around the twin barrels of the gun, how the tendons tauten. His eyes blink furiously and I know that he is looking for that moment of courage, that still place in his mind where he can leave himself behind and pull the trigger. He doesn't. As he pulls the gun out of his mouth his body convulses and is racked by sobs. I know that this is my chance to sneak back upstairs safe from detection under the cover of my father's cries.

Like My Own

It is two days before I leave. I am in bed. The room has that empty hush that night brings with it. I have spent the last hour or so trying to sleep. Soon I will leave this place and rejoin the world. I know that it will be difficult. I tell myself to trust what has happened in the last few weeks. I don't remember falling asleep, but I must have done, because when I open my eyes again I know that time has passed. I sense him before I see him. He feels like a soft July wind brushing against my skin.

He looks like me. I know that he has been watching me sleep. At first I tell myself that I'm dreaming. Maybe I am, sometimes I can't tell, that has always been my problem. He is younger than me, not in his body, but in his eyes, they are alive with hope and joy plays in them like a foal stretching its legs for the first time. It unsettles me. I shift in the bed and try to speak to him but he shakes his head as the words begin to form in my mouth. He smiles, he knows that I am afraid and he is trying to reassure me. I have spent the last few weeks fighting my way back from the dark land where drink took me, where thoughts spiral into madness and pain and the last thing I need is to go back there. This time I think I will never come back, but wander there among the black clouds like a bird that has lost sight of land.

He begins to speak to me. I recognise the voice. It is like my own but softer and it reminds me of the days in my youth when the world was like a meadow in summer, fierce with flower and colour. He speaks of my fall and how it began when the long winter came and held our house in its icy grasp. He shows me the pain in my father's heart by pointing to his own. He talks of my mother and my sister and how they did the best they could. He says that I was wilful, and that I was made to be broken, just like everyone else, he told me.

He says that madness had saved me and that now it was time to let it go, to let everything be. Don't fight, he says to me, stop fighting. He tells me that my journey has been like so many others that he has seen and that the skies are full of falling souls. He says that he can't stay but that it was important that we met again. You don't remember? I shake my head no, and he smiles. It was in the rain a while ago, he said. I called you my twin and you called me the devil.

The Last Day

This is not how I saw this day when I thought about it in the last four weeks or so. When I wake I feel the usual sense of foreboding lying across my heart and have to cajole my mind into coming to. I have breakfast as usual and then join the others for the morning check-in. New people are arriving all the time. I look at their grey skin and their bloodshot eyes, and remember my first days here. Alf is taking the roll call and he sits at the head of the room and gently explains to the newcomers to listen and not to feel beholden to speak, we are here to look after you, he says. When it is my turn, I introduce myself and say that it is my last day. I get a round of applause, Greg slaps me on the back. I smile and afterwards I make my way to my room to finish packing. No. I expected at least some sunlight to herald the beginning of my new life, but all I see is rain, the sky seems to be full of it. I could feel Alf's eyes on me as I spoke in the recreation room. I know that he wanted me to say it, to spit it out, that I was an alcoholic, but I didn't. I think of the number of times in the last few weeks when they have all had a go at prompting me, at goading and cajoling me. You'll use again, they all said, you'll end up back at square one, or worse. I think of that day when Thaddeus hunted me down in group therapy and I faced him down. I remember Greg and how he had stuck up for me.

I think of the places my mind took me to and how by the

end I believed every image it sent me. Some things I remember, some I don't, and my curse will be that over the next few months these things may come to haunt me. I want to see my son again, to hold him in my arms and to reassure him that the other man has left for good. I am nervous and I can feel my legs wobble slightly as I make my way to reception to leave my case there. I have one more session with Thaddeus and my wife will be there, then I will leave this place.

I walk across the large garden past the bench that I have sat on so many times in the last four weeks. I recall when they moved me from the lock-up ward, escorting me across the wet grass, making sure I did as I was told. I stand for a moment and think of the man I was when I arrived. I imagine I see him moving towards me, I see the vacancy in his stare and the way his hands fidget at his sides as if at any moment he will be broken by the thoughts that shoot around his mind. I watch as the men on either side of him glance at him making sure that he doesn't make any sudden movements. As he approaches I see the animal that lurks in the corner of his gaze and I know that this is the most important day of his life although it will take him some time to see it. He looks heavenwards. I know that he is searching the sky for his shape as it falls towards the earth. As he passes I find myself praying for him. At first this takes me by surprise but then I realise that when a man is dying he will take anything he can get.

The Quiet Friend

My wife is looking at me. For the first time since I care to remember there is something like love in her eyes, but there is also pity, which I don't care for.

'I didn't know,' she said. 'My God, I didn't know . . .'

'I couldn't tell you . . . I couldn't tell anyone . . .'

I get up and walk to the window. I have spent the last hour speaking about my father, how he came to my bed and ripped the love for the world from my heart. Thaddeus is with us as always. He had quietly spoken to my wife before I began, asking her to listen and under no circumstances to interrupt until I had finished. She had nodded and looked at me as if to say what is all this about? Then she had sat opposite me, put her hands in her lap and licked her lips as if she was about to eat a meal she wasn't sure about. I know that my stay here has been leading up to this, that if I wanted to get on with my life in any ordered way I would have to break the back of these memories that have enslaved me since I was a child. I look back at my wife and see that Thaddeus is leaning over her, whispering to her. I am not crying; it surprises me. When I thought of this moment in the last few days, I always saw myself shaking from the horror of what I had lived through, my speech halting and raw with emotion, and my eyes full of tears. But it's not like that; the truth when it comes is a quiet friend. It tells you that the world is simpler than you thought, that pain equals pain and that hurt people hurt people, just as my father had hurt me and I in turn had hurt my wife, and my son, and anyone who had ever reached out to me.

I see my father differently now, my mother too. I know that they were frightened just as I am. I feel sorry for him, for the man he became. I know that I am luckier than he was, that I have a choice, that I stand at a crossroads. He never had that chance. He had been broken by the beast that he had been given to tame.

'Gabriel?'

Thaddeus is standing beside me. His eyes are warm. He gently runs his hand across my left shoulder.

'How are you feeling?'

'I'm . . . I feel relieved, Thaddeus.'

'Good man.'

Yes, the truth when it comes is gentle and steady. It enters the room without fanfare. It sits beside you, patiently waits for you to recognise it.

My wife and I spend the afternoon together. We don't speak much, there is no need to, there has been too much talking recently. We sit and watch the parade of winter clouds across the sky and the crows as they flit between the threadbare trees. I like the stillness that has settled over me. It is clean and it is pure. I can look at this scene in front of me and not want to change it or myself for that matter. I know now that this is my story, and that others have theirs. And your story will always ask questions of you, and it will keep asking you until you reply. We are all broken, we all need fixing. Some people never heal. I think of Clive and his eight or nine stays in treatment, always bolting whenever he came near to the dark secret that had caused him to poison his life and the lives of those around him. Maybe I will fall again, I don't know. In this second as I look at my wife's profile and the lines around her mouth that age is putting there, and see the strong force in her gaze, I realise that for so much of my life I have missed these things, the glow in someone else's eyes that says that the world is not as lonely or as terrifying as you think. I want to put that right. I tell my wife and she smiles at me. For the first time she doesn't throw it back in my face, or question what I've just said. She just lets it sit there between us, for what it is, a hopeful wish from a man who has spent too long in the dark. She tells me that my son misses me, that he always has. She puts her hand on mine and I let it stay there, feeling her warmth. She says that the future is waiting for us both. I nod and suggest we try and walk some of it together. She says nothing for a moment. The she looks at me and says: 'We'll see . . . We'll see.'

'Cathy?'

'Yes?'

'My name is Gabriel . . . And I am an alcoholic.'

She squeezes my hand and I see the beginning of a tear in her eye. When she holds me I can feel the heavy patter of her breath on my neck.

After an hour or so we leave the grounds of the hospital. Thaddeus comes to say farewell. He puts his arms around me and holds me in a tight hug. As he lets go he tells me to look after myself.

'And don't you dare forget me,' he says.

I nod and hold his gaze for a moment before turning to say goodbye to Alf who has joined us too.

'You were a stubborn old bastard,' he says to me.

'Thanks, Alf. So are you.'

'See you in the rooms.'

'Yes.'

As we walk through the gates I think of the previous few weeks and how I've changed, it scares me to think of how far down I went. The mind is a universe in itself. Thaddeus was right when he had said that all of the heavens and all of the hells are within us. I have been to each of them in my time.

Some Kind of Peace

I am on my way to Thaddeus's funeral; I am with Greg in his car. It was he who rang me to tell me the news. We left Newry about forty minutes ago. The burial is on the outskirts of Dublin, we are in good time. In spite of everything we have both stayed sober in the last five years. Others have not been so lucky; Clive, we later found out, returned to the United States and was arrested for shoplifting in an off-licence in the small town in Arizona where he grew up. Josey ended up back in lock-up twice, the second time she slashed her wrists. She survived, just. After that she moved, some people said England, some Canada. Wherever she is I hope that she has found some kind of peace.

Shortly after I left St Pat's I phoned Jeff and arranged to meet him. I remember how I sat in the front room of his house unable to speak to him, maybe it was pride, maybe it was fear. Eventually I said: 'I see the ceasefire is holding.'

'Yes,' he said. 'And it's all because of us,' he continued.

I laughed and then looked down at the floor and quietly said: 'Thank you, Jeff . . . Thank you.'

'No need, Gabriel. The fact that you are sober is thanks enough for me.'

Frank became my sponsor, my mentor. He steered me through my early days of sobriety when the desire to drink would rise in me like a tidal wave, so high and so sudden that

I feared that I might drown. I stayed with him for a while in his small flat and we went to meeting after meeting. It took six months for my wife to take me back. I remember the feeling as I stepped over the threshold of my home, I felt as if I had come back from a war. My son John was standing in the hallway to greet me, gently hopping from foot to foot with excitement. It wasn't easy at first; there were many wounds to heal. There were times when we both nearly called it a day but something kept us there. Words like forgiveness and goodness crept into our vocabularies. I often shook my head in disbelief when I recalled the madness that had engulfed me. I kept away from bars, in the beginning I even crossed the street to avoid walking past their doorways with their warmth and their sweet promise. My sister and I began to reclaim some of the ground we had lost when we were children. We would meet for a sandwich in the town and quietly talk of the past and the need to move on. Seamus and I even went fishing from time to time and sometimes we would remember to comment on the beauty of the world around us.

When I was one year sober I found work in a new school that had only been open eighteen months or so. It was thrilling to teach again. Slowly but surely I became more comfortable in the skin I had been given to wear. Sometimes though the black clouds would steal across my soul like they did so many times before, except this time I knew that they would pass.

I didn't see Thaddeus for a long time but I thought of him often. One day shortly after my second sober birthday I was in Dublin and arranged to meet him. I smiled when he answered the phone and immediately heard the familiar authority of his voice, and the strong unwavering self-belief. We met in a small café in the centre of the city; he was already there when I arrived, sitting in a corner watching the world around him going about its day. He rose to shake my hand and said: 'Still sober?'

'Yes, Thaddeus. Still sober.'

He made a fist with his left hand and gently punched the air.

'We're still here.'

'Yes, Thaddeus, we're still here.'